SAVAGE CITY

Also by L. Penelope

Earthsinger Chronicles

Song of Blood & Stone

Breath of Dust & Dawn

Whispers of Shadow & Flame

Hush of Storm & Sorrow

Cry of Metal & Bone

Echoes of Ash & Tears

Requiem of Silence

The Eternal Flame Series

Angelborn

Angelfall

Other Romance

The Cupid Guild Complete Collection

Writing As Leslye Penelope

The Monsters We Defy

BOOK ONE OF THE BLISS WARS

SAVAGE CITY

L. PENELOPE

HEARTSPELL

Heartspell Media, LLC

ISBN: 978-1-944744-25-0 (eBook)

ISBN: 978-1-944744-26-7 (trade paperback 1)

ISBN: 978-1-944744-27-4 (trade paperback 2)

Cover design: James T. Egan of Bookfly Design

Chapter One

TALIA

THE FIRST TIME I DIE, my life doesn't flash before my eyes in a rush of images. All I see is a single moment from the past: me, sitting on a hospital bed, my feet a long way from reaching the ground. I had on the pink sneakers I'd begged Mom for, but the pristine white toes were splattered with blood. Adults spoke around me in loud voices. One of the ladies had a tone so high pitched and sharp that it reminded me of the screaming. I sang a song in my head, to drown out her voice.

A cast in the same pink as my sneakers weighed down my right arm. I picked at the edge of it, at the gauzy white bit, trying to unravel a thread. The cuts over the rest of me were slowly turning into scars, the bruises becoming mottled and gray. I was obsessed with scars back then—how they were made of the same stuff as regular skin, but transformed. How some animals don't scar at all—they can completely regenerate, regrowing skin and organs as good as new. In my mind, scars were tougher and stronger, a protective shell covering a vulnerable interior. But Mom told me that they were just a part of life. Scars meant you'd seen some things, been through some things, and you were different now. Forever changed. My new scars were inside and out.

I was remembering my mom—how she looked when she laughed—when a pair of loafers stepped into my field of vision. I tilted my head up to find a man, tawny-skinned with dark, hazel eyes. A short, neat afro topped his head, cropped with laser-like precision. His mustache was similarly well-groomed. He looked down at me, and something about his face was familiar.

"Talia," he said, his voice like bitter chocolate.

I looked up at him and he looked down at me, and the corners of his mustache drooped with his frown. I looked up with hope and he looked back with an expression I was destined to see often on him. Eventually, I came to understand it as dismay.

"Who are you?" I asked, curious but not afraid.

"I'm your father."

The image fades, but the rest of the day rushes back to me in a swirl of memories. My father leading me from the hospital and into his maroon sedan the day I met him. The back seat already taken up with two brand new, never used car seats. Me squeezing in between them and fumbling around for the seat belt with my good arm while he started the engine. The drive seemed like it took days, but in reality it was only a few hours. I tried to scrape the blood off my shoe using the edge of the front seat. It didn't come off.

My eyes open slowly, overwhelmed by the brightness of the light surrounding me. I lick my lips and wince at the soreness in my throat. Nearby, someone hums. A woman wanders into my field of vision, smiling and grandmotherly in pink scrubs.

"Where am I?" I croak out.

"Shock Trauma," she says, holding a plastic cup of water with a straw for me to sip. "A car hit you while you were crossing the street, honey. You flatlined, but they brought you back." She smells of cinnamon and cloves. The water soothes my aching throat. "You'll be sore for a while from the intubation. But you're breathing on your own now, so that's a good sign."

Another hospital. I shiver. Another car accident, though this time I'm not trapped inside a metal coffin for hours with the echoes of screaming rattling around in my head.

While I can't really move any of my body, nothing hurts. I must be on the good drugs. "My father?" I ask, unable to keep the hope from soaking my voice.

The nurse's lips turn down; discomfort enters her eyes. "No visitors so far. But someone sent you flowers."

She points to a glass wall. I slowly turn my head to find an enormous bouquet on the other side, its vibrant blooms already wilting. "They're not allowed inside the ICU rooms." Her tone is apologetic.

I close my eyes again for a moment—or an hour, or a day —wondering how many times I will cheat death. When I wake again, it's to chaos.

My body looks far away but magnified, like I'm viewing it through a telescope. People in scrubs buzz around the bed speaking curtly to one another. It's not like on television. No one yells "Stat!" Someone does mention the word *embolism*, followed by a string of curses.

Eventually, a single, low tone beeps and the vision fades to darkness. I'm no longer looking through a lens at anything. Rushing air passes by my skin, but I can't see anything. It's almost like I'm flying. I'm excited to discover what the afterlife holds. Is there a heaven? Hell? Will I be reborn as someone new and get a chance to do things over? There are so many things I wish had gone differently.

The darkness soon turns to gray, and the flying feeling turns into the sensation of falling. A free fall through overcast skies. I reach out to touch the clouds with my fingertips. My hand slips through the insubstantial mass, leaving my skin coated with moisture. With eyes burning from the speed, wind whipping at my hair and tearing it out of its braids, a bubble of fear opens up within me.

My teeth chatter, and even though I can't see anything other than a thick, gray mist surrounding me, I don't think this could be heaven. I'm still considering what's happening and where I really am when I hit the ground.

The impact takes the wind out of me, but given the speed I was falling, I really should be lying shattered on the cold earth as a pulpy, bloody mess. However, I'm not even bruised. I lie staring up at the gray sky and catch my breath. Then I sit up and look around.

Wherever *here* is, it's foggy: the pea soup kind where you can't see more than a few feet in any direction. There's dirt, an empty stretch of soil with nothing growing on it at all. Hell is looking like a strong possibility—this place is bleak and cold and lifeless.

I stand and cringe as sharp little pebbles cut into my bare feet. I'm only wearing a flimsy hospital gown. It's snapped closed in the back so my ass isn't hanging out, but it's no warmer than fifty degrees here and shivers rake over my body. A blood-curdling, animalistic shriek shreds the air from not very far away and I forget the cold and discomfort.

I have no idea which direction the sound came from, so I don't know which way to run. I crouch down, scanning around me for anything I can use as a weapon, but of course there's nothing. Just dirt and rocks too little to be useful for more than jabbing my naked feet.

I swallow thickly as my throat starts to close. Sucking air into my lungs is getting harder and harder as panic reigns. A roar sounds, louder and closer. Was that a different creature or the same one? It reminds me of one of the bears in those endless nature documentaries my stepsister used to watch.

More animal calls ring out, growls and howls and—was that a wolf? Then a squawk like some kind of war bird. I hunker down because the sounds are coming from all around. I'm a shivering, quivering mess when a hulking form bounds out of the mist, heading straight for me.

I get a glimpse of red eyes and sharp, jagged teeth, and then I'm sprinting in the opposite direction. I was never particularly athletic and I haven't run since high school gym class, but I guess the adrenaline pushes me forward because whatever that thing is doesn't immediately catch me. I dimly recognize that each step is painful—I'm shredding my feet—but I keep running as the thing behind me bellows its dinosaur-like roar.

What I need is to put on a burst of speed—isn't the human body capable of miraculous things when under duress? I think of the story of a mother lifting a car to save her child, but apparently my body didn't get that particular memo because I'm slowing down with a painful stitch in my side, muscles failing too soon. I dig deep, but my tank is empty. I know I'm not going to get away when I actually feel hot breath on my neck. I squeeze my eyes tight—I've already died at least twice…is my hell going to be new and innovative ways to be killed over and over again?

Pain slices down my back as the creature roars again. I topple over, crashing to the ground and getting a face full of dirt as I'm blinded by agony. My throat is suddenly sore again and I realize it's because I'm screaming. How long I've been screaming, I don't know. The realization makes me stop. I draw a deep breath and the snarls and snaps of animals fighting reach my ears. They're close, but I don't turn my head to see. Something is battling the creature that took me down, and I really hope it wins. At least I'm pretty sure I hope it wins, though with the way things are going, this new thing may want to eat me, too. The theme of my life thus far—twenty-three years of going from the frying pan into the fire. Why would my afterlife be any different?

An intense wind picks up. I'm flat on my stomach without

even the strength to curl up into a ball. It's like someone flayed my back and then poured acid on the wounds. I might have started screaming again, but I'm not even sure. My eyes are closed and dizziness swamps me, spinning me around in the darkness like a top. Hair flies all over my head and bits of dirt and debris hit my searing back, kicked up by the crazy, gale-force winds and intensifying the already unbearable pain.

Another roar and then there's heat, an explosion of heat blasting somewhere very nearby. Fire crackles and sizzles and smoke clogs my nose as something burns. Something that howls in torturous pain as it fries, its flesh turned to flame and then char. The pops and hisses and odor of burning meat are making me feel like I'm at the worst barbecue of all time. I gag and squeeze my nose closed, gasping air through my mouth.

My mind is telling me to get farther away from the fire—the instinct for self-preservation hasn't left me. The heat kisses my skin, uncomfortably warm and far too close. But I can't move. I can't drag myself anywhere, not just because of the pain but because I literally can't move. My limbs have turned to stone. I'm paralyzed—did that thing hit my spine and damage it? My eyes blink open—they still work—but my thoughts are starting to muddle into mush. The ground vibrates as heavy footsteps come toward me, walking into my limited range of vision.

They're not shiny black loafers but scuffed, thick-soled boots. They stop an inch from my face, and I can't turn my head to see who they belong to. I can't even keep my eyes open one more second. But before things go dark, I do notice that they have what looks like blood splattered across the toes.

Chapter Two

RYIN

THE TOP of the wall is wide enough for three men to stand shoulder to shoulder, with only one of them at any great risk of falling off. I'm already standing at the edge about as far as I can get when two Nimali soldiers march by, one brushing against me and nearly pushing me over. My teeth grind and I swallow the shout that wants to fight its way past my lips. My eyes burn with the need to push back at them, but I press the feeling down, hard, and channel that energy into my mission.

Other than the assholes surrounding me, I don't mind duty at the wall. On a clear day, from here I can almost see my home in the Greenlands, a place I haven't set foot in for over three years. Of course, now it's nearing sunset and the fog that descends around the city is too dense for me to see much of anything. I peer out into the murky gloom to the south, into No Man's Land, but can barely see the base of the wall thirty feet down.

Up here, surrounded by my enemy, forced to pretend subservience to them, I refocus on my true duty: monitoring the movements of the Nimali soldiers. I commit to memory those who are stationed here so I can bring the information back to the others and add it to the communal database of knowledge my fellow Fai are building. I take note of who trains and how hard, who slacks, who notices, and a dozen other things that will help us one day gain our freedom.

Until a screech rends the air and ice rolls down my spine.

"Revokers!" someone shouts from the ground. The Nimali on the wall snap to attention, readying themselves for a potential battle. My daimon would love to be let out to fight—it hasn't had so much as a skirmish for three years—but it will have to wait a bit longer. That doesn't mean I don't call to it, keeping the spirit that shares my body within easy reach inside me. If the growling and snarling rising from No Man's Land are any indication, a fierce fight is going on down there, obscured by the fog.

On top of the wall, silence reigns as the soldiers wait for word. We all stare toward the ground, anticipation a dark cloud suspended over us as sharp eyes scan the gloom for either a member of the scouting team that went out an hour ago or a Revoker, red eyes flashing and fangs covered in gristle and blood.

The first person who runs into view is tall and familiar and very much Nimali. His armor is blood spattered, but he appears uninjured. Others sigh audibly in relief, but my jaw tightens. Prince Shad. I wouldn't have minded if he'd been grievously injured. My daimon silently chastises me for the unkindness, but I can't help it. There are only two Nimali men who could have killed Dove, and he's one of them. Until I'm certain it *wasn't* him, I have to act like it was.

A bear and a lion are close behind him—part of the prince's honor guard. The bear's gait is hampered by a pronounced limp, though she still eats up the ground with long strides. Then my focus returns to the prince. He's carrying something—someone—over his shoulder like a sack of beans. His bounding steps cross the distance easily, and then he's at the rope ladder a soldier threw down. He climbs it with one arm while holding what I can see now is an injured woman.

Blood pours down her back from gashes that I'm sure were made by a Revoker's claws. Her clothing is odd. A short, loose dress, oddly patterned and flimsy—I've never seen anything like it before, not on a Nimali or a Fai. Why anyone would go into No Man's Land without battle armor is a mystery, but the woman is also barefoot. Begrudging respect bubbles up from my chest for the way the prince is able to negotiate the climb with that much dead weight, carried awkwardly. He could have shifted into his other form and flown up, but his own claws might have further injured her. And he is definitely treating her like something special.

The reason becomes clear when he finally gets to the top and one of the soldiers reaches out to help him with his burden. Prince Shad shakes his head and gently lays the woman down on her side, revealing her face.

I'm too far away to see at first, but when the soldiers in front of me gasp and immediately kneel, I get a glimpse. Princess Celena lies there, bloodied and battered. Her rich, chestnut skin is ashen, taking on an almost gray pallor. I'm frozen in place for a moment viewing her small form, her strange, tattered clothing, the odd way she's braided her hair.

Then I'm shoved hard from behind, stumbling forward through the kneeling men and women.

"Where is the healer?" Prince Shad roars, but I'm already there, crouching down beside the princess. My daimon joins me seconds later, eager to fill me with its essence and lend me its healing power.

Celena's back is ravaged, the wounds already bubbling with the poison from the Revoker's talons. They look fresh, so it's not too late to heal them if I'm quick about it. I hold out my hands and close my eyes, letting my daimon fully take over.

Its energy flows through me, using my physical body as a conduit for its power.

Through my daimon, I sense the damage, the torn flesh and the toxins that have already entered her bloodstream. The healing energy pulls the poison out, a sticky black substance that leaks onto the stone of the wall. The flesh, layers of muscle and skin, is knit back together until there isn't so much as a scar left. I silently thank my daimon and it retreats. Then I open my eyes.

Prince Shad is staring down at his sister. When the blue light of my power retreats, his dark eyes flick up to mine.

"I removed the poison," I tell him.

"All of it?" I nod. His lips flatten into a grim line. "We're taking her back to the Citadel. Come with me; the king will want to be sure."

My muscles grow rigid before I nod again. An audience with the king is the last thing I'm interested in, but of course, I can't disobey a direct order from the prince, or any Nimali, really. I might grind my teeth into dust before I'm free of these people.

The princess stirs, rolling over from her side to her newly healed back. The breaths of the half-dozen soldiers gathered around us catch as she blinks her eyes open. She meets my gaze and her brow lowers. She gasps for air and her face clears before breaking out into a joyous expression.

I've been in the presence of the princess many times before. I've healed her and been the subject of her scrutiny, but I've never felt the breath leave my body when she looked at me. I've never seen her lit from within with pure happiness.

Her smile as she sits up is a beam of sunlight in the darkness. "Victor?"

I swallow, unable to answer, but disappointment crashes into me—which makes no sense. "My name is Ryin, Your Grace."

She tilts her head as her gaze roams over my face and

body, then returns to my eyes. Her joy dims somewhat. "Victor," she repeats, more uncertain. "Are we really in heaven?" Her voice is different, brighter, even in her doubt.

Behind her, Prince Shad frowns deeply, troubled by her confusion. He clasps her shoulder and she turns around, noticing the others for the first time. Her mouth drops open with shock. She must still be processing everything she's gone through. The trauma. The injury. And healing can take something out of a person. She'll need rest.

"Celena," Shad says.

She scrunches up her face. "Who?" She looks around again then down at herself. Then she seems to notice that she's on top of a thirty-foot wall.

She was already sitting in the middle of the platform, but still she scrambles closer to me, brushing against my legs. I slide out of the way—it's forbidden for a Fai to touch a Nimali. The princess is too discombobulated to even notice.

"Wh-Where am I?"

"You're back home," Prince Shad says slowly. "In Aurum. We found you outside the wall just as Revokers attacked."

No light of recognition for him or his words shines in her eyes. Shad looks at me with worry in his gaze. "Did you sense something amiss when you healed her?"

Celena's head snaps toward me, her eyes peering intensely.

"No, Your Grace. But I would not be able to sense a missing soul."

"Soul?" she screeches, curling into a ball and wrapping her arms around her legs.

Shad sighs and runs a hand over his face. "You've been missing for two weeks, Celena. And it seems in that time, you have lost your memory soul."

Celena's eyes widen and her head darts all around in jerky movements as she takes in everything. When she looks back at me, it's like she's expecting me to contradict the prince's words, or…Or like she's turning to me for comfort.

I can't gainsay the prince, nor would I, as his assessment is correct. She appears to have no knowledge of herself, her stepbrother, or anything else she should know. I didn't see any trauma to her head that would explain missing memories, and if they are missing completely, then that could only be explained by the loss of the soul that controls memory.

But when she looks at me like this, dark eyes rounded and fearful and seeking solace? *From me?* For the first time, I feel sorry for a Nimali. The emotion is brief and I shove it away the way I suppress the anger and rage, because just like them, it will do me no good. I must squash any sympathy for my enemy, for not a single one of them would show anything similar for me. I am not here to reassure her or ease her path, not after what her people, her own father, have done to me and mine.

I tear my gaze away from hers and lower it, faking deference. A hiss escapes her lips. Shock? Dismay? It doesn't matter. The princess needs nothing from me but what I have already provided. I saved her life, and it's more than she deserves.

And if her eyes haunt me, the sadness brimming in them gutting when I catch another involuntary glimpse, I ignore that as well. I must.

Chapter Three

TALIA

I STARE AT VICTOR, my head still spinning. Victor all grown up—which is something he never had the chance to do. The darkness and the cold fade away. I can't tear my gaze away from him.

As a kid, he was a little awkward, sort of gangly, already six feet tall at the age of thirteen with dark freckles and a giant, reddish-brown afro that was perpetually lopsided. I was absolutely smitten. He was the son of my father's housekeeper, and for a few months they lived in a little apartment above the garage. I used to spy on him through my bedroom window as he shot hoops in the driveway until my stepmother complained that the bouncing gave her a migraine. He and his mother found their own place after that, and I would only see him every once in a while, on school half-days or holidays. Then, when he was sixteen, he was in a park with some friends and was killed in a drive-by shooting.

If he'd lived, he'd be twenty-eight, and that's about the age of the man next to me—the one with Victor's face and a different name. He's still lean, his hair still tinged with red. But there is no light of recognition in his gaze. I'd thought for a moment, blinking to look up into his eyes, that I was in heaven and would be reunited with people who were important to me, like the pre-teen crush I never quite got over. But that spark of joy flickers and dies. If this were heaven, would he have kept growing older?

A shiver races through me, cutting through the thin fabric of my gown. And heaven wouldn't have me somehow on the top of a giant wall surrounded by men and women who dress like futuristic renaissance faire cosplayers. They're all in black, the material tough and leatherish and fitted with reinforced shoulders and elbows and knees. It's pretty badass, and I wouldn't mind an outfit like that too. Looks warm. The only other person not dressed like Mad Max meets King Arthur is Victor—no, not Victor, *Ryin*. Who's dressed all in dark gray, his clothes softer and less armor-like.

He won't look at me anymore, and I miss his attention. He's the only familiar thing here, and even if he's not Victor, his presence is still a grounding rod in the electrical storm that has become my life—afterlife, whatever.

The man on my other side stands, extending his arm to me. After thinking about it for a second, I take his outstretched hand and he helps me to my feet. Which are not cut up anymore. The pain in my back is gone as well. I stretch my shoulders, surprised to find that I feel good, with not so much as an ache anywhere. Weird.

I stare up at the man who hasn't let go of my hand yet. "Who are you?" I whisper.

He winces, but recovers quickly. "My name is Shad. I'm your stepbrother." He searches my face, maybe for recognition, as I search his in turn. I'm speechless, thinking of my actual stepsiblings: the twin girls with ash blonde hair born just a few weeks after I went to live with my father and his wife.

"Shad." I repeat his name. He towers over me, at least six-foot-three or -four. His dark hair is cropped short, and he reminds me a little of a classmate whose mother was Korean and father was Black. Maybe he has a similar background.

Behind me, everything is still. I peek over my shoulder to find a half-dozen people still on their knees in rows of two.

"Are they okay?"

Shad cracks a small smile. "They can't rise until you tell them to, Your Grace."

He looks at me expectantly. Your Grace. That means royalty, right? Or at least nobility. I think back to all the historical romances my stepmother kept in boxes in the basement.

"Does that mean I'm like a duchess or something?"

"It means you're a princess. And your father, the king, will be extremely eager to have you home. Come with me, please. We'll figure all this out."

Just then, an enormous golden eagle swoops down from the somber sky to land at Shad's feet. It's bigger than I'd ever thought an eagle could be, standing almost waist high. I think of the squawking and screeching after I was attacked and tense, gripping Shad's hand tighter.

He gives me an odd look, then gently disentangles himself and crouches near the creature. I'm no bird expert or anything, but I didn't think they'd be okay this close to a bunch of humans. This one seems to have no problem with it, though. Can you train an eagle?

Shad reaches for something gripped in its claw. I take a step back instinctively, but there's literally nowhere to go because I'm on the top of a fricking wall that's crowded with people. I can't see much to the left, either, but I think it might be a city over there. A low breeze stirs the air, and I can barely make out tall buildings rising in the gloom.

The eagle spreads its massive wings, making me turn back to watch. My breath catches and a fresh wave of cold washes over me as its wings beat, carrying it silently into the air.

"Are you ready?" Shad asks as if that whole thing didn't

happen, or as if it happens every day. Maybe it does here.

"I think so?" My voice is pitched up because I really have no idea. I have so many questions that I don't even know where to start. Where am I? How did I get here? What attacked me? Why do they think I'm their princess? I should tell them I'm not, but what happens then? Being mistaken for a princess isn't the worst thing that could happen. It's better than being mistaken for a criminal or something, but unease still coats my skin. I didn't get a choice in any of this, and the possibility that it's all some sort of elaborate hell hasn't left my mind.

Shad offers his hand again, and I pause before taking it. As he begins to stride away from the others, I tug on him to stop, then turn around.

"Um, you all can get up now," I tell the kneeling men and women. They rise as one, all staring at me. I shift from foot to foot, uncomfortable with this attention, and flinch as the cold stone cuts into my bare feet.

Shad looks down at my toes, then his head snaps up. "Sergeant, give the princess your boots." A blonde woman, her hair cropped in a cute pixie cut, immediately begins unlacing her boots.

"Oh, that's—" I begin, but Shad cuts me off.

"Are you cold?" His quick manner seems more efficient than rude. I've been warmer, but I don't want anyone else to lose an item of clothing, so I shake my head.

"Healer, you're with me," Shad says. And Victor—Ryin—approaches, his features grim.

It's weird, and vaguely cringe inducing, sticking my feet into the still-warm shoes someone else just removed, but they're a perfect fit. The soldier stands in her socks, pride shining in her eyes.

"Thank you," I tell her, and she looks surprised before bowing to me.

"You're very welcome, Your Grace."

Shad seems to be in a hurry, so I follow him with Ryin a few steps behind us.

"Will she be okay without shoes?" I ask.

"She's a soldier, she'll be fine." His words are clipped but the tone is reassuring.

I look back, realizing that while all of these people are soldiers, none of them appear to be armed. I haven't seen a single gun or rifle. I'm still pondering this when we reach another pair of soldiers, a man and a woman, standing at the base of one of the giant light posts that line the wall. Both snap their four fingers to their chins and then straighten their arms back to their sides in precise movements that suggest some kind of a salute. Then they bow low at the waist.

Shad acknowledges them with a brief nod. "Ladder," he says, and they rush to unfurl a rope ladder that ripples down the city side of the wall.

"We have to climb down?" There's a tremor of fear I can't keep from my voice. Shad squeezes his large hand around mine.

"Yes. But it will be perfectly fine. I'll go first."

I try to clamp down on the shaking that's taken over my limbs while ignoring the pitying looks the two soldiers are giving me. Ryin's face is carefully blank. That's also how I know he can't be Victor. He was mischievous, full of laughter and lightness, a class clown. Ryin seems like the light has gone out of him. He's stoic and his energy is heavy. I look away when he catches me staring.

Shad steps onto the flimsy rope. If they're up on this wall all the time, why haven't they built permanent steps? Why do they rely on rope ladders to go up and down? I press my hands to my belly and take a deep breath.

"Come on, Celena," Shad says, face tilted toward me. "You can do this."

I'm willing my courage to be up to the task and peer over the edge of the wall. The fog down there is so thick I can barely see how far I have to fall. That should be comforting, but it's not. I smile at him, a little shakily, and step onto the ladder.

The thing is more stable than I thought, made of no kind of rope I've ever seen before. But whatever the material is, it bounces less than expected. Still, it's no picnic climbing down. Ryin is above me and I get a good look at his boots—thick-soled shit-kickers just like everyone else here has.

I just keep climbing, humming to myself as I go to keep the crazy away. My arms are jelly and my legs are noodles but, amazingly, they hold up.

Finally, I get to the ground, where Shad is smiling at me, proud. But I don't take a full breath until Ryin jumps down the last few rungs. More soldiers are gathered down here, some warming themselves around a trash can fire. They snap to attention when they see Shad. When they see me, eyes widen, jaws drop, and low bows follow.

"The princess has been found," Shad announces. "I need air and ground support back to the Citadel."

Eight soldiers salute before breaking off into a run and disappearing around a building. I look around wildly; are there helicopters here? Then Shad leads me across cracked asphalt toward a crumbling brick building and into what looks like a garage. As we step farther inside, flickering blue lights come on showing a much larger space than I was expecting filled with trucks and SUVs. But I don't recognize the makes or models of any of them. All insignias are completely foreign. Now I do stop walking.

"Where did you say we were again?"

"Aurum," Shad says. "That's what we call the city."

He leads us to something very similar to a Jeep Wrangler on four giant wheels with a soft convertible top. It's Ryin who opens the passenger door for me, but he doesn't offer a hand to help me into the high seat. I climb up myself before he shuts the door.

He settles in the back and Shad slides behind the wheel. Instead of a key, he shoves what looks like a screwdriver into the ignition.

"Are we stealing this?" Surprise cuts through my voice. He looks over at me, brows high. "You don't have a key." Now he looks like I have antenna growing out of my forehead; I sink further into the seat cushion. "Never mind."

His screwdriver thingy engages the engine and then we're off. We rumble out of the garage and onto a pockmarked street where the fog isn't quite as thick as before. It eases even more as we drive, giving me a view of the street: craggy and cracked, not maintained at all. The city is abandoned, dead even. As we crest a hill, the mist rises even more, revealing a postapocalyptic wasteland.

The buildings within sight are in various states of decay: houses, shops, apartment buildings, all crumbling. There are plenty of lots that are nothing but piles of rubble. Abandoned, rusted, windowless cars line the streets. Some intersections are full of cars, as if there had been a massive traffic jam too big to clear and folks just got out and left their vehicles behind.

In other places, someone has made a path through, literally slicing cars in half and pushing them out of the way. Vegetation rises from the long unused sidewalks and side streets. Nature has reclaimed much of the area that isn't being actively used as a throughway.

I'm waiting for the zombies to appear.

I take in as much as I can through the haze. But I sit up straighter when something that looks a lot like Coit Tower rises far off to the left. But the famous landmark couldn't be here, right? My gaze sharpens and I squint up trying to get a look at any street signs.

Most are missing, but we make a turn and a sign dangles from a cable on the side of the intersection. Market Street.

"San Francisco?" My voice is incredulous. "We're in San Francisco?

Chapter Four

RYIN

THE PRINCESS LEANS over in her seat, pressing her nose to the glass of the window. I view her in profile, amazed at the emotions playing on her face. Her widened eyes are full of wonder, and her voice is awed. Gone is the stoic woman with the chilly demeanor who I've seen marching through the Citadel for the past three years. Without her memory, she is much changed. I've never encountered the like before in one who lost a memory soul; it is fascinating to witness.

"San Francisco is what they called the city before the Sorrows," Prince Shad says, hope coloring his tone. "Do you remember that?"

Princess Celena mumbles something under her breath and lifts both palms to the glass. Then I'm thrown forward as the car screeches to a halt. The seat belt cuts into my chest. I peer through the windshield to find three people—two men and a woman—standing in the center of the street. Their eyes glow blue with daimon power.

"Get down!" Shad cries, reaching for the princess's back

and pushing her toward the floor. She's belted in so she can only fold forward.

With his free hand, the prince wrestles with his own seat belt. He probably wants to exit the vehicle so he can shift—something he cannot do in the car, especially with his sister so close. I stay silent and motionless as the copper-haired Fai man in the center breaks off from the others to approach the driver's side window. He taps on the glass politely, then grins as Prince Shad growls at him.

"Your Grace," the man says, sketching a mocking bow. I recognize him now. Von Nyallson. He's all sharp cheekbones and wiry, coiled strength ready to strike. He scans the interior of the vehicle, eyes catching on me but not lingering, thank the tors. No need to advertise to the Nimali that we know one another; instead, a presence seeks entry into my thoughts, like a mental knock upon a door. I let him in.

Are you well, brother? he asks. Von is an Air Fai, his daimon giving him the power of telepathy—something I wish I had—among other things.

As well as can be expected. You seek to capture the prince? I ask.

We'd intended only to create a little mischief. The prince is an unexpected bonus. He does not usually travel by road.

As we communicate, the vehicle becomes surrounded by my brethren, fellow Fai united with their daimons, eyes glowing with their spirits' power. My cousin Xipporah is there. She leans a hip on the hood of the car, eyes shooting daggers at the prince.

Von taps the window again, and when Shad refuses to move to lower it, the man's fist punches through, sending shattered glass spraying through the interior. Celena whimpers, still folded over.

Von leans in casually, resting his arms on the jagged glass, ignoring the fact that it cuts into his forearms. I recognize a fellow Fire Fai among those gathered who will be able to heal anyone injured. "Who do we have here?" A sneer twists Von's voice.

"No one you need to be concerned with," Shad says. Von chuckles and raises a brow.

Princess Celena is returned, I tell him. *She was found injured in No Man's Land.*

Von pauses, staring at me now. Then he peers more closely at Celena's curled figure. Faster than an eye blink, his arm shoots out, hand gripping the prince around the neck and squeezing. Joined with his daimon, Von is infinitely stronger than the prince's human form.

Shad gasps and grabs for Von's arm, releasing Celena to scrabble at the hand choking him, trying to pull the man off. The princess pops up, shaking. She screams and lunges for Von as well.

"Stop! Why are you doing this?"

Tears burst from her eyes, something that makes both me and Von freeze. Such a display of emotion from a Nimali—a princess, no less—it's unbelievable. His glowing eyes wide, Von releases Shad, whose wheezes are the only sound for a long, long moment.

Then the shock leaves the Fai man's face and a wide grin replaces it. The smile is slightly feral and Celena sits back, as if trying to get farther away from him.

"Princess Celena. You have returned."

I don't know Von well—he's a few years younger and was part of the Air Corps when I was captured. He must have risen through the ranks, though, if he's leading a raiding party this far into the Independent Zone.

"We haven't formally met before, of course. But the pleasure is all mine." His voice oozes with a counterfeit version of the pomposity the Nimali aristocracy are known for. But the calculating gleam in his eye puts me on alert.

What are you thinking, brother? I ask.

The princess returned much changed, has she not?

It seems she's lost her memory soul. She is not herself.

The man's smile widens. *This is something the GenFi can use.*

Use? How?

"Enemy incoming," Xipporah calls out. Her gaze skims across me without hitching. I wish I could greet her properly, but though we cannot acknowledge one another, it is good to see her again. My heart aches being so close to my people. So close to freedom.

I could open the door now and step out of the vehicle. Be embraced by my brothers and sisters once again. Return to the Greenlands with them and be home. The urge to leave is so strong, it has me actually resting a hand on the car door's handle. Pulling it is all it would take.

And I would be dead by morning.

We will speak again soon, brother, Von says to me. "Without Fail!" he shouts.

"Without Fail!" the other Fai respond in unison, repeating the Genus Fidelis—GenFi—motto and battle cry. Then he rises into the air.

Celena sucks in a breath—of course, she does not recall having seen this before, the power of the Fai. Von's Air daimon, a crow, gifts him the power of flight without having to transform as the Nimali do.

I sigh and release my grip on the door handle, letting my hand fall back to the seat. True freedom remains elusive. For now.

The ground begins to rumble like thunder walking, shaking the vehicle. Von darts away, shouting orders that I don't catch. Other Air Fai rise as well, floating upward and turning to face the oncoming threat. The remaining Fai who surround the car, those who most likely host Land and Water daimons, pull away as well, readying for battle.

My hand tightens into a fist, and the urge to join them and fight is strong. But I push it back.

"W-What's going on?" Celena asks, her voice thin and terrified.

The rumbling grows closer until it is a stampede. I turn to peer out the back window and find that all the noise is caused by a relatively small number of Nimali soldiers. Racing toward us are an elephant, two bears—a grizzly and a polar bear—and a handful of wolves. The screeching cry of a hawk sounds from the sky, and an eagle circles once before diving to meet a female Fai soldier who flies directly toward it.

"What's happening? Shad?" Celena is panicked, turning this way and that in her seat, peering out the windows.

Shad lets out a groan of frustration, then grips the steering wheel tightly and stomps on the gas pedal. The vehicle lurches and picks up speed, racing away just as the fighting begins.

Chapter Five

TALIA

THE JEEP DARTS along the overgrown streets, but I can't get those sounds out of my head. The growls and roars of animals mixed with human shouts and war cries. I press my palms into my eyes and shake my head, willing myself to wake up. What did I do to deserve this as my afterlife? I wasn't religious, never went to church a day in my life, but I was a good person. Kind. Caring. Never cruel, even with all the shit that life threw my way.

I scrub at the tears streaming down my face and curl up on the seat, trying to catch my breath. Trying to make sense of it all.

The glowing eyes. The flying people. The animals attacking.

"Maybe I'm in a coma," I whisper. "This is some kind of fever dream."

Shad skids around a corner and I peek over at him. His face is fierce, and his grip on the steering wheel looks punishing. He pulls out something from a side pocket of his pants. It sort of looks like an old flip phone, but thicker. He taps it, negotiating the streets one handed, and the device glows blue, just like those people's eyes.

I grip the bar on the door, seriously considering opening it and trying to get out. Of course we're driving too fast, but I'm already dead, right? Can I die again? Would that take me somewhere even worse?

"Your Grace?" a voice on the end asks in a clipped tone.

"The princess is safe and we're headed to the Citadel. Where was our air escort? The ground support?" The last sentence is practically shouted.

"The enemy created distractions to the west and south to peel off your guard, sir."

Shad sighs deeply, sounding more pained than angry now. "They will have to deal with the king."

The person on the other end is silent for a long moment. "Yes, Your Grace."

"We're eight minutes out."

"I've doubled the air guard," the voice says. "You will have no further incidents."

"Good." Then he taps the thing again and it fades back to a dull gray color.

Out the window, a number of large birds fly overhead. All my curiosity and wonder about being home—but not home— is gone, leaving behind a sick, cold terror that's infused itself into my bones. I need to get out of here. Is that even possible?

"Your people grow bold, healer," Shad says, peering into the rearview mirror.

I turn to find Ryin staring straight ahead stonily. "You would have them sit idly by while their brothers and sisters are enslaved? While our enemy does its best to destroy us? Your Grace." His affect is flat, but I hear a slight sneer as he uses the honorific.

Twisted around in the seat, I'm suddenly unable to move.

"You're…you're a slave?" Visions of my ancestors in chains fill my mind. Stolen away from their homes to toil and be tortured on this land.

I look to Shad, accusatory.

"He is a prisoner of war," he says tightly. My confusion must show on my face. He scrubs a hand over his head then his shoulders slump.

"Those people who attacked us are Fai—a rival clan. Our clan, the Nimali, and the Fai have long been enemies. Since the Sorrows, however, our conflict has intensified. When your father began his rule, he also began the practice of taking prisoners of war to work as drudges in the Nimali settlement. To demoralize the enemy and weaken them."

I look back at Ryin staring stoically out the windshield. The different clothes and the heaviness of his demeanor make sense now. Demoralized, yes, but weak? I'm not sure. There is a certain defiance to Ryin that shines through the surface-level deference.

I want to apologize, though I haven't had any part of this. And I don't want any part of this. "I need to tell you something—" But the words die in my throat as we turn a corner.

There are lights. And civilization. We've crossed into the Financial District, and it's like a switch has been flipped. One minute we're in the future of the Terminator movies, and then the next block is *almost* like the city I remember.

The buildings here have been rebuilt or restored. Electricity is flowing. Streetlights shine down on quiet, lovely, manicured streets. Darkness has fallen, but there's no fog here. We pass shuttered coffee shops and restaurants and businesses, even a theater. The area comprises just a few blocks and beyond that is darkness, but it's all so recognizable that I spend a little while just taking it all in.

We pull up to one of the city's most iconic locations, the Transamerica Pyramid. It's a tall, narrow pyramid-shaped building that defines the skyline. In front of the building, several blocks have been razed and a large grassy plaza that doesn't exist in my world stretches out. Benches line the sides, and replicas of old-fashioned gas lamps light up the park with blue-tinted light. It's so charming and picturesque that it nearly makes me rethink the whole "being in hell" thing. And then I flash back to the animals screaming.

Shad pulls the jeep up to a circular driveway at the bottom of the tower. Two armored trucks are parked ahead, and soldiers clad in black are stationed outside the front doors.

"This is the Citadel," Shad says, cutting the engine. "This is home."

That snaps me out of it. *This* isn't my home and can't be. He moves to open the door and I grab his arm to stop him. "Shad. I am not Celena. My name is Talia Dubroca, and I realize I must look like your princess, but I promise you I'm not her. I...I didn't know what to do before...I was still a bit shell-shocked back there on the wall. But if she's missing, you should probably keep looking for her. I'm not her."

I'm trying to will belief into him, but his expression grows concerned. He turns to Ryin. "Are you sure you checked her for severe trauma? She didn't have any head wounds?"

I roll my eyes and blow out a breath.

"No, Your Grace," Ryin says without emotion. "Everyone deals with the loss of a memory soul differently. Confusion is often a side effect." He's not looking at me, only Shad.

I take a deep breath, forcing the exasperation to manageable levels. These men aren't listening to me. I probably shouldn't have even gotten in the vehicle, but what other choice did I have? "Listen, I don't know what a memory soul is, but I remember my life just fine. I'm just... not from here," I finish lamely.

"Check her again," Shad bites out. I'm half afraid his forehead is going to get stuck with permanent frown lines because he's scowling so hard.

Ryin bows his head with great patience and closes his eyes. A moment later, when they reopen, they're glowing electric blue. I yelp and jump back, slamming into the dashboard.

His hands are surrounded by the same bright, blue light, and he holds them out toward me, leaning forward between the gap in the seats. I shrink away but he doesn't try to touch me. I feel nothing—no heat or cold or anything else from him. No darts of magic or energy sizzle out from him to me; he just holds his hands out staring with that eerie gaze. Then, he lowers his hands and leans back. His eyes close, and when they open, they're normal again; dark brown and filled with sadness.

"No head trauma. No other injuries. But..." He frowns deeply.

"But what?" Shad asks.

"Older injuries. Ones that must have been healed during her disappearance. I fear she was..." He swallows and looks directly at me, expression laced with pity. "I fear she was tortured. Her arm was broken, and there are other scars."

Shad's fists tighten. "But daimon healing leaves no scars."

"I know. I cannot explain it."

Both men gaze at me, and I wonder if they will finally believe. Confusion tangled with dread is all I sense from Shad. Ryin is still implacable. If there was pity there before, it's gone now.

"Leave us, healer." Shad's voice is clipped.

Ryin exits the car without a word and goes to stand several feet away. I turn back to Shad, whose gaze is thoughtful. "You truly are not Celena?" he asks, and hope flickers to life within me.

"I promise you I'm not. I remember my entire life. I...I died, and then I found myself here and was attacked by that... thing out there with the red eyes."

He takes a deep breath and rubs a hand over his face. His

eyes close for a long moment. When they open, determination shines in them. "You can't tell anyone else."

"What?"

A tap at his window makes me jump. A young Asian man in the black soldier's uniform stands there. Shad holds up a finger indicating the man should wait and lowers his voice to an insistent whisper.

"Tell no one. You must be Celena for now. It is the only way you will survive. I will explain more as soon as I can." Then he opens his door and is gone.

My door opens too and another soldier is there, an older dark-haired man whose eyes widen when I turn to him. He takes a step back, then bows, and offers me a hand to help me exit the vehicle.

"Your Grace," he says reverently. "Welcome home."

Shad comes around to stand next to me. I search for Ryin and find him a dozen steps away, arms clasped behind him.

"The king is inbound," one of the soldiers says to Shad, who nods.

"Come," he tells me. "We cannot keep him waiting."

I shake my head, unwilling to keep on with this ruse. Surely this Celena's own father will know I'm not his daughter. "Shad, listen—"

A roar rings out overhead, drowning out my words. I drop to the ground and crunch into a ball. Another attack? Shad is by my side, reassuring me. He grips my arm gently, telling me to look up. My ears are ringing and I don't want to, but his calm demeanor edges into my panic and curiosity wins out. I look up.

All the lights around the plaza leave the sky illuminated, so it's not hard to make out the beating of huge wings circling the towering building. A monster, a gigantic beast, flies overhead and lets out another cry.

It grows closer, the flapping of its wings and the tornado

they almost create seeming familiar. As it descends, I'm able to make out the animal's features and my mouth goes dry.

I sit on the blacktop of the driveway, staring up, mouth hanging open. It takes a second to find my voice and when I do, it's just a croak.

"Is...is that a dragon?"

Chapter Six

TALIA

EVERYONE IS REMARKABLY calm about seeing an actual dragon flying around the airspace of a major American city. However, my muscles are leaden and my blood has turned to wood. The dragon glides down to land on the grass of the plaza, the ground shuddering slightly beneath its staggering weight.

The creature is red and gold, its iridescent scales catching the glow from the street lamps. Two large, spiky horns run the length of its head, with smaller protuberances running down its face. Golden eyes blink once and then a bright blue light flashes, blinding me momentarily. A sort of sulfurous smell, like when you strike a match, blasts my nose but then is gone quickly.

When I can see again, the dragon has disappeared and a man dressed in red stands in its place. I blink, eyes adjusting after that bright flash. When he steps forward across the grass, I nearly lose my shit.

"Dad?" I say, eyes so round they almost hurt. My father smiles at me so warmly. Like he's overjoyed to see me. And that's how I know he isn't my father.

Rows of soldiers have suddenly appeared on the plaza. They are saluting, fingers on their chins, and Ryin is kneeling, and Shad is bowing, and I'm staring. At my dad. Who is not my dad.

He's of average height, about five-foot-nine—still half a foot taller than me—and he stands straight and proud, eyes shining with love. His complexion is the color of oak wood with golden undertones, and his hair is cropped much shorter than I've ever seen it before. Gone are the carefully coiffed waves he kept in place with a can of sticky pomade he forbade anyone else to ever touch. His mustache is the same, thick and neatly trimmed but now with a few gray hairs showing. He's dressed in a crimson version of the same uniform Shad and the other soldiers wear.

He steps to me, arms open and reaching, his face filled with joy, and I walk over blindly, not caring that this man was a dragon a moment ago. Not caring about anything else than this crazy impossibility that my father actually wants to hug me.

"Celena, my girl," he says, wrapping me in warm arms. I even ignore that name and that this embrace was meant for another. He smells of night air and fog and something coppery and tangy. Something I push out of my mind because his arms are tight and warm and squeezing me like his life depends on it.

"Dad," I repeat, a little guilty. My resolve to be done with this ruse crumbles to ash as he squeezes me tighter.

After the longest hug in the world, he finally pulls away and looks me over with tears in his eyes. "My little girl. Words cannot express how much I've missed you."

My heart thumps rapidly, joy and wonder flooding my veins. I'm still thinking of something to say when he turns away. "Shadrach, report," he says, voice full of authority and command.

Shad straightens. "King Lyall. As I relayed, we found the princess across the wall. She'd been attacked by a Revoker."

The king's eyes sharpen and harden. He takes another look at me and then turns me around as a growl rattles from his chest. Everyone nearby tenses as the sound grows louder.

"I'm okay. I'm fine now," I rush to reassure him, alarmed by the sound.

"The healer removed the poison and knit her wounds. He assures me that she is otherwise unharmed." Shad's voice is tight. I'm glad he omitted the mention of possible torture. I don't think this Dad would react to that well. "Aside from her memory soul, of course."

"And the Revoker who dared to injure my daughter?"

"I burned it myself."

The king narrows his eyes at this, and a strange tension hums between them. Shad continues. "I left two of my best men there to comb the area and sent a team of trackers to find out where the princess came from." Shad's manner is oddly detached and formal, especially since my father is apparently his stepfather. But King Lyall doesn't seem to have any sort of paternal affection for him, either. The whole situation is so strange and strained.

Lyall stares Shad down, more like he's an enemy than a family member, before turning back to me, his expression instantly softening. "You don't recall anything of where you've been, what could have happened?"

My gaze involuntarily shoots to Shad, whose lips thin as he stares at me. I recall his words. *You must be Celena for now.* Pretend to be a princess, enjoy the warm and loving father I never knew. It's like a dream, or at least it could be. But it isn't real.

I catch a glimpse of Ryin through the ring of soldiers surrounding us. His face is grim, but his attention is on me as well. How can I stay here as a royal in a world and society that enslaves its enemies? I have to tell the truth.

Just as I turn back to the man who looks like my father, shouts rise from down the plaza. The soldiers tighten around me and Lyall whips his gaze around. I can't see anything because I'm shorter than just about everyone, but booted feet march closer and the shouts and pleas grow louder as well.

"Please! Don't!" a woman cries. "No, I've done nothing wrong!"

Apparently, the men and women around me have determined that the threat is low, so the knot of protection loosens to the point that I can now see what the fuss is. Six soldiers frog march two handcuffed people, a middle-aged man and woman. The pale woman wears a dark brown version of what Ryin has on. Her salt and pepper hair is in a bun and her shouts cease when she catches sight of the king. The captive man has deep brown skin and a long, scraggly beard. He's emaciated, with sharp cheekbones and sunken eyes, and is dressed in layers of rags. The group draws to a halt in front of us.

"Captain, report," Lyall barks.

A flinty-eyed woman in black steps forward and bows precisely. "Your Majesty. This one was found scavenging in the waste receptacles." She jerks a thumb at the obviously malnourished man. "And we caught this one giving him food." She motions to the woman in brown, who begins whimpering and shaking her head.

The starving man's dull eyes stare only at the ground. He hangs limply between the two soldiers on either side of him, like he would collapse if they released him.

The king takes a step forward. "You are an exile, are you not?" he asks the man, who doesn't respond. Lyall sniffs and then focuses his gaze on the woman. His back is to me, so I can't see his face, but judging by her expression of abject terror, maybe that's for the best.

"And you. Sharing resources with an outsider. What would

impel you to commit such a crime?" His tone is neutral, the query almost casual.

The woman's jaw quivers, but she visibly composes herself. "H-He was my sister's husband. And a good friend. Before." Her head lowers, but Lyall draws closer and tilts it up with a finger to her chin.

"A good friend and a criminal exiled for just cause. Breaking these ties is difficult, I understand, but necessary." His hand drops from her face, and she exhales in visible relief.

Lyall turns and begins walking back toward me with a contemplative look on his face. My body is drawn tight like I'm ready to run at any moment. Tension thrums through me and a cold wind picks up, reminding me that I'm just in a thin hospital gown. Just as a shiver raises goosebumps all over my skin, Lyall turns around again.

"You were taking them to the locker?" he asks.

The captain nods. "Yes, Your Majesty."

"No need. Let us dispense with justice right now. The penalty for an exile returning to Nimali territory for any reason is death. And just to prove that I am not the heartless king you think me to be," he addresses this to the woman, "*you* may carry out the sentence in my stead."

My stomach drops away. How is that not heartless?

Her eyes widen, and she shakes her head. "Your Majesty, I've done nothing wrong. I took nothing from anyone else. I shared only my own food with him. I've stolen nothing."

"You have broken the law. That food was not yours to give, it does not belong to you—it was merely given to you for your use. Nimali struggled and suffered to create the food you so carelessly give to an outsider. It is only for Nimali, and this man is no longer one of us."

The man in question hasn't moved this whole time. He stares at the ground in obvious defeat. The woman, however, is now trembling where she stands and continues shaking her head.

"I cannot kill him. It…it would b-break my covenant. My daimon would abandon me."

The king tilts his head. "Not necessarily. The covenant forbids the killing of those who are not actively harming you, but I assure you, this exile is harming you and every other Nimali. Scavengers, outsiders, threaten our entire way of life; they steal our vital resources. If we allow this sort of anarchy to persist, we would still be scrabbling our way back to civilization as we did after the Sorrows. Your daimon may interpret the law as mine does, and if so, your covenant with it will remain intact."

She's still refusing, even trying to back away, but with the soldiers holding her, she has nowhere to go.

The king smiles. He's half facing me so I can see the expression, and it chills me even further.

"My ruling has been given," he says, speaking just as pleasantly as he has this entire time. "Carry out the sentence I have ordered, or face my wrath. My covenant demands I be obeyed, and you are well aware of the punishment for disobedience." His eyes are diamond sharp and deadly. The woman's quaking intensifies.

I actually take a step back, but Shad is there at my side. He grabs my arm, holding me steady. He lends warmth to my chilled body, but it doesn't penetrate.

I want to call out and try to stop this, but the words die in my throat. I know less than nothing about this world and what goes on here. I have no idea what this covenant is they're talking about, but the idea of crossing the king locks up all of my muscles. This man is a dragon, after all. Polite voice and loving hugs aside, the dread of the prisoner and taut wariness of the gathered soldiers all point to a man that should not be crossed.

The captured woman lowers her head. Tears stream down her face and her entire body is racked with sobs. My heart goes out to her.

Lyall crosses his arms over his chest and plants his feet. No one else moves.

"I...I have no way to do it," she finally says, holding up her bound wrists. Defeat is evident in the slump of her shoulders, the softness of her voice.

"Captain, a knife."

The soldier produces a long knife from the belt of her uniform. So they *do* have weapons, though these look more utilitarian than those meant for combat. She hands the blade to the woman, who reluctantly grips it.

"Your Majesty, please. Hasn't he suffered enough? Please don't make me do this."

The king merely stares. The soldiers holding the woman push her forward. She stumbles on the flattened grass and approaches the exiled man, whose head is still lowered.

Then he raises his head and nods slowly at her. It's the only evidence that he's been aware of what's happening.

My belly churns. I haven't had solid food in longer than I can remember, but whatever's in my stomach feels ready to come up. Tears stream down my face as the woman's sobs begin again. Her hold on the knife is so tenuous that I'm afraid she will drop it. But she swallows and her grip tightens. With a cry, she slashes out. I shut my eyes tightly and bury my face in Shad's arm.

A soft thud sounds as a body hits the ground. The woman wails, heart-wrenching cries that speak of misery.

Then she stops so suddenly it's jarring. A bright glow lights up even the darkness behind my eyelids. I open my eyes and gasp.

The woman's head is thrown back. She's caught in a silent scream as light shoots out of her mouth and ears and eyes. It's something from a horror movie, like she was possessed and then exorcised. Then it's over and she slumps to the ground boneless. I think she's dead until a moan rises from her crumpled form.

The soldiers pick her up again none too gently. The dead man's blood pools at their feet.

"I suppose you were right after all," Lyall says, dropping his arms. "Your covenant is broken. You are Nimali no more. Exile is your punishment. If you are caught in Nimali territory pilfering any of our resources, you will be killed." All of this is said in a matter-of-fact voice that holds no malice; he almost sounds bored.

He motions to the captain and she and two other soldiers march away, the woman in tow. "Clean this up," he orders to no one in particular with a wave of his hand. Then he faces me again.

I'm still plastered to Shad's side, unwilling to leave, ever.

Lyall frowns at my reaction. "Celena, are you well?" He takes a step forward and I shrink further into Shad.

"Oh my dear girl." His eyes are liquid pools of concern as he stalks forward and plucks me away from the prince, wrapping me in an embrace that I don't want. "Without your memory I understand that what you saw must have been a shock. But I assure you, it was very necessary. Our way of life is in constant peril and must be protected at all costs. It is not always a pleasant task, but as king I must make many difficult decisions. Your memory will return when you leash a daimon, but until then, you have much to relearn. Just trust that I do all of this for our well-being. To protect the territory that you will one day rule."

He pulls away, and I'm glad of it. There was something too warm, too comfortable in his hug. Something my traitorous heart is nearly willing to ignore atrocities in order to feel.

"Your memory may be gone," he says, "but I know that I saw recognition in your eyes. Earlier, when I first arrived."

I swallow and blink, clearing my mind. What to tell him? What is the safest thing to say? "It's true. You're...familiar. But

I don't know anything about my life or...or this world." I refrain from staring at the dead man being dragged away.

"You have a strong heart, my girl. And your souls are mighty as well. Whatever ordeal you have faced will only make you stronger. For you are my daughter and there is nothing you cannot overcome."

His words cause fresh tears to come to my eyes. He is so sincere and so full of love and admiration. Those words coming from that face—familiar but utterly foreign. My mind is a jumble. In some ways, this is everything I've ever longed for during lonely evenings seated at the edge of the couch while a happy family of four chats about their day. But the scent of blood still fills the air. The woman's screams ring in my ears. Exiled for feeding a family member.

There's obviously no way to tell this man, this king, that I'm an imposter. An outsider, not one of his beloved Nimali, and not his treasured daughter. But continuing this deception...it could be even more dangerous.

You must be Celena for now. It is the only way you will survive.

I'm in an impossible situation. The truth will likely kill me, but the lie—how can I pull it off?

I turn to Shad, who stares at the blood pooling on the grass with a pinched expression. Ryin still stands several feet away. His face is carefully clear, but for a moment there, just a split second really, I catch a glimpse of something he can't contain. A tear in the fabric of a mask that conceals pure hatred.

In an instant the expression is gone, the rip repaired, but the memory reverberates through me. If I do this, if I play along, then I'm complicit. I'll be a part of the suffering of Ryin and every other Fai "prisoner of war" held by the Nimali. Of the exiles and those punished for reasons I don't really understand.

I will be a part of it and that hatred he feels will be for me too. And I'll deserve it.

Chapter Seven

RYIN

THE ECHOES of the Nimali woman's screams still resound across the plaza. My hands curl into fists. The struggle to play the part of the obedient servant is difficult on a good day. When I have to face the barbarian king, it's nearly impossible.

In my head, I repeat to myself what's at stake if I lose my temper. If I burst forward on my daimon's power and try to rip his vile throat out. The personal cost is one I would bear if it didn't also mean a cost for my people, both those locked here in the Citadel and back home in the Greenlands.

So I bite my tongue until it's bloody and make an unholy effort to keep the rage from my face. I think the princess sees it, though. Her eyes round and her gaze darts away. This timid, strange creature who returned from across the wall is mysterious.

What happened to her out there? When she first disappeared, the Fai were blamed, of course. All the drudges in the entire building were lined up and questioned. Two were trammeled for nothing, just as a way for our captors to flex their power over us. To remind us what happens if we go astray.

Then a scrap of her clothing was found near one of the mines —a place no Fai in their right mind would dare tread—and the investigation was refocused.

But lost princesses aren't my concern. And the outrage that flared when I realized she must have been tortured has no place here. It was likely an echo of my daimon's pity. Its sympathy radiates down the bond we share, twisting my emotions. No Nimali would care if a Fai were brutalized. I must harden my heart against her.

King Lyall clutches his daughter close to him in a one-armed embrace. She looks awkward and uncomfortable there. Of course to her, this man is a stranger. A cadre of royal retainers in their crimson uniforms have joined him on the plaza, bowing and scraping when they arrive.

"Now that that unpleasantness is over," the king says, as if he wasn't the cause of the *unpleasantness*, "we will celebrate. Let it be known to all, tonight, at the tenth hour, every man, woman, and child in the territory will gather on the plaza to welcome my daughter back home. My greatest treasure is back where she belongs and we will all rejoice."

Cheering commences, and my teeth gnash. When it ends, some signal for dismissal has been given. The soldiers and retinue retreat back toward the Citadel. I'm not sure if I'm dismissed as well, but Prince Shad catches my eye and motions me to stay.

Soon it is just the four of us—the king, princess, prince, and me—alone on the grassy lawn, though a dozen soldiers stand just out of earshot. Unease tightens my skin, but I stand tall at attention, clearing any emotion from my mind or expression.

"Healer," the king says, his gruff voice turning up the temperature of my blood. "You will be assigned to Celena for the foreseeable future. I do not want her taking a step without you there behind her. We do not know what was done to her or by whom, and her health and well-being are of the utmost import, so you will be her *shadow*." A cruel smile plays upon his lips at that last word, and my heart clenches.

Celena turns to her father. "Is this really necessary? I feel perfectly well. I'm sure others will have need of a healer."

The king sends a kind smile her way. "Dear girl, there are slow-acting poisons and other insidious inventions that can be injected and released into the bloodstream, timed to attack at a later date." The blood drains from her brown skin, leaving her looking ashen.

"I would not leave you at the mercy of these unknown villains, so until we know exactly who took you and what their agenda was, your health and safety is my highest priority." She nods, appearing shaken.

The king's dark eyes pierce me. I meet his gaze, holding back the fire licking through me that wants to incinerate him. "If she so much as suffers from the prick of a thumbtack, I will have you trammeled so quickly, your mind will be mush inside your skull and you will spend the rest of your life mining bliss with the other puppets. Do you understand me, Fai?"

I unclench my jaw. "Yes, Your Majesty."

Next to him, Celena's complexion turns even more wan, a grayish tinge reminiscent of when she was unconscious. She appears rigid in her father's hold, her shoulders nearly reaching her ears.

"You must be tired, dear one," the king says to her. "Why don't you go to your rooms and rest?" It's amazing how quickly his normally icy demeanor defrosts when he speaks to her.

He's a glacier again when he looks up. "Have food brought to her. And Shadrach, you stay. I want a detailed debrief."

The prince bows. King Lyall embraces his daughter once more then walks away without another glance, toward the Citadel, with Shad on his heels.

The princess blinks several times, then visibly pulls herself together, color returning to her skin. She meets my eye and gives a brief, watery smile. I motion with my arm to the building; protocol dictates that I follow at least three steps behind. Celena squares her shoulders, appearing to gather her strength before moving forward.

The back of her odd clothing is blood stained and ripped from the Revoker's claws, but she still manages to look regal, although still somehow different than before. She was always a quiet, cold beauty living in the shadow of her father's vicious cruelty. But she had never *reacted* to it. I can't recall seeing her flinch or recoil at his harsh statements or the quick changes in his demeanor. Perhaps that was a skill built up over many years and without her memory it will take more practice to renew.

It doesn't matter anyway; the princess is not my concern. But having to follow her around every waking moment for the foreseeable future definitely puts a wrench into my plans. My duties for the GenFi will have to shift. I have no idea how the princess spends her days, but I'll no longer be able to monitor the soldiers now.

We pass the support columns of the building and the guards stationed at the front doors open them and usher the princess through. She marches, head high, across the narrow lobby and toward the elevator bank. More soldiers line the space, another reason that this building is so defensible. It not only houses the royals and most Nimali aristocrats, but it is also the military center of their territory as well.

At the elevators, Celena hesitates. She clasps her hands in front of her so tightly her fingernails change from pink to white. Her anxiety is bleeding through, but I don't understand the cause. She clears her throat. "I, ah…I don't know where we're going." Her voice shakes.

"Only these two go all the way up, Your Grace." One of the two soldiers before her motions to the last two cars at the end of the short hallway. He presses the call button and the doors immediately slide open.

"Could we take the stairs? I'm sure I could use some exercise." The soldiers share a startled glance, their surprise almost comical. "There are stairs in the building, right?" Celena asks, hope lifting her tone.

The taller man recovers quickly. "Yes, Your Grace. But they are generally used by the drudges. Besides, your apartment takes up the entirety of the forty-sixth floor."

Her shoulders collapse. Warily, she walks into the elevator car. The pair of soldiers enter behind her and I follow. I'm nearest to the panel and press the button labeled forty-six.

The car rattles as it climbs and Celena gasps slightly, then clutches the bar behind her in an iron grip. The soldiers eye her curiously but do not comment. She is afraid. The realization comes over me suddenly. But why would she fear an elevator?

Moments later, the doors open revealing a short, brightly lit hallway ending in a door guarded by two more soldiers. They come to attention as Celena leads the way out of the elevator, which soon takes the other two guards away. The princess's steps are slow and uncertain, but there are no other visible doors on this level.

She stops before the soldiers and nods at them, then stares at the door for a long, awkward moment. Does she not even remember how to operate a door? Her memory can't be that incomplete—she can still walk and talk and seems to have retained her intelligence. None of the memory drudges has shown this level of loss.

"Your Grace?" the steely-haired woman on the left says, brows politely raised.

"There's no doorknob." Celena waves a hand at the smooth panel, inset into the wall much the same way the elevator doors are.

The guard motions to the circular indentation to the right

of the door, about waist high. "It's a sensor. Place your palm there and it will open. You control access to your suite." Her voice is patient, but the other guard, a rangy man, narrows his eyes at the princess.

Celena smiles. "Thank you so much." Both blink at her, and even I jerk at the display of gratitude.

She tentatively touches her hand to the sensor, then startles when it turns blue and the door slides open. She chuckles, then turns to me with a brilliant smile on her face. It's the unfettered glee of a child who's discovered a hidden trove of candy, and it does strange things to my chest. Her expression falls quickly when I don't respond. Something catches within me as she turns away.

I follow her into her suite, nearly bumping into her before the door slides shut behind me. She's stopped just at the threshold, staring at the sitting room.

The princess's suite of rooms is opulent in true Nimali style. A patchwork quilt of rugs of varying sizes, colors, and patterns cover the floor. Furniture of all kinds fills the space: There are half a dozen couches, even more love seats, armchairs, recliners, and other seating of different sizes and materials, along with console tables, coffee tables, end tables, and a long twelve-person dining table along the far wall.

The walls themselves are covered with artwork: paintings, photographs, posters, mirrors, sculptures trapped in glass. The Nimali love excess, and the aristocracy loves it more than the rest.

Celena turns in a full circle. "It looks like a furniture store vomited its warehouse in here."

I can't help but smile at the sentiment, because her voice drips with disgust. She turns to face me, her expression horrified. I try to smooth my face, but she's so comical I can't help the curve of my lips. Then she shakes her head and begins to laugh.

"This is the most hideous, cluttered thing I've ever seen. Is my taste *that* bad?"

The truth would probably get me trammeled, so I stay quiet, but inside I'm laughing as well.

"I mean, that's an orange mid-century modern sofa next to a pair of Louis XIV red upholstered armchairs. My eyes!" She covers her eyes with her hands dramatically and shakes her head.

When she drops her hands, she's still smiling. I get myself under control and flatten my lips. I think she looks disappointed, but I can't be sure.

"Do you know where all of this came from?" she asks.

"Most of it was salvaged from different parts of the city."

"I guess that makes sense."

"Pre-Sorrows furniture is a status symbol for the aristocracy." I didn't need to add that...maybe it's my daimon's sympathy bleeding through again.

"What exactly are the Sorrows? People keep talking about them, but I don't understand what they were."

"They were the end of the world. Are you hungry?" I'm not here to answer all of her questions and the king ordered that she be fed, so even if she has no desire for it, I'm duty bound to at least request food. I ignore her startled expression at the abrupt change in topic and cross the room, moving to where the servant's door is hidden. I press my hand on the sensor, then tap the pattern to call Noomi.

"Um, I guess I could eat. But I can get it myself if you just show me where."

I turn at that, but her focus is on the walls, staring at the vintage movie posters and formerly priceless artwork liberated from museums around the city after the Sorrows.

The servant's door slides open and my cousin Noomi is there, arms clasped before her. Celena spins around then comes over, picking her way carefully through the maze of furniture.

"Hello," she says, a bit uncertain. Noomi is stunned. Her eyes slide to me, brows raised. She tilts her head as if to say, *It's true?* I nod.

"This is Noomi, she's the drudge assigned to your suite."

"Hi Noomi, it's so nice to meet you. I mean, I'm sure we've met before, but I don't remember, so it's like meeting you for the first time."

Noomi's eyes just grow wider and wider. Celena blinks and then looks chagrined. "Sorry for the word vomit, I just want you to know I'm grateful to you for all your help—in the past and the future, I guess."

I'm worried Noomi might faint on the spot and so I step in. "You must have lost your whistle, Your Grace." At this, Noomi shakes off the stunned expression and digs into her apron pocket to retrieve a whistle. "This is how you call her."

Celena looks horrified. "A whistle? Like for a dog? Absolutely not." She actually takes a step back from Noomi's outstretched hand.

I look back and forth between the two women. "It's how the Nimali call the drudges."

"I don't like that word, either. I know cooking and cleaning and all that definitely feels like drudgery, but you're a person." She shakes her head.

Noomi's confusion has turned to fear. She pleads at me with her eyes.

"All Nimali use the whistles," I say simply, not sure how else to explain it. "If you don't…We will be punished." Noomi shoots me a fear-filled glance.

Celena catches it and takes a deep breath. She holds it for several seconds before letting it out in a gush. "Is that what you really want? For me to use that thing to call you?"

Noomi nods her assent, and Celena's brows lower. "Do you not speak?"

"She doesn't. She can't."

"Oh." Celena looks again at the whistle on the delicate

silver chain in Noomi's palm and finally takes it. Noomi's shoulders sag with relief.

Thank you, my cousin signs to me. At that, Celena perks up. "You use sign language?"

I nod briefly and she lights up, her smile knocking me back a step again. "Oh good, you can teach me. How do I say, *Hello, it's nice to meet you*?"

I'm sure Noomi and I wear identical looks of confusion. "She can hear you just fine, Your Grace."

"Oh, yes, of course. I know. But then how will I understand what she says to me?"

"What she says to you?" I blink, not connecting the dots.

"How can we only have one-sided conversations?"

"She's your drudge. You tell her what to do and she does it. The Nimali do not converse with their drudges."

Celena swallows, a stricken expression coming across her face. She turns to Noomi, her gaze sorrowful and pitying. "Is that how I treated you before?"

Noomi is frozen, likely unsure what response is best and how to deal with the woman the princess has become. For her part, Celena seems at a loss for words, shaking her head and staring down at her hands.

Finally, she finds her voice. "I'm so sorry for that. I suppose my recent experiences—whatever they were—have changed me. But you're a human being, not a *drudge*." She makes a face like the word tastes bad. "I'm sure you work hard and you don't deserve to be treated like a dog or a silent beast of burden. It isn't right."

Noomi tilts her head, peering at Celena through soft eyes for a long while. *Hello, it's nice to meet you*, she signs.

Celena blinks, then looks at me. I repeat the signs, speaking them aloud at the same time. The princess radiates happiness as she repeats the movements, working to commit them to memory.

"Now, how do I say, 'I'm hungry and would love something to eat'?"

I haven't seen hope in Noomi's eyes for years, not since her voice was taken away and she was conscribed into service in the Citadel. But as Princess Celena stretches and curls her fingers, taking the time to learn a few phrases in the language of the Fai voice drudges, a light begins to glow in my cousin's eyes. And though I don't want it to, though I lost the ability to truly hope a long time ago, a spark of it comes to life within my own chest.

Chapter Eight

TALIA

THERE ARE NO WINDOWS HERE. At least not in my apartment. There's plenty of light coming down from globes on the ceiling, all of it with that blue tinge that everything here seems to have, but there's no fresh air or natural light. Which is odd because the outside of the building is entirely made up of windows. There must be hundreds of them, but so far, they all seem to be covered over and blocked by walls on the inside. Still, I don't feel the terror of being suffocated to death like I did in the elevator. The space is big and bright and though it's cluttered, I have room to breathe.

I perch at the head of the enormous dining table while Ryin sits a few feet away in a very uncomfortable looking plain, wooden chair in the corner. I tell him he can sit at the table and keep me company, but he gives me a look that politely indicates he thinks I'm a mental patient. Noomi disappears and returns a short while later with a covered tray.

The idea of being served by her still rankles, especially since I know she has no choice in the matter. While it's hard for me to even imagine that type of slavery, the work of a drudge is something I know all too well.

My stepmother wasn't evil, but once she gave birth to her twins, she had little time or energy for a grieving eight-year-old. My dad wasn't the father of her babies. He was just the man who fell in love with a pregnant woman running from an abusive ex and agreed to raise her children as his own. Some would view him as a hero. Those people wouldn't include the biological daughter whose mother he'd abandoned before she was born.

But I'd had nowhere else to go and so I made the best of it. Tried to fit in and help out and not be a burden. I changed diapers and heated bottles. Cleaned up, learned to cook, doing anything and everything I could to be useful. To be accepted. But none of it could make me fit. I was the square peg in their neat little round holes. My father's caramel skin tone was not light enough for him to pass for white, but all the same, no one seemed to question his status as the father of my pale, blue-eyed stepsisters. Framed with their tall, equally pale and blue-eyed mother, they were quite the picture. In our family photos, I was always off to the side, an afterthought. People mistook me for the nanny or the maid, and some days I felt like that's all I was good for in that family.

The smell of food brings me back to the present and makes my stomach rumble. Noomi uncovers the tray, and I freeze, not recognizing anything on the plate. But, hungry as I am, I'm willing to try anything. The pink cubes with the consistency of tofu taste sort of like corn. A long, purple, rectangular mass that's oddly Jell-O-like reminds me of a fish-textured chicken. It's all edible, hopefully nutritious, but so, so strange. The bowl of little gray pellets looks the least appetizing, but it turns out to be the most tasty. Sweet and crunchy, I'm tempted to ask for more, but I'm actually pretty full right now.

"What time is it?" I ask once the dishes are cleared away.

"Half past the eighth hour," Ryin responds.

"How do you know that? Is there a clock somewhere?" I look around and find several on the wall, but none of them actually work.

"The Fai have an internal sense of time."

"Must be nice. I'm always running late."

His brows descend, and I realize I've revealed having some knowledge of myself, of my past. Ice fills my veins, but Ryin doesn't make any mention of my slip, and I press my lips shut. I need to be Celena or else face the king's wrath, only I have no idea how to be her. Everyone assuming I've lost my memory soul helps, but I'm not sure that will be enough to really pull this off. I need more information. I need to talk to Shad.

A ringing bell, soft and musical, startles me. I turn to Ryin, a question in my gaze. He doesn't speak, merely rises and crosses over to the front door of the suite. His movements are graceful and liquid but manage to hold a swagger even as he's dodging armchairs and end tables. I'm unable to look away. Until now he's always been behind me, so I haven't yet gotten a chance to ever watch him walk and it's...I blink and tear my gaze away, feeling guilty for ogling him.

At the entrance to the suite, he must press some hidden button because the door slides open. His broad shoulders block the doorway, preventing me from seeing who's on the other side.

"The princess will require a new comm, Your Grace," Ryin says, voice and manner stiff. Then he turns around, heading back to his seat. Behind him, people begin to stream into the room, Shad at the lead—exactly the person I need to talk to.

He's changed into a red outfit, similar to the one he wore earlier. Three women in flowing, glittering dark blue dresses and a young man in a lighter blue outfit follow him. They stay on the far side of the living room, but Shad crosses over to the dining table. "How are you doing? Have you eaten?" he asks, concerned. Deep lines frame his eyes—worry lines. He's only got a couple of years on me, but his eyes look older, like he's seen too much already.

"Yes, I stuffed myself. And I feel fine." I offer a tentative smile and he nods.

"This is Filomena, your personal stylist, and her staff." He waves behind him and the women bow. Filomena is in her fifties, with sharp cheekbones and a severe bob. The two other women are twins, slightly younger, and curvy with chestnut hair. The thin, dark-skinned guy looks like he might still be a teenager. All stare openly at me, making me self-conscious.

"They're going to get you ready for the evening's reception," Shad adds.

I nod wordlessly and the four of them disappear around a corner. I crane my neck to see where they're headed.

"Have you explored your suite yet?" Shad asks. I shake my head. "Well, let me show you around." He extends his arm like he's going to lead me across a Victorian ballroom and I take it. But I throw a glance over my shoulder at Ryin, who's still in that hard-backed chair, face impassive. He doesn't look like he's inclined to move anytime soon.

As soon as we turn the corner and are out of earshot, I drag him down the hallway. "You said you would explain," I whisper. "I need some answers. I don't think I can pull this off."

Shad looks around us warily, then gently wraps a hand around my wrist and raises my palm to an indentation in the wall. A door I didn't even realize was there slides open and he tugs me inside. This must be Celena's bedroom, all done in grays and pewters and thankfully holding the normal amount of furniture a bedroom should.

He takes a few steps into the room then sighs. "We don't have much time, and honestly there isn't much to tell. Do you have any idea how you got here?"

"No." I relay to him what I do remember: waking up in the hospital. Dying again. Flying through the air and then being attacked by that red-eyed creature. "You know the rest."

He places a hand against one of the upholstered armchairs near the door and leans on it. "I've never heard of anything like that. Maybe it was a spirit summons or some kind of new use of the bliss." His brow is furrowed in confusion, and my heart sinks. "We can try to figure it out—I have some ideas on ways to research. Once we know how and why you got here, we can hopefully find a way to send you back— but only if you're alive."

I swallow. Go back? I nearly snort. Back to what, to death? To the afterlife I should have had? But I stay quiet. "So your idea is for me to just pretend to be her until we figure this out? I don't think I can."

He comes toward me, arms outstretched, and places warm hands on my shoulder. I never had a big brother, but I think he'd make a good one.

"You've seen what the king is capable of. Things here are much worse than you know. The Nimali and the Fai have been locked in a cold war for years. Celena's disappearance nearly ignited a full-scale military conflict. At first, we thought they'd taken her."

"The Fai?"

He nods. "But all evidence disputes that. Whatever happened to her, if she went across the wall, she's almost certainly dead. She didn't have a daimon to protect her. Your presence just might be the thing we need for peace."

"I don't understand."

"There isn't time now to explain. But Lyall listens to his daughter. She can exert influence on him. You can give me time to work to avoid this war. To save thousands of lives. Is that something you're willing to do?"

My mouth opens then closes. "Of-of course. If I can. But you're a prince, can't you influence him too?"

"Celena is the king's daughter. I am family by adoption and...marriage." The pause before the last word leaves me with questions, but Shad is closed up tight and I sense that topic is painful. And no one has mentioned a queen.

"Is my mother...?" I can't bring myself to finish the sentence.

"She passed into the Origin when Celena was young."

I swallow and nod. I hadn't really hoped.

"My mother is gone too," he adds.

I take a deep breath. "So, I pretend to be her. And influence him...to do what?"

"He's distracted with your return. He will want to spend some time with you, ensure himself of your well-being. That's enough for now."

"And what will you be doing?"

He turns toward the door. "I must get you to the stylists. You'll need to look like her for tonight's celebration."

His avoidance of my question feels significant somehow.

"My life is in your hands, too," he adds, before stepping toward the door. I nod. Either one of us could out the other to Lyall, who doesn't seem like the merciful sort.

We're back in the hallway and crossing to the other end. Shad leads me into what looks like a mini beauty salon. All of the stylists are here looking busy, stacking creams and powders and warming up curling irons.

Shad stays in the doorway. "I'll be back to escort you to the event," he says. Then he gives me a short bow and retreats.

"Right here, Your Grace," Filomena calls out, beckoning me toward the plush chair. "Let's get you all fixed up for your welcome home celebration."

I sit and she flicks a cape around my neck. Then she pauses, staring at my hair. "Who did these braids, I wonder?"

I almost tell her I did but keep my lips pressed shut. From her tone I assume Celena didn't know how to braid—doesn't seem very princess-like, I guess. But Filomena doesn't linger on the topic; she just gets to work unbraiding then washing, drying, straightening, and curling my hair.

All the while, the same words repeat in my head over and over again: *What would Celena do?*

I'm tempted to ask the stylists about her—me—but they're maddeningly quiet. They don't chatter and gossip like at the salon back home. Everyone is respectful and professional, but it's so sterile that my teeth are set on edge.

While Filomena works on my hair, one of the twins gives me a manicure while the other attends to my pedicure. Then they start on my makeup. After that, I'm handed off to the young man in charge of wardrobe. We head to the giant walk-in closet, which takes up a space approximately the size of the bedroom and has racks and racks of clothing all in shades of red.

This must be Celena's favorite color, though it's not mine. Of course, neither is this life, and I sigh as the kid leads me to where he's selected several gowns for me to choose from. One is sort of a bloodred color, but still gorgeous. I reach out to touch a fabric that doesn't exist back home. It's soft and strong, velvety and satiny at the same time. So strange, but it feels like butter against my skin.

"Do you like any of these, Your Grace?" The kid's voice barely rises above a whisper. I have to lean in to hear him.

"Which one do you suggest?"

His gaze darts up at that before lowering again quickly. "I...well, I would say this one." He points a shaking finger at what is truly the prettiest of the options. It's a deep, dark red, edging into mahogany with a corseted bodice and a skirt of ruched fabric. I take it to the dressing room within the closet and pull it on.

"I think I need some help with the fastenings," I say, and then he's there helping close up the back, encasing me in the truly gorgeous gown.

It's then that I make an uncomfortable discovery.

Though Celena and I are apparently identical, our waist sizes are not. I suck in a breath as he cinches the bodice tighter, caging me inside. When he's done, I can breathe, barely, and look down at myself, surprised at the amount of cleavage this dress has created. I've never dared wear a neckline so low. But this bodice really pushes the girls up and puts them on display. It makes even my meager assets look kind of impressive.

I swallow down the shyness. Of course a princess wouldn't be a prude.

Filomena comes into the closet and I turn around. "Am I allowed to see myself yet?"

The little beauty salon, oddly enough, had no mirrors. My tone is playful, but she blanches and bows deeply. "Of course, Your Grace. Follow me."

I feel bad, suddenly wondering if Celena is more of an "off with their heads" type of princess. Filomena leads me into the hallway and grabs a small cameo hanging on the wall. It has a crack on the face of the woman in profile, and when she turns it, the entire wall begins to slide up. Underneath is a giant floor-to-ceiling mirror that finally reveals my reflection.

No. Princess Celena's reflection.

Talia Dubroca, unwanted daughter and sometime waitress, bartender, and dog walker, has left the building. In her place is someone else. Someone I barely recognize.

The makeup makes me look older and less friendly. Viciously beautiful, like a rose with sharp thorns. The dress I'm squeezed into accentuates curves I didn't realize I had. It makes me look taller somehow, but also dangerous.

One of the twins holds out a pair of high-heeled boots—stilettos, the heels of which are metal and very pointy. I'm not entirely sure I can walk in these things, but I sit on the bench in the hall and let her put them on my feet.

"You all have done an amazing job," I say, still a little startled at my reflection. The stylists preen and I hope I've smoothed over whatever fear I accidentally instilled.

Through some magic of engineering, or maybe actual magic, who knows here, the shoes are actually comfortable. I wobble a bit at first, but find them amazingly stable—I don't think I'm in danger of falling to my death in them.

I walk around the corner, back to the living room where Ryin sits, testing them out. He's still on the far side of the room, but I feel his stare as if he were touching me. He stands then bows low, and when he straightens, his gaze is colder than ever. A frigid, icy wind comes from his general direction.

It's not like he was exactly friendly before, but I definitely feel the change. In the few hours I've known him, his detachment has hovered around a nine on a scale of ten. Now it's been cranked to eleven.

I get it. I looked like me before, and now I look like her.

I swallow, wanting to say something. Wanting to apologize, but I stay quiet. What is there to say? And why does his change in demeanor mean so much to me? Is it just because he has the face of the boy I had a crush on when I was young? Whatever the reason, the frost from him settles into me, making me shiver.

The doorbell rings again and one of the twins answers it. Shad walks in and gives me a once-over. "You look exquisite, Your Grace." His expression is hard to read, but his words are kind.

"Thank you."

He frowns slightly and steps closer to me, lowering his voice. "Nimali do not say, 'Thank you.' Not to those of lower rank." He extends his arm again, bent at the elbow in that chivalrous way.

"Well, you're the prince. Don't we share rank?"

"Adopted, remember?"

I grab hold of him as we head toward the door. I can already tell that figuring out and remembering all of the rules of royal behavior is going to be a bitch and a half. Behind me, I sense Ryin's presence drawing nearer. He's my shadow after all, but right now he feels like a black hole, sucking up all the light and energy in the room with his displeasure.

Then we're stepping into the elevator and it takes all my mental energy to endure the ride. I squeeze Shad's ample biceps as if my life depends on it. He peers down at me curiously and pats my hand gently like he's soothing a child. But it's Ryin's sharp gaze arrowing in on my anxiety that actually gives me comfort. There's a crack in the ice as he looks at me, struggling to breathe normally as sweat pools in my armpits and trails down my back. Through that crack, I witness his alarm. I shoot him a wan smile, hoping to convey that I'm not having a medical crisis that will incur the king's wrath.

Ryin's expression warms a few degrees, but he doesn't take his eyes off me for the entire ride.

I like that more than I want to admit.

Chapter Nine

TALIA

I HEAR the crowd before I see it. As we cross the lobby, the people roar like thunder, like a storm beating against the shore. Like the fans at the arena that time we all went to see the Golden State Warriors play. My dad had gotten tickets to a fancy luxury box from a client of his. I was there to watch the twins, just toddlers then, and make sure they didn't run wild and tip over the champagne buckets or something. A wall of glass separated us from the chaos, but then someone flicked a switch and it slid away, replaced by a wall of noise.

So many people in one place. So much energy and joy. The cacophony of it all sank into my bones and nourished me. My life was so quiet and small, but in that moment, I realized that it could be big and brash and full of laughter and shouting. I always wanted to go back, but we never did. All the screaming gave my stepmother a migraine.

Now, as I step out onto the plaza, the faux gas lamps charmingly illuminate the space and a crowd nearly as raucous as any horde of basketball fans greets me. Hundreds of people fill the square. The Nimali population in this small area of reclaimed city is larger than I thought.

My grip on Shad's arm tightens as I stare out in wonderment. "They're all here for me?" I whisper, but what I'm thinking is there's absolutely no way I can pull this off.

Shad just chuckles and leads me to the raised platform that's been erected sometime in the past couple of hours. It's fairly small, only large enough to hold the two thrones sitting upon it. One of them is bulky and awkward looking. As we get closer, I realize that it's actually made of bones. Giant bones.

My dinner roils in my stomach, and I jerk to a stop. At least the bones are too large to be human, but the sight is disturbing to say the least.

"All right?" Shad asks, and I'm not really sure. We are completely surrounded by soldiers in black. The first few rows of people in front of the throne are also soldiers, straight backed and somber. Then the cheering crowd stands behind them. But everyone is watching me. I finally nod and we keep walking, my jaw tense and my teeth clamped together.

What would Celena do?

The smaller seat on the stage is made of normal throne materials, wood and dark red fabric, very decorative and very pretty. Too ornate for my taste, but more palatable than sitting on bones. Shad leads me to it and I stand gaping out at the people as the noise grows louder. Clapping, screaming, cheering. It fills the night, echoing off the buildings around the square and vibrating through my body and draining away my nerves.

The adoration lights me up inside.

I know they're not really cheering for me. They're cheering for the woman I look like. The woman whose life I've stepped into. The woman who is probably, even now, lying dead somewhere beyond the wall. A victim of one of those terrible, red-eyed beasts. My heart goes out to her. And I should be ashamed at myself, stepping into her life like this, not allowing those who love her to grieve. Part of me *is* ashamed, but the other part just soaks in the people's love like a dry, cracked sponge does water.

I perch gently on the princess's throne and look for Shad, but he's climbed down from the platform. There isn't a seat for him here, underscoring his words from before. He takes a position on the ground with the other soldiers. All the civilians wear shades of red or blue or brown. The only other colors in sight are the gray outfits similar to what Ryin and Noomi wear. These must be the other Fai drudges. Rows of them stand on the sidelines and, aside from the soldiers, they're the only ones not cheering.

The warmth inside me cools. How could I forget that some of this world is built on their backs? People who have no choice about where they are and what they're doing. I swallow. But this deception is meant to help them too. Give Shad time to do…whatever it is he's planning to do to get peace. I straighten my back as the noise on the plaza dims, revealing the sound of boots marching in lockstep.

A dozen guards flank the king as he exits the Citadel's main doors. Lyall's presence dampens the enthusiasm of the crowd. The soldiers lead him to the platform and he comes to my side. He opens his arms and the expectation is clear. I rise and embrace him, my emotions a jumble within me.

I can't remember my father ever hugging me. Burrowing my head into his chest should not feel so good, so comforting. I know he's not a good man, but he wraps me tightly and I allow myself to enjoy it. I imagine Celena must have.

When I pull back, two Fai men are dragging a large box to the front of the stage. They open it and heave a big translucent cube onto the platform at our feet. It's the size of a small trunk or footlocker, and once it hits the stage, the whole thing glows blue.

Everything is silent now. Hundreds of people wait, voices hushed, the quiet oppressive in its completeness.

Lyall smiles widely and takes a step forward with one arm still around my shoulders. "The princess is returned!" he cries, his voice magnified by the glowing box at our feet. It rises and echoes across the audience and the cheers ascend again, louder than before. People applaud and whoop and scream. At first I think it's just because Lyall basically ordered them to, but I'm close enough to the front rows to see the real tears streaming down the cheeks of the people there.

"Come, let's greet the people," Lyall says, extending his arm in the same old-fashioned way Shad does. The guards surround us, two deep on all sides, as we step off the platform and head into the crowd, which parts before us like magic. But even with the buffer of soldiers, the people still call out to me.

"Your Grace, we're so happy you're home again," a woman says, tears overflowing.

"Your Grace, I made this for you in hopes of your safe return." A teenage girl holds up a silver and crimson tapestry with a beautiful floral design stitched into it. I reach for the fabric, but Lyall tugs my hands away. Instead, a guard grabs it, folding it into her hands.

It goes on like this for what seems like hours. These shoes were not really meant to traipse across the grass, but the raw emotion focused on me from these people erases my aches and pains. At one point they all just start screaming the princess's name over and over again like I'm a rock star or a celebrity.

"Celena! Celena!"

I'm nearly dizzy from it all. People share their hopes and the little trinkets they've made. This must be some kind of ritual or cultural practice that I don't understand, but it's very sweet. Guards collect all the items and I hope they won't be thrown away.

After a few automatic *Thank You's* when people engage with me, Lyall rubs my arm. "I know your memory is gone, dear, so there are some things you will need to relearn. But a Nimali princess does not give gratitude—she accepts it. Never lower yourself before those beneath you. You have no need to be grateful to them for giving you what is your due."

I nod at him, sobered and angry at myself for forgetting this lesson so soon. Lyall maintains a calm and placid expression. Shad, Ryin, and a group of aristocratic looking men and women in red trail us. They all stay behind the soldiers who encircle me and the king, and all maintain remote exteriors. I work hard to do the same, though it's difficult.

The crowd is gathered by the color of their clothing. People in red are up front, then those in shades of blue, then brown. The colors must represent a type of class system, because it's obvious those in blue are not as well dressed or well fed as those in red, and those in brown are worst of all.

Deeper grooves line the faces of those in the back of the crowd. Their thinner cheeks and sunken eyes show how much more they've been weighed down by life. But their delight at my presence is no less real. In fact, as we pass through the lines of those lower in class, the fervency actually increases. I don't believe they're faking their enthusiasm simply because the royals are here demanding it. These people really love and care about Celena. It makes me wonder why—is it just that she's a beloved princess, or does she actually do things that endear the people to her?

We finally make it to the opposite end of the plaza, where a vehicle idles on the street—a jeep with the top down. Lyall motions me into it and sits beside me in the back seat. Two soldiers are sitting up front already, and once we're settled, the driver accelerates—very slowly.

We drive around the plaza like a single car parade. I watch Lyall carefully for clues; should I wave and smile? But he does neither—just looks on impassively as drums begin beating. I can't see the drummers, but they play a cadence that has a hypnotic quality to it. Then, a song rises from the audience.

A chorus of voices in harmony sing a haunting tale of losing their homeland and searching for another. Of wandering until they find a city on the sea and settling there. The entire crowd sings and the music imprints itself on my heart and grips it tightly. It's sorrowful and lilting and tears spring to my eyes again. I blink them away, willing them not to fall.

The jeep ends its tour in front of the Citadel once again. We pile out of the vehicle and are escorted back onto the stage, where I sit on the plush throne waiting for me. The song continues, every Nimali taking part, many with their eyes closed, a hand over their heart, taken somewhere else by the music. The Fai stand silently on the sidelines, staring out in front of them.

The last verse causes goosebumps to rise on my flesh. The purity of the melody doesn't change and the poignancy of the voices in unison remains, but the lyrics speak of an enemy who encroaches on this new homeland. Of how they must break this enemy's back, rout them from the land, and remove them even from history.

I look to my left, past Shad, to find Ryin standing solemnly. As the last notes of the song echo across the plaza and the voices die, I catch his eye. He holds my gaze for a long moment before turning away, almost like he's dismissing me. I face forward again, grip my hands together, and tremble.

Lyall stands beside me now; I didn't even notice him moving. He gently cradles a delicate, jeweled circlet in his hands. It's crafted of thin strands of silver woven together. At first I think they're meant to look like tree branches, but as he shifts it, I realize they're actually shaped like bones.

The bodice of my dress suddenly feels tighter, and I struggle to suck breath into my lungs.

Quiet reigns throughout the square as the king smiles down at me. He places the crown upon my head and the cheers are deafening.

Chapter Ten

RYIN

AN EAR-SHATTERING roar shreds the air, vibrating off the crumbling structures around me and rumbling through my prone form. The pavement beneath me is cracked with gaping holes, and more chunks disintegrate under the force of my fists slamming against it.

I'm pinned beneath a slab of concrete, my shattered bones still in the process of healing. All of my daimon's power is focused on restoring my body—I don't have the necessary strength to get myself free. My sister's soft boots come into view, and her thin fingers pull at the wall that collapsed onto me.

"Get out of here!" I shout through gritted teeth, swatting her away. But she just moves out of my reach and keeps tugging uselessly at the slab.

"I'm not leaving you," she cries, tears and snot streaming down her face. Meanwhile, the growls and snarls of beasts grow closer.

I reach toward her and groan as my broken back flares in

agony. "You have to run, they're almost here!" Down the street, the squad of howling Nimali draws closer.

"Go!" I shout again. "Please, Dove. Please get to safety. I'll be able to move in moments. I'll be right behind you."

Her expression is pure misery. Round, freckled cheeks tremble as she shakes her head stubbornly. Another roar shakes the earth—closer this time. Finally, she seems resigned. "You better be," she says before dashing away.

The ground quakes from the hooves and paws and claws drawing near to my location. I keep my head turned in my sister's direction as she heads toward one of the hidden tunnel entrances. Once she makes it to safety, she can hide deep in the underground network of passageways our people mapped after the Sorrows. She can get back home, this doomed scouting mission a thing of the past.

My spine is now reconnected and all the internal damage healed. Finally, my daimon's strength can be funneled toward lifting this wall off me. I groan and twist, pushing up onto my hands and knees with a yell until I can shove the slab to the side, and then I'm free. And I'm flying.

I rise off the ground, staying relatively low. Chasing after Dove as she nears a manhole hidden by a pair of rusted-out cars.

A wolf leaps for me, hot breath grazing my neck, but I dodge, shooting up higher only to have to turn at the last minute to evade a swooping crow. The bird moves out of reach, flapping overly large wings. But the wind that rises is out of proportion to even this giant Nimali animal form's wingspan. Violent gales create a thunderous assault against my skin. The wind whips into a frenzy accompanied by the steady *thump, thump, thump* of wings that are even larger still. I don't have to look up to know what flies above me.

A blast of heat sears the top of my head, singeing off my hair. Fire surrounds me. Everything is flames. They shoot in an arc, consuming my body and moving down the street, getting closer to the nimble figure dashing away too slowly to elude them.

Ignoring the pain of my own burning flesh, I put on a burst of speed and dive on top of my sister, tackling her smaller form and covering it with my body, doing my best to smother the flames engulfing her. But dragon fire is hotter than any other kind. And Dove is too young to have a daimon to help her.

I push the spirit within me to heal her, ignoring the stench of my own skin and muscle as it blackens and crisps and makes me gag. I'm not even aware of the pain—it's progressed from agonizing to nonexistent, my nerves destroyed. Everything else is a haze. Everything but my sister's form in my arms, so silent and still.

I grip her motionless body to me as the sound of footfalls grow closer and closer. The steps are as loud and jarring as the beating of wings.

Thump. Thump. Thump.

The banging wakes me from the dream—the memory of the day that will haunt me for the rest of my life. The reprieve is welcome, though I'm disoriented for a long moment when my eyes first open.

I'm splayed on a narrow cot. Across from me is a long countertop, and the blue glow of bliss lighting flickers on when I move. Servant's quarters. Princess's suite.

The lighting sparks a flare of anger within me. So much waste and excess here, but the banging on the door begins again before my thoughts can spiral. I make my way to it and wrench it open. Servant doors all have normal handles—no need for fancy biometrics here.

A surly looking Fai man stands on the other side scowling, probably because he must have been knocking for quite some time.

"Enzo," I say, greeting him.

"Meeting's starting," is his gruff reply.

"But we just had a meeting two nights ago."

"New blood came in today. Tried to ambush the prince."

I'm fully awake now. "Who'd they get?"

"Von and Xipporah."

"What?" It comes out much louder than I intended, especially since it's the middle of the night.

Enzo shrugs, looking even more put out. "They're waiting for you. Asked for you specifically."

"I'm on assignment." I point to the door leading into the suite and in the vague direction of the princess.

"Her royal highness requires your presence while she sleeps?"

I sigh deeply. According to the king she does. Before she was abducted, I wouldn't have dared abandon the princess once I'd been commanded to stay near her every waking or sleeping moment. But without her memory I'm in far less danger of her wrath. She doesn't seem to have any wrath. And it's unlikely she'll wake up and need me.

Besides, I need to know what Von and Xi are up to. There's no way they got caught unexpectedly; they're both too skilled as soldiers for that. I was too, once upon a time.

"Fine, let me get my shoes," I say, and within a minute, we're off.

We climb down fourteen flights of steps to the thirty-second floor, one of several earmarked strictly for Fai use. The drudge floors include kitchens, laundry, and maintenance facilities, along with our dormitories. I pass the dorm I usually sleep in and nod to the woman serving as lookout, then enter the east kitchen, where the meeting will take place. It's just after the third hour of morning, and soon the Fai cooks will be up to begin preparing the morning meal. For now, the immense space is quiet, no steam hissing from pots or delicious aromas floating through the air.

About a dozen others have gathered here tonight, fellow Genus Fidelis members—mostly soldiers who refuse to give up the fight. Drudges are all prisoners of war, but we are not all soldiers. My cousin Noomi is one of many civilians the Nimali captured in dishonorable raids on our places of worship. But she's here as well, brave as a warrior, even though her daimon's gifts are not martial.

The space is so dark that a few have called their daimons to them, so their eyes glow blue, giving off a little light and allowing them to use their enhanced vision. A short and thickly muscled woman stands before a handful of stubby candles, clicking a firestarter over and over again. It must be out of fuel, for no flame comes out.

"Let me help," I say, and she moves away. I call my daimon to me then inhale deeply, purse my lips, and blow a thin streak of fire over the candle wicks. Were there any Nimali present, I wouldn't have dared.

I help to position the candles on the counters and greet the others with grave bows in the Fai tradition. I thought Enzo and I would be the last to arrive, but the door opens once again, revealing Von and Xipporah.

Noomi gasps, then races across the room to embrace her sister. It's been years since they've seen each other, and they cling to one another like vines. Tears stream down Noomi's face. Xipporah is more stoic—she merely closes her eyes and squeezes tighter.

Noomi is a smaller and more delicate version of her older sister. Both share the same wide-set eyes and wear their hair in long, thickly coiled locks that tumble to their waists. Their skin is as dark as the rich earth back home in the Greenlands. Their reunion brings back the emotions of my dream and remembrances of family. A bittersweet ache fills me as I pace over to Xi and throw an arm around her.

"Guess you felt like being captured today, huh?"

She grins and nudges me with her shoulder, still embracing her sister. "Something like that."

"Can't say I'm glad to see you, though. You're lucky they

didn't take your memory soul." I shudder to think of what it would have been like to see her after all this time and for her to have no recollection of her past. It would have destroyed Noomi.

"We were both reasonably sure our memory souls weren't our dominant ones. And you just might be glad I'm here when it's all said and done." Her cryptic words pique my interest. But Von breaks away from a pair of middle-aged soldiers and claps his hands together, calling us to attention.

He moves his hands to speak and a pang of sadness punches my chest. Earlier today, his voice was intact, but when he was captured they must have taken his voice soul.

"I know you all have questions about folks from home, and Xipporah and I are happy to answer them, later. Suffice it to say, life in the Greenlands remains as always. Our home is secure and our soldiers battle the Nimali when they encroach upon our territory. We guard and protect the bliss from the invaders."

Murmurs and nods of approval rise from those gathered. "I also wanted to assure you," Von continues, "that the Crowns have sanctioned this mission. I was able to speak with the Air Priest and he has blessed our path."

Everyone here presses their palm to their heart and drops their head in a display of reverence. To converse with the priest telepathically over such a distance—halfway across the city—Xipporah or someone else with a Land daimon must have aided him. Their daimons often serve as amplifiers for the powers of others.

"The Crowns are very interested to learn more about the return of the princess." Von turns to me. "I told them this might be the opportunity we need, and they agreed."

"Opportunity for what?" I ask.

"To exert leverage." His eyes flash in the flickering candle-light. "The barbarian king's most prized treasure is his daughter. When she disappeared and he blamed us, the Crowns realized that we had missed an opportunity. If we actually *had* kidnapped her, what would he have done to get her back?"

Noomi and I exchange a glance. The same wariness within me is reflected on her face.

"I suspect something terrible happened to the princess," I say. "She may have been tortured. She has scars and healed breaks in her bones that she did not have before. She's come back...changed. More fragile."

Noomi pipes in, her fingers flying. "If there is an opportunity with her, it's to change her mind. She is more gentle now. Kinder. That is what we can use."

"Use her kindness?" Von's expression is almost mocking, and Noomi stiffens. Xipporah does too.

Noomi continues, her movements precise as if she wants no misunderstandings. "She has no recollection of the war or any hatred of the Fai. Her mind is no longer poisoned against us. She sees us as equals. As *people*, not drudges. She won't even use the whistle. That is someone we can turn to our side. Imagine having such a powerful ally."

"Ally?" Von shakes his head, and most of the others present seem skeptical as well. But they haven't been around her. They haven't seen the affront she displayed when she learned of our capture and servitude. I'm not entirely sure that the princess can truly be turned to our side, but she is certainly not the same enemy she used to be.

However, could she be a new kind of enemy?

That is yet to be seen. Von moves on, outlining new mission priorities handed down straight from our leaders, the Four Crowns of the Fai Court. Instead of gathering information on troop movements to find a weakness in the defenses for an external attack, they want us to prepare an attack from within.

One of the more battle weary soldiers, a woman with gray stubble covering her shaved head, speaks up. "We are too few. And as soon as we make any move, they will trammel a handful of us in retaliation. Besides, what good is attacking them if we can't get our souls back? We won't survive for a day if we're too far from the souls they stole from us."

"There is a plan," Von signs. "If we follow it to the T, then we will have our souls and our freedom. We could be home by the Gloaming Festival."

The mention of the yearly event that all in the Greenlands look forward to silences any further protests. I don't want to allow myself to hope for such a thing, but hope is like a virus and we cannot always choose when it will take root in us.

The meeting ends shortly after that, but Von catches my eye, motioning for me to wait. Once the others leave, I blow out most of the candles, leaving only one lit so as not to waste the precious wax. Von's crow daimon gives him excellent vision during the day, but unlike me, he has no advantage at night.

I lean against the counter facing him. "You truly got captured on purpose to put this into play?"

He nods.

"How did you know they wouldn't take your memory soul?"

"We have a test now, brother. Back home. We can tell which soul is dominant."

At least he knew what he was getting himself into. The dominant of a person's three souls is the one that's taken by the Nimali's soulcatchers. He tilts his head, peering at me as if he's staring into my two remaining souls. His intensity is unsettling.

"You want to know about the princess," I guess.

He grins. "Everything. How she was found, where she was found. Anything you can tell me."

"So you can use her in some way?"

"Use her to get to her father. The beast king nearly lost his mind when his precious daughter disappeared. We have been searching for a weakness in all the wrong places, and this chance we have is too good to miss."

The idea that Celena is a weakness of any kind feels wrong to me. Then I bristle at the thought and work to make sure it doesn't show externally. There is no room for sympathy for a Nimali in my heart—even if she reminds me more of an injured creature now than a hardened beast.

Plus, as much as I hate to admit it, he's right. Celena would be excellent leverage against her father. I push past the strange reticence that has no place within me and begin telling him what he wants to know.

But every word that comes out of my mouth feels like a betrayal.

Chapter Eleven

TALIA

I WOULD HAVE THOUGHT that a princess's bed would be luxurious and soft, a paradise of cloud-like comfort, but Celena's mattress is lumpy and hard. I wake with a crick in my neck and an ache in my back. Plus, I'm oddly disoriented because I'm so used to the sun peeking in through the blinds greeting me in the mornings. No blinds here and no windows. I have no idea what time it is, so I groggily decide it must be time to begin the day.

I stumble out of the torturous bed and cross the enormous bedroom to the equally enormous bathroom, also decorated entirely in gray. After washing up, I put on the robe hanging on the back of the door and emerge into the hallway to find Filomena and the crew setting up in the preparation room.

She assures me this isn't the everyday routine; I only have to withstand the stylists when I'm scheduled to meet a large number of my royal subjects. Fortunately, the beauty regimen is abbreviated this morning.

Hair and makeup fly by, and then the quiet teenaged boy is stuffing me into another too-tight outfit where my boobs are practically spilling out. Today's selection: a ruby-red bustier made from the leather-like material, which is honestly pretty bad ass, and a pair of form-fitting leggings. Instead of yesterday's stilettos, he holds up a pair of knee-high boots in a slightly darker color. He motions for me to sit on the bench in front of the mirror wall.

"I can put these on myself," I tell him, but he shakes his head, looking affronted. Resigned, I step a foot into the boot and then look on in awe as he takes the laces and whips them back and forth, catching them on the grommets with precision and lacing them all the way up in seconds. "Never mind. You do that much better than me."

The stylists all smile and coo in approval when I'm done, and I try not to let it go to my head. They bow their goodbyes and file out, and then I head to the main room, where Noomi and Ryin wait for me. This morning, her dreadlocks are piled on top of her head in a bun, and her eyes sparkle with light. She has what I've always thought of as Disney princess eyes, doe-like and wide set, along with a little button nose and an overall fey quality that seems almost magical. She's in stark contrast to Ryin, who has dark, heavy clouds hovering over him. His expression is the same implacable mask as usual, but I can somehow sense a darkening in his mood compared to yesterday.

After their obligatory bows, Ryin retakes his seat on the same hard chair, which ignites a spark of anger within me. At the very least he could have a comfortable chair while he waits for me; there are plenty around.

I sit at the dining table and try to act nonchalant. "Ryin, would you mind moving that chair for me, please?" He looks startled, and I hold back a smile as I dig into my breakfast: a black porridge-like substance that tastes like strawberry jam.

He stands and I have him swap out the plain, wooden chair he sits on for one of the ornately carved, golden, gilded Louis XIV monstrosities. It looks kind of heavy and I feel bad for a moment, but he has no trouble lifting the thing and carrying it across the room. Now it sits in the corner near the dining table and he stands next to it expectantly.

"That's all," I say. "Please have a seat."

The soft huffing sound of Noomi's laughter lights me up inside. I glance over at Ryin, who looks completely ridiculous sitting rigidly on the throne-like chair. He shoots visual daggers at Noomi and then veils his features before turning to me. His eyes narrow but I just grin at him, then toast him with my glass of amber peach-cran-grape drink.

Victor would have laughed. Ryin shows no amusement, but I think I see a crack in his armor. I decide to make it my goal to lighten him up a little. It always helped me to focus on the rays of joy breaking through the clouds of misery. Maybe I can bring a little cheer to counteract all the pain.

"You've eaten, right?" I ask him.

His head jerks in surprise, but he recovers quickly and nods. "We have our rations, Your Grace. Fai are not permitted to eat Nimali food."

I purse my lips. Of course not.

Then the doorbell chimes with a much longer ring than yesterday. Noomi disappears into the servant's room, a haunted expression on her face, and the door slides open without needing anyone to open it. When King Lyall saunters in, it makes sense. He must have access to anything he likes.

Something in my chest lifts when I see him, a sensation quickly followed by guilt. But the cavernous crater inside me that always longed for a father's love wins out, especially with the joyous expression on his face when he looks at me. He crosses the room, and I rise to meet his embrace.

"Celena, my girl," he says, still beaming. "I trust your breakfast was pleasant."

"Wonderful, everything is wonderful."

"Good." He settles himself beside me, still smiling, but

flicks a hand at Ryin, who quickly makes his exit. His sudden absence is the space left by a lost tooth, tender and throbbing.

"I have a present for you." Lyall pulls a small object wrapped in a red bow from his pocket.

A memory of last Christmas flashes before me. The twins both received new cars, months before they were even legally able to drive. Identical white Mercedes convertibles with red leather interiors. Meanwhile, I was puttering along in the twenty-year-old Hyundai I'd driven since high school. A hand-me-down from my dad that he claimed he'd kept for nostalgia. There had been a box under the tree with my name on it— Dad gave me a sweater fit for a nineteenth-century librarian. High neck, pearl buttons, the whole nine. Meanwhile, my stepmother had spent some money, too much money, on the ugliest Louis Vuitton handbag I'd ever seen. I'd smiled and thanked them and actually put on the horrible sweater, taking our yearly Christmas Day photos in it.

I desperately hope Lyall has better taste in gifts.

I slide the box toward me and open it. Nestled inside is an object about the size and shape of a man's wallet, black and smooth, its texture silky. "What is it?"

Lyall chuckles. "It's a comm. Here." He motions for it and I push it back over to him. "Just open like this." He pulls the edges apart and it opens on a hinge, changing the device's shape from flat to a prism, with the newly revealed section made of glass. He hands it back to me, and I turn it around in my palm.

Then he pulls out a similar device from his pocket and opens it. "Ping Celena," he says, and his comm lights up. The one in my hand starts pulsing blue light and rattles to get my attention.

I gasp and look up to him. "How do I answer?"

"Just say, 'Accept.'"

"Accept," I speak into the device, and the pulse settles into a solid glow. Then, Lyall's head pushes out from the glass in a monochromatic display. The image is a little scratchy, definitely not high-definition video, but what it lacks in quality it makes up for in depth.

I rotate the comm in my hand to find that the face is three-dimensional, extruding out of the glass. "This is fantastic," I whisper.

Lyall's blue-tinted image shakes his head and smiles. "Now, this is just a temporary comm." His voice comes from both across the table and the device in my hand. "It was all the engineers had available this morning. But I've commissioned the artist who created your last one, and she will have a custom model ready by this evening."

My mouth opens on an instinctive *Thank you*, but I snap my lips shut before I can speak, not sure of whether that's appropriate.

"We only have short-term bliss cells available," Lyall says, his demeanor growing serious. "Unfortunately, all the larger cells are being diverted for critical usage."

I tear my gaze from the magic 3D video phone to face him. "What is bliss?"

He smiles again, the brief darkness fading away. "It is the reason the Nimali were able to claw our way back to civilization after the Sorrows. After the human electrical systems failed, and war and weather and disease basically destroyed their race."

He closes the comm with a snap and spreads his hands apart. "Bliss is the energy that runs through the spirit world. It breaks through into our world in places called matrices. Our city, Aurum, is home to several such matrices, and we have developed ways to mine bliss. That is how we've reclaimed this city and our way of life."

He motions to the lighting overhead and the comms before us. "Bliss powers everything."

I'm still stuck on the whole "spirit world" part of it. "Is this technology or magic?" I breathe in wonder.

"A bit of both. But it is also the reason we fight the Fai." His expression grows thunderous again. "Those zealots worship bliss and believe it's better stored in a temple than used in our lights and technology. Their territory to the west includes several rich matrices that they deny us access to. Even as our mining supply dwindles."

"So the matrices, they can run out?"

"Yes, certainly. But there is plenty of bliss in Aurum, hoarded by the Fai."

I choose my words carefully. "But if you do get access to their matrices, at some point we would mine them until they're empty. What happens then?"

He tilts his head at me looking thoughtfully, then grins widely. "Come, it's time for your tour of the city."

He stands and pockets his comm. I do the same, mindful that he never answered my question. Ryin appears and follows us out of the suite to the elevators, where a lean, bald man in a well-fitted cherry-red suit is waiting.

"Your Majesty. Your Grace," he says, bowing low.

"Lord Jovi, you have a report for me?" Lyall commands.

"Yes, Your Majesty." He holds up a thin, rectangular-shaped object that reminds me of that children's handheld game where a clear plastic box is filled with liquid and you tilt it this way and that to make the fish inside move around. The thing in his hands is filled with blue liquid that moves slower than water, with floating dark beads inside it.

Lord Jovi slides some of the beads around, then turns the device and presents it to Lyall. As the king peers at it, I ask in a low voice, "What is that?"

"A data tablet, Your Grace."

"Like an iPad?"

He tilts his head, reminding me of a confused puppy with his long face and droopy eyes. "We store data in liquid bliss. These devices allow us to access the information." I see nothing but beads in blue water, but I guess I'll have to take his word on it.

"Come with us," Lyall says, handing the device back to him. "I'm accompanying Celena and her retinue on a tour of the territory. We can discuss further."

The elevator ride leaves me dizzy, with sweat drenching my back and underarms. I haven't figured out the deodorant situation here, so I keep my arms close to my sides, my fists gripping my skirts as if that would help if this thing were to plummet to the ground. Ryin is in front of me and in the corner so he's unable to witness my reaction, for which I'm grateful. He's way too perceptive, and I don't think there's anything his magical healing abilities can do about my claustrophobia.

When we finally make it down to the first floor, Lyall and Lord Jovi exit first, deep in a conversation I had no extra mental energy to expend listening to. All my focus is on walking upright and breathing deeply while leaving the rattling death trap of an elevator. The rides are not getting any easier with repetition, but at least the things have been running smoothly so far, not stoking too much fear of becoming trapped in a broken down car.

That thought jars me and I miss a step, tripping over flat ground. An arm reaches out to steady me and I look up into Ryin's stern but concerned face. I'm overcome with gratitude, opening my mouth to thank him when I hear a hiss.

One of the soldiers who rode down with us is staring daggers at Ryin. He withdraws his hand quickly, but I reach out and grab hold of his arm again, leaning heavily on him.

"Your Grace?" the soldier asks.

"Just a bit light-headed. I deeply appreciate the healer for not letting me fall."

The soldier sniffs and looks away. I squeeze Ryin's biceps, noting the firmness of the muscle and honestly needing a little stability as I move forward, legs still wobbly. Based on the guard's reaction, I'm guessing Ryin isn't supposed to touch me, but I also know that no one will naysay the princess. And memory loss has made Celena a bit more touchy feely. Also, Ryin's steely arm under my hand has short circuited a few of my brain cells. The last thing he needs is me groping him, especially since he's here under duress, so I reluctantly let go.

But my fingers itch to hold onto something as I walk toward the unknown, surrounded by guards. Today will be my first real test at being Celena, and so far I'm doing a terrible job. A tour of the city will help me learn more about this place and hopefully how I can pull off this deception.

Chapter Twelve

TALIA

OUTSIDE, the morning is gray, but warmer than I'd expect from this city. I realize I have no idea what month or season it is. Not that it matters much in San Francisco—the weather could be anywhere from cold and rainy to even colder and overcast any time of the year, but I am curious. "What's the date?" I ask Ryin, who walks a few paces behind me.

"It's the fifth day of the Weed Month, year fifty-three Post Sorrows, Your Grace."

Oookay. "Thanks," I tell him, then wince and press my lips shut.

In the circular driveway in front of the building, a line of young women stand in a perfect row waiting for us. They're all wearing shades of red and smile brightly as we approach. Shad is there too, just off to the side with a handful of soldiers. He greets me with a bow.

"Celena, these are your courtiers. I'll let them reintroduce themselves." He melts away and they all curtsy as one and begin the introductions.

Elayne is short and curvy, in her early twenties with

straight black hair and cool blue eyes. She's the most effusive, making sure I know how much she missed me and hoped for my safe return. Alaya is lean with wild curly hair. She looks Latina, is maybe seventeen or eighteen, and her smile is the warmest and most sincere. Ofelia is a skinny younger teenager with mousy, lank hair. She keeps her eyes downcast and practically whispers her greeting and how happy she is to have me back home.

Last is the queen bee. I can tell by the way she holds her shoulders and meets my eyes with no fear and very little deference. She's not tall, about my height, and thin in a way that still seems strong and powerful. Her skin is a beautiful, rich chocolate, so smooth she's probably never gotten a zit in her life. Her name is Dominga, and I'm not sure if she's Celena's best friend or greatest enemy. The look she gives me just about slices me in two, it's so full of rage and joy—I've never seen an expression like that. I want to avoid her, but I think I should keep her close.

"I'm sorry that I don't remember any of you," I say. "But I'm glad to be back and I'm happy you're all here. I'm not sure we can pick up where we left off"—I look at Elayne here; her eager beaver energy is a little off-putting—"But friendship is so important, and I'll need your help navigating the unfamiliar."

My little speech has shocked them all into silence. Courtiers are friends, right? This is, like, Celena's squad, or at least I think it is, but their reactions have me questioning that. I have no idea how I should act in order to more effectively be the princess. She's quite obviously nothing like me—maybe I should lean into that.

King Lyall finally pulls away from his advisor and addresses everyone present. "Today is a day for the people to see Princess Celena retaking her duties. To show them that the blood of dragons is strong and we are not easily daunted."

Everyone is quiet, showing great submissiveness to their

leader. Lyall spins around and soon we all fall into step with the guards creating a wall around us. Shad walks ahead with the soldiers. Lyall is on my right, and there's a brief flurry of activity to my left until Dominga emerges the victor, claiming the space at my elbow with Elayne just beside her, visibly pouting. The younger girls trail us, chatting amongst themselves. I can't find Ryin, though I know he's not far away.

"Was it very awful?" Elayne leans around Dominga to ask.

"Was what?"

"I heard you were attacked by a Revoker."

Dominga rolls her eyes. "I'm sure it was an absolute delight."

Elayne's curiosity seems pretty bloodthirsty. "I don't remember it," I respond. "And I'm still not exactly sure what a Revoker is."

Elayne looks only too happy to offer details. "Demons. Creatures with wings and scales and claws and sharp teeth. They're horrifying." She shudders dramatically, and I stifle a laugh.

"They sound like dragons." Well, that was the wrong thing to say. Both girls slide horrified gazes toward Lyall, who is once again ensconced in conversation with Lord Jovi.

"They're nothing like dragons." Dominga's voice is clipped. "Revokers are covenant breakers who feast on human flesh. Their poison makes you die a painful death, then their daimons harvest what's left of your body to increase their numbers. They're a vile scourge."

"I keep hearing that word, what is a daimon?"

Dominga eyes me a bit confrontationally. Elayne takes this as her cue to explain. "Daimons are spirits—they're our counterparts in the spirit plane. It's one of my favorite stories. The legend goes that many generations ago, the daimons grew curious about the mortal world. Spirits have no physical forms, but their world connects to ours in many places—the bliss matrices—and they wanted to be able to explore but had no bodies to use.

"A human brother and sister, both powerful seers, were the first to communicate directly with the daimons. They made a pact to share their bodies with the spirits and allow them to experience life through their eyes. In return, the host would receive strength, powers, and other gifts at will. That was the first covenant."

Elayne gesticulates wildly as she tells the story. "The brother and sister could not agree on how humans should host daimons. She believed the physical form should change to match the daimon's essence. But her brother thought it best for the human to retain his natural form and only take on the qualities of the daimon. And so the feud began."

"The feud?" I ask.

"Between the Fai and the Nimali. The disagreement was never resolved and the followers on either side became the two clans. We Nimali transform into animals that match the essence of our daimons, while the Fai keep their own bodies, but take on the daimon's powers."

"And are you born with a daimon?" I wonder if I'm supposed to have one inside me—will that be a dead giveaway that I'm an imposter?

Fortunately, she shakes her head. "You have to go through the trials, but only once you reach adulthood and can fully consent."

Dominga crosses her arms and seems to grow more agitated, but Elayne plows on, ignoring her.

"You have three attempts to leash a daimon—leashing is what we call it. The Fai call it something else, right?"

"Joining," Dominga spits out.

"Right. So you get three attempts, usually starting at around age twenty-one or so."

"And what happens if you fail?" I ask.

Dominga glares at Elayne, who has finally taken note of

the woman's deteriorating mood and clams up. Dominga answers, enunciating each word carefully. "Each failure results in the forfeit of a soul. You can survive without two, but if you fail a third time, you die."

"So…we have three souls?"

"Memory, voice, and shadow."

"The first two seem self-explanatory, but what happens when you lose a shadow soul?"

"You lose your shadow." Her tone is like she's talking to a preschooler. Then she points to the ground beneath us. The overhead sun has created shadows for everyone around.

Everyone except me.

I stumble, but recover quickly. My breathing grows shallow. I wave a hand around but there's nothing. No movement at all.

"Your souls are restored when you leash your daimon," Elayne chirps. But I barely hear her. How is this even possible? I'm not Celena, I'm from a place where shadow souls aren't even a thing—at least I don't think they are—but here I am with no shadow. Did I lose a soul when I was brought here?

"So I've tried before?" The whisper is so quiet I don't think they can hear it, but Dominga nods. No shadow. No memory—though that at least isn't true. My memory is perfect even if virtually no one here understands.

I'm still reeling from the revelation that my shadow is missing when the soldiers stop walking. Lyall turns to me. "It is important for our subjects to see your strength, dear girl. You are unbowed and unbroken. No one here is your equal. They're barely worthy of setting eyes upon you and should treat this opportunity as the great gift it is."

I blink, surprised, but nod as if I've understood. Lyall moves forward and the sea of guards parts for him. I follow the king into the lobby of a brick building facing the plaza. It turns out to be a fabric mill and clothing manufacturer.

Inside, the workers are already lined up waiting for us.

There's a giant showroom with curtain-length swatches of fabric hanging from the walls in dozens of shades of red and blue, along with a handful of browns. That's it. The fabric comes in different textures from satiny smooth to the leatherish texture of my own outfit.

The managers show off their wares with pride, but fear tightens their expressions as Lyall marches over to a display and brushes the cloth with a hand. Tension clogs the air as he affects a thoughtful expression. Then he releases the cloth and wanders away.

"This is all so lovely," I say, to cut through the thickness in the air. "I can't wait to go shopping." The factory owners release a collective breath and smile.

"We'll have some bolts sent over to the royal seamstress immediately for you, Your Grace," the woman says.

I'm about to deny the offer—I definitely have more than enough clothes—but Dominga catches my eye and gives a swift shake of her head. A thanks is on the tip of my tongue, but she narrows her eyes, so I bite my tongue and simply nod. The woman in blue beams.

The tour continues, focused mostly on the buildings surrounding the plaza. We meet business owners and crafts-men, engineers, scientists, and a troupe of actors rehearsing in a small playhouse. We tour a hydroponic farm that takes up the entirety of a tall building at the far edge of the park. Apparently, there are several like it scattered across the reclaimed part of the city and they provide all the city's produce.

Everyone we meet is dressed in either a red or blue color palette until we reach our final stop, three blocks off the plaza. It's a building that reminds me of an old bank, with half a dozen roman columns holding up the front portico. There are words carved into the cracked white stone. I can just make out *Reserve Bank* and smile to myself.

The inside has been completely redone and is now a

honeycomb of rooms, each filled with children all wearing shades of brown clothing that is ill-fitting and obviously of lesser quality. Joy seems in short supply here. The children are polite and well groomed, but there's no laughter ringing through the halls. There doesn't seem to be a playground or play area at all.

"The Umber orphanage is one of your favorite charities," Elayne confides in me as we stroll down dark hallways. Every building we've been in has covered all the exterior windows from the inside. The interior light always has a blue cast to it, giving everything a sheen of iciness.

Everyone is obviously afraid of King Lyall. He hasn't lost his temper once, hasn't snarled or threatened, but each person we meet seems wholly focused on his reactions. After their initial welcomes and expressions of gratitude for my safe return, I'm largely ignored, an afterthought, which does tell me something about the princess. She must have existed in her father's shadow; no one here is afraid of *her*.

I think I've done okay so far. I've been cool and somewhat remote, nodding regally instead of being effusive with my thanks or praise, and no one has commented or seemed surprised. Shad's promise to help is never far from my mind— I need to talk to him in private again so we can figure out how I got here and if I can go back.

But the more people I meet, the more I wonder if the princess can do more to help. It's clear that this place has a whole set of problems, my new father included, and if my presence here can be beneficial in any way, shouldn't I help to change things? If I can.

We exit back onto the plaza, ready for the next stop on the tour, when an alarm blares. Every building seems to be equipped with a speaker; the high-pitched sirens leave me covering my ears and crouching as the guards surrounding me draw tighter.

People are shouting and then Shad is there, holding me by the elbow and urging me forward. "To the shelter!" he yells.

"What is it? What's happening?" I ask as soldiers form a protective circle around me and we hustle forward.

"The lockdown alarm." Shad's voice is barely audible over the piercing bleats. "There's been a breach somewhere in the city. We need to get you to safety."

We run to the nearest building, an astonishingly modern, silver mass of smooth shapes that reminds me of the Disney Concert Hall in Los Angeles. The shiny metal is reflective and looks like someone bent a few sheets of steel into different directions and set them down. It definitely didn't exist in my San Francisco.

The wide double doors open on their own and we rush in, though some of the guards who were with us peel off and stay outside. I don't know what I was expecting of the interior, but a giant, empty room was not on the list. The entire first floor is a wide expanse of gray slate flooring—no furniture, no walls, nothing. But I barely have time to register the oddness when I'm led to the corner where a stairwell lies.

My retinue is down to Shad, Ryin, and three other guards. They draw to a halt just in front of the stairway entrance, which is dimly lit with bliss lights. Concrete steps descend into darkness, with the low blue glow barely bright enough to make anything out.

Shad releases me and takes a step back. "Go with them down to the shelter where you'll be safe. I'll come back to get you once the all-clear sounds." With that, he jogs away, and in a brilliant flash of light, transforms into a dragon—this one blue and silver with a wingspan so wide I can't even fathom it.

My jaw is slack. I've really only seen a shift once, when Lyall did it, and my brain is having a hard time catching up to my eyes. Shad takes flight, right there inside the building, and heads toward the ceiling. Some sensor must turn on, because part of the roof retracts and then he's through it, disappearing into the blue of the sky.

I continue staring up at the space he just occupied, but the soldier to my left, a tall South Asian man, his long hair caught in a low ponytail, urges me forward. "We must get you to the shelter, Your Grace."

I nod and turn back to the stairway of doom and start down, my body still shaking from shock. I'm sandwiched between the two men and one woman with Ryin bringing up the rear.

"Is everyone here a dragon?" I ask, my voice echoing.

"No, Your Grace. Only the king and prince."

We descend into the depths of the building. There are so many steps that I'm breathing hard and sweating by the time we finally reach the bottom. It's cool and damp and more than a little creepy. A wide, rusted metal door that looks like it hasn't been opened in centuries is set in the middle of a cinderblock wall. Next to it, the smooth panel of white looks out of place. But when the soldier who spoke to me places his hand on it, the whole thing glows blue and the door pops open with an ominous creak.

"Your Grace." He motions me inside the room, and I step through the doorway on rubbery legs.

"All the buildings in the plaza are fitted with these shelters," he tells me. "It's protocol when a lockdown alarm is given."

The darkened room lights up when I step inside to reveal gray cinderblock walls and a small space about ten by ten with a cot sitting along the far wall. The only other furniture is a metal bookshelf stocked with canned food, a first-aid kit marked with the familiar red cross, and a few other unlabeled boxes. A covered silver can about two feet tall sits in the corner. I hope that's not a toilet—then again, I hope it is.

This place is narrow and coffin-like, and I balk at the

thought of spending any time entombed here. "About how long do the lockdowns last?" Panic edges my voice.

"Generally no more than a few hours, Your Grace."

"Hours?" Now the panic isn't just along the edges—it's all throughout. I shake my head. I can't stay in this tiny box for hours. The walls already seem to be sliding inward. "There's got to be another option."

"Other than the Citadel, these shelters are the safest places to be during an attack." His voice is patient, but his eyes are strained.

"Five adults cannot possibly spend multiple hours in this tiny room."

"The shelters are for the highest-ranking Nimali present. Only the healer will be with you. We will stay outside to guard the exterior."

I swallow and feel tears stinging my eyes. At some point Ryin slipped in; I feel his silent presence at my back.

"It's the king's orders," the soldier says, and my resistance melts away. There's no way I can ask one of them to go against the king. I have no doubt that Lyall would deal very harshly with them, so I nod mutely and the soldier bows before closing the door in my face.

Locking me into my nightmare.

Chapter Thirteen

RYIN

Princess Celena hasn't moved from her spot in front of the door for minutes. I would call out to her, but the drudges are prohibited from speaking unless spoken to—those of us with our voices intact, at least. However, the princess doesn't recall the rules. And by now I know that the version of Celena who returned from across the wall would not punish me for breaking protocol. Especially seeing as she does so herself regularly.

"Your Grace?" A shudder ripples through her; my voice seems to have broken her spell. She turns around, the pallid tone to her usually vibrant complexion making her appear waxy.

"You're ill. Please sit down." I motion to the bed and she shakes her head but sits anyway.

"I'm not ill, I'm just..." She sucks in a staggering breath. Her head swivels, looking from wall to wall, agitation palpable. "I don't like small spaces."

I'd gathered as much from her reaction to the elevators. Compassion surges from my daimon and, begrudgingly, from me. Was she held captive in some small prison? Her body may remember even with her memory soul lost.

"I'm sorry to say that is not something I can heal." I don't know why I add this, but she looks up, surprised.

"I wouldn't think so." She frowns. Tilts her head. "How does your healing work? What kinds of things *can* you heal?"

"My daimon can manipulate the physical form, heal wounds, change temperatures, force sleep or waking."

She nods, but I'm not entirely sure she's listening. Her eyes are glassy, her breathing labored. I move across from her to lean against the wall but she slides over on the cot.

"You can sit," she says. I eye the space next to her dubiously. "Please. It would help me. Besides, it's cold here." She punctuates the statement with a shiver.

I take a deep breath, cross the few feet separating us, then sit beside her on the cot, leaving a healthy distance between us. Her gaze strokes the side of my face, almost like a touch. My daimon urges me closer. Goosebumps rise on her skin, but she incongruously begins fanning herself as if she's warm. Then she leans over, face between her knees, breathing in and out very loudly.

My daimon rushes forward to investigate, brightening the space with its glow. We search her body for the cause to this reaction, but there's nothing. No physical injury, just the rapid pace of her heart and her frayed breathing. Instinctively, and against all common sense, I place my hand on her back and rub circles to try to calm her. She wraps her arms around herself and, slowly, the trembling subsides. My hand stays where it is, and even though she's bent forward, she seems to lean in to my touch. My daimon retreats, satisfied I have the situation in hand but ready to lend aid when needed.

"I'm sorry. I'm trying to keep it together here," she says, voice muffled.

"Take your time." She cannot control her claustrophobia.

I have known seasoned soldiers who would be hard pressed to withstand this type of mental stress.

"Can you talk to me? Take my mind off it. Where—where are you from?"

To share anything of home with a Nimali feels profane, but she seems relatively nonthreatening sitting here. And all of the differences between how she acted before and how she is now form an avalanche in my mind that loosens my tongue.

"The Fai home in Aurum is called the Greenlands. It lies to the west and overlooks the ocean. It is a beautiful place, not of concrete and stone, but of greenery. After the Sorrows, we did not try to mimic the human life we had lost—we saw an opportunity to become closer with nature. The Nimali mine the bliss and wrangle it into their technology. We revere the bliss and hold it as sacred and it blesses us."

"So you pray to it?"

"Not as such, but we believe bliss is sentient and divine. It's part matter and part spirit and connects our two worlds. Using it as the Nimali do is enslavement and moreover wasteful. They mine the bliss and when a matrix is used up, they move on to another. It isn't sustainable. The bliss in an empty matrix will never return."

"You're conservationists," she says with a smile in her voice. She's breathing more normally now, though still bent over. I continue to smooth circles against the fabric of her top, but when I brush against the soft skin on the back of her shoulders, I pull back. Celena lets out a sound of protest.

I slide farther down the cot. "Fai are not allowed to touch Nimali. We're not allowed to speak unless spoken to."

"That is such bullshit." She sits up and turns to face me. "I know you're a prisoner and you're basically enslaved. But when we were on the wall—I mean, what keeps you from escaping? Why not just run away? Those were Fai who ambushed us in the jeep. You could have left with them."

The urge I'd had hits me again just as strong. "When the Nimali capture prisoners, they take one of our souls."

Her eyes widen. "They *take* one." She blinks rapidly. "You still have your voice and your memory." She looks down to the floor and the wall, to the shadows cast by the shelving and the bed. "They took your shadow." Her voice is a whisper.

"It was my dominant soul—that is the one you lose first. When a soul is taken, we must stay near to wherever it's kept or else our daimons will weaken and eventually die, and us along with them. If we leave Nimali territory, our lives are forfeit."

"So if you lose three souls, you die, and if you go too far from your stolen soul, you also die...But how is it that I'm alive? If everyone believes I've lost my memory soul?"

"You have no daimon. To unite with a daimon is to share your body and your souls. The two of you are connected. But the daimons are much more sensitive to soul loss than a human is."

Her brow crinkles. "And is it a problem, that I don't have a daimon?"

"You will need one in order to be queen. Your father will want you to undergo the next trial soon." It feels strange to be so forthright with the princess, but she appears to appreciate it.

"But he loves...me. He believes I only have one soul left. I don't think he would risk my life like that." But she doesn't sound sure.

"He loves ruling. Loves being a dragon. Loves his legacy." I want to add more but hold myself back. Even with her new openness, it wouldn't be wise to disparage the king out loud.

"But isn't Shad...he has a daimon. He's a whole dragon. He can be the legacy."

I shrug. Their internal family structure and lines of succession are not my business or my concern, but the topic troubles her a great deal, I can tell.

She sucks in a breath and her gaze darts around the room before centering on the floor. Her heartbeat speeds again— she's growing more anxious. "Can all Fai heal?"

"No. Your abilities depend on your daimon. They come in four aspects: fire, land, air, and water. I have a fire daimon."

She tilts her head, birdlike. "What kind of animal?"

My lips press together. "We do not share that with Nimali." A sharp pain pricks my chest when her face falls.

"And what qualities does your fire daimon give you?"

"Mainly healing." I cannot tell her the rest. Many of our powers we have carefully hidden from our captors.

"And Noomi? Am I allowed to ask what she can do?"

"She has a water daimon. Hers allows her to cleanse and purify, among other things."

Celena nods, deep in thought. I think I've successfully distracted her from her distress again. All of her physical symptoms have abated, for which I'm grateful. Not just because if the king heard of it he'd have my head, but I think I'm starting to care about the princess's well-being. Her reaction to the revelations are not what I would have expected from her even a day ago. Celena was always a remote, icy creature. Eager for knowledge and not particularly warm or kind. Not unkind either, per se, just distant.

But the returned Celena wears her heart on her sleeve. I think again of Von's plan to use her and it leaves me cold.

She falls quiet after that, as do I. I don't know that I've spoken so much in the past three years. But the changes her experience has wrought on her seem to be deep. And she seems so sincere and earnest. I seriously consider Noomi's statement—can this Celena be an ally and not an enemy?

Chapter Fourteen

TALIA

RYIN and I sit in companionable silence for a while. As long as he talks, I can keep the panic at bay, but I don't want to force him and he seems like more of the silent type. However, in the quiet, focusing on the sound of his breathing proves to be calming. I shut my eyes and imagine I'm in a wide, open space —a football field, a desert, Antarctica, somewhere with no walls at all—and listen to his steady breaths.

I relive the sensation of him rubbing soothing circles on my back and bite back a request for him to do it again. Even if I'm not technically ordering him to do something for me, the power differential is clear in my mind. Any request is de facto a command. But enduring this space is getting hard again, and as the minutes tick by, my breath grows shakier. I squeeze my eyes tightly, desperately grabbing for that fleeting sense of peace that I'd held just before. But it's gone.

I'm dizzy in the darkness behind my eyelids when the door opens. I jump up and race past the surprised faces of the guards, then lean against the cold cinderblocks sucking in deep breaths.

Murmurs sound behind me—Ryin's low voice and the lead guard, probably talking about my condition. Once I feel better, I turn to face them.

"How long were we in there?"

"Forty-five minutes, Your Grace," the blond man answers.

I gape at him. It felt like hours.

My eyes close on a long blink before I snap them open again. "And what was the source of the alarm?"

"A Revoker breached the secure area. That's all we were told." This from the female guard who towers over me.

"What...what are your names?" I don't want to keep referring to them as "ponytail" or "the blond one."

The woman looks to the others as if unsure whether to answer. The South Asian man answers. "I am Harshal, this is Callum and Zanna. We are part of the prince's honor guard and will be providing your security."

"Thank—" I catch myself about to thank them and screw up my lips. How much does Shad trust them? Has he told them the truth about me?

"Are you allowed to tell me what animals you turn into?"

"Certainly, Your Grace. My daimon is an eagle." I recall the giant bird who swooped in on the wall. Was that Harshal?

"A lion," says Callum, straightening proudly. He's pale with curly, sandy hair and a kind face, like it would rather be smiling than holding any other expression. He's in direct opposition to the Amazonian next to him, Zanna, with her golden-brown skin and a braid as thick as my wrist going down to her waist. A scowl seems to be her go-to.

"Bear," is her terse response.

"Were all of you there when I was found?"

As one, they nod in assent. "And the prince, he confides in you?" I'm testing the waters here, unsure of what I'll find.

Harshal shoots the others a warning look, then glances from the corner of his eye at Ryin behind him. "He does, Your Grace." Then he sweeps an arm toward the steps, and I get the point. He doesn't trust Ryin, and while I don't want to believe the Fai man would betray me, if he ever learned the truth, he likely wouldn't have a choice.

Zanna and Callum precede me up the steps. We emerge back into the big empty room just as Shad enters—human again—talking on his comm. He ends the call as we approach. I'm glad to see that he's okay. If he had a run-in with a Revoker, there's no evidence of it.

"You weren't injured, were you?"

He seems surprised at the question. "No. The...situation was handled. No one was harmed."

I nod, grateful. "I would prefer to never do that again," I tell him. "Since I've...*returned* I find that small spaces do not agree with me."

His eyes widen a fraction. "Each building is equipped with an emergency shelter; however, in the event of another alarm, we will make an effort to return you to the Citadel where you can move about freely in the event of an incident."

"I would appreciate it." I pause, looking around the vast space. "What is this building used for anyway? Storage?"

"This is the library."

"What?" I look around with wide eyes. "But it's empty. Where are the books?"

Shad shrugs. "Books are fragile. Any paper text that survived the Sorrows was stored in the stream so the knowledge could be kept forever."

"The stream?"

"I can help you with that, Your Grace," a gravelly voice grits out from behind me.

I turn and stare and keep staring until I know I'm being rude. My eyes probably dry out and crust over I stare so long, but I just can't bring myself to do anything else.

"You're an elephant." The first words that come out of my mouth aren't what I intended to say, but they come out none-theless. And they're not really rude...I mean, he's not just a very large man who might derisively be called elephant-sized. He is a literal elephant. A small one, I think, at about ten feet high, with gray skin and ivory tusks and intelligent, dark eyes. And very light on his feet, because he totally snuck up on me, but an elephant just the same. One who can, apparently, talk.

"Yes, Your Grace. My name is Akeem. I am the librarian."

The elephant bows deeply by straightening his front legs and dipping his head. His trunk curls upward and his ears flatten. I've witnessed a dragon turn into a man and a man turn into a dragon and people with glowing eyes floating into the sky, so you'd think I wouldn't be surprised at anything that happens here. But I am. I slowly gather my wits and close my mouth. Then try to affect a regal demeanor. "It's very nice to meet you, Akeem."

I pause for a long moment and then decide to just go for it. "Would it be unforgivably rude for me to ask *why* you are an elephant?"

He huffs in what might be a laugh. "You mean, why I do not shift back into my human form?"

"Sure."

"You are the princess, you may ask what you wish." His voice is a deep rumble that I can feel in the soles of my feet. But it's not unpleasant.

"Yes, but if the subject is somehow uncomfortable to discuss, I don't want to cause you pain."

His eyes widen a fraction. "You are all kindness, Your Grace. The covenant I struck with my daimon is different than most. It loves knowledge, and I allow it to stay present in its physical form and soak it all in. Most shifted Nimali cannot speak, but it's given me that gift as well. My natural body is frail and unhealthy and it is easier for me to stay as you see me."

"Oh," is all I can say.

"Healer, you may wait outside," Shad says to Ryin, who bows before exiting. I watch him walk away then raise my brows at Shad. He pulls a little box from his pocket, about the size of an ice cube. When he taps the side of it, the thing starts to glow blue.

"This is a dampener; it ensures we won't be overheard," he says, responding to my silent question. "If you must speak inside a building of something you don't want others to hear, you'd be wise to use one."

I swallow and look around the vast room. Could there be hidden microphones somewhere? Who's listening? I take a step closer to Shad.

"Akeem here, as well as my honor guard, has been entrusted with your secret."

Callum smiles a little, while Harshal and Zanna remain impassive. "These are my closest confidantes," Shad continues. "I have trusted them with my life on many occasions. And Akeem is our best option for understanding how you came to be here and how we can get you back to your home."

My stomach knots at the statement. Home. Is that what it was? "I appreciate your help. All of your help, and I'll do what I can to help *you*. Though it might help to know what exactly you all are doing."

"We are trying to prevent a war." Shad's voice is matter-of-fact.

"Yes, but how? You want me to distract the king, but Lyall doesn't seem like he's going to be spending all of his time with me. I'm not sure how much I can do."

Harshal scratches his chin. "Do you think she can influence him to entertain peace talks with the Fai?"

"Perhaps," Shad replies, though he looks dubious. "But it must be done naturally, motivated by something tangible. The real Celena was not a proactive proponent for peace."

I straighten. "What was she like?"

"Difficult to know. Quiet, aloof, fairly apathetic."

My heart sinks as Zanna pipes in. "She kept *you* at arm's

length because of her father's machinations." She turns to me. "He wanted to see them wed."

"B-But you're her stepbrother."

Shad shrugs.

"Did you want...?"

"No. Neither did she, and honestly it's not something we spoke of. I believe she resented me for my position and my daimon. She desperately wanted to leash a dragon daimon." A tinge of bitterness has crept into his tone.

"But she leashed none at all," I whisper, looking at all the shadows on the ground and swallowing. "Well, I do want to help."

"First," Akeem pipes in with his great rumble of a voice, "it would behoove you to learn more about this world and what you're up against."

I smile, liking the way he thinks. "Good thing we're in a library. Will you show me how this place works?"

"Of course. Please follow me."

"I will leave you to it," Shad says. "We will speak again after dinner." He taps the dampener, turning it off, then pockets it.

I wish we could talk more now, but he seems to be in a hurry. I wave goodbye and follow Akeem. He's incongruously graceful as he walks across the empty room. My three guards spread out to defensive positions around the room. The sounds of flowing water capture my attention.

Liquid has begun gushing out of the ground about a dozen feet away. It whirls like a cyclone, and at the top, it spreads out horizontally in a flat disc then falls back in a curtain. It's like a three-dimensional column of water with a tiny tornado at the center. I can't stop looking at it, tilting my head trying to understand exactly what I'm seeing. It's not really water, being tinted blue like mouthwash—liquid bliss, Lord Jovi said, same as the liquid in the data tablets.

"What is that?" I whisper, a little in awe.

"That, Your Grace, is the stream." He sweeps his trunk toward the swirling liquid. "The stream is how we store information using bliss. In its solid form, bliss fuels our technology and provides light and power. But in its liquid form, it is the perfect medium for holding the collected knowledge of the Nimali."

"But how do you...? What's the interface?" I took a coding class in high school but can't wrap my mind around how this possibly works.

"Let me show you. Please, stand here." He motions with his trunk to the center of a large slate square directly next to the fountain. I stand where he says, expecting to feel the splash of the liquid bliss and surprised not to.

"Now simply make a query of the fountain." His voice is a gentle vibration.

"I just ask the water a question?"

"Yes, Your Grace."

They all come to my brain at once and I have to pick one of the many vying for prominence. I decide to start small. "When are we—in time?"

Four walls of water shoot up all around me, along the borders of the slate square, coming from dozens of tiny jets that must be embedded in the ground. I jump as the stream blasts well above my head and flows very precisely, entirely self-contained without splashing at all. A voice comes out of the liquid, a voice that sounds very much like Akeem's throaty rumble. "Today is the fifth day of the Weed Month, year fifty-three Post Sorrows."

"Great. Super helpful." I try another tack. "What planet is this?"

"This planet is called Earth."

The water disappears as quickly as it came, leaving only the still-gurgling fountain in the next square. I breathe out a nervous laugh and swallow, feeling like my eyes are going to pop out of my head.

"How many Earths are there?"

The water shoots up again, caging me, surprising me even though I'd expected it. "In the universe or the multiverse?" it responds in Akeem's low baritone.

"Um, the multiverse?"

"There are infinite Earths in the multiverse."

The water dies down again and I whisper, "This is so crazy." I spin around, delighted and astounded, and grin up at Akeem. "Why does it sound like you?"

"I am the librarian," he replies simply.

I shake my head. "Are there visuals at all?"

"Certainly. Ask the stream to show you something."

I focus back in and come up with a question. "Please show me a map of this Earth."

The stream shoots up and one of the four sides surrounding me resolves itself into a screen of moving, calm liquid. A glowing image emerges from the flow in monochromatic blue. It's a map showing the world I know, but with some big differences.

Eurasia has split apart through what I think is Iraq and Western Russia, and Africa is more like a gigantic island adrift in the Atlantic—much farther west than in my world. In North America, Maine and Florida and much of the East Coast are missing and a wide sea separates California, Oregon, and Washington from the rest of the country. Central America is a tiny, thin strip of land and Australia is just a small blob in the South Pacific, barely bigger than New Zealand.

"This was rendered from the last pre-Sorrows satellite image," the real Akeem says. "All satellites ceased functioning at that time and no more recent images are available." The image slowly fades, the liquid lowering again.

The next question pops into my mind suddenly. "How do you travel between the different Earths?"

"Interdimensional travel is not possible," the library says.

I look to Akeem. His eyes crinkle in what I think might be a sad smile. There's such a gentleness about him, so much comfort in his tranquil energy, that it seems to sink into my bones. "Yes, Your Grace, there are limits to the knowledge that we've gathered."

"You know you don't have to call me that—Your Grace. Not when it's just us."

"It is habit, and I should hate to forget when it is not just us." He winks and I nod, chagrined.

"Of course."

"I have some other resources that I will consult regarding your predicament. Use this time to better familiarize yourself with this world. There is not much information on Princess Celena, however. But there is a wealth on many other topics."

"That's too bad. I feel like I'm doing a terrible job at being her."

"Very few knew her well, and the loss of a memory soul affects each person differently. I'm certain you are doing a fine job. There is, after all, no reason for anyone to suspect you are not who you appear to be."

His reassuring words wrap around me. "Thank you." I can't hold back the gratitude in this moment.

"I will leave you to it, Your Grace. Just call out if you need me." He turns slowly and moves to the far side of the room, then taps a spot with his trunk. A portion of the wall slides open, revealing an enormous elevator. Convenient for him.

Once he's gone, I turn back to the fountain, careful not to shift too much on my square of slate. I forgot to ask how to take notes; I haven't seen paper or pens anywhere here and I guess they don't use them, but for now, I'm determined to soak up as much information as I can. So I begin asking questions. I have a whole memory soul's worth of knowledge to replace.

Chapter Fifteen

TALIA

WHEN I RETURN to the Citadel, a guard in the lobby informs me that the king would like to see me.

"Please head to the forty-seventh floor, Your Grace," the young woman says. "The healer's presence is not required."

Ryin bows before disappearing around the corner, headed away from the elevator bank. For some reason, I feel more comfortable when he's around. I don't want to look into those feelings too much, so I stuff them down and pour all of my energy into withstanding the elevator.

Harshal, Callum, and Zanna ride up with me in silence and if they notice my distress, they don't draw attention to it. When the doors finally open, I release the air trapped in my lungs in a gush as we step out of the metal box.

The hallways in the Citadel look just like any office building I've ever seen: bland and tan with thin carpeting underfoot. Of course, there are the biometric doors and the glowing blue orbs in the ceiling giving off bliss light—spirit energy. I'm still trying to wrap my mind around that.

A hallway leads off to the right, but Harshal stops just outside the elevator, where two guards are stationed on either side of a door. Instead of the single handprint sensor that leads to my suite, this doorway has three different indentations.

"What is this place?"

"The royal vault, Your Grace," Harshal answers.

The second elevator dings and the doors slide open, revealing Lyall with his own guards. The short hallway is quite crowded now, mostly with soldiers. They take up positions along the wall, shoulder to shoulder.

"Celena, my girl!" Lyall booms, again overjoyed to see me.

I swallow, hating the fact that his greeting warms me inside. "Everything's okay now, right? Shad said that Revoker didn't hurt anyone."

He tilts his head as if I've said something odd. "Our soldiers dealt with it. Nothing for you to worry about. You were never in any danger."

He approaches the one door in sight and presses his hand to the lowest indentation in the wall next to it until it pulses blue. Then he leans his head to the second notch, which appears to scan his eye, and finally, he again presses his hand to the third and highest one. When he pulls back, a bead of blood is visible on his palm.

"Only you and I have access to the vault," he explains. "It is tuned to our blood—our living blood pumping through our veins. No one can steal blood from us to open these doors. The sensors also test for the presence of adrenaline and will not open it if we are exhibiting a fear response like we're being forced to open it. Ingenious, really."

Pride wafts from him like smoke. The door slides open and it's thicker than the other doors I've seen: nearly three times as thick. No drilling through it either, apparently.

We step into a small vestibule with a round table and two

plush chairs. Beyond is a dimly lit room bearing rows of shelving. The closest ones reminds me of a safety deposit box room in a bank, with rectangular lockers taking up all of the space.

"So bliss makes all of that possible?" I ask, waving back toward the door we just came through.

"Our scientists innovate the usage of bliss every day. It is the key to keeping our people happy and successful. It is part of the strength of our line." Lyall makes a fist and holds it up to indicate strength.

I want to shrink away from him, from the violent gleam in his eye, but I hold steady, mindful of my role. If I'm going to try to push him toward peace, I need to move slowly...plant seeds, and hopefully watch them bloom.

"So the Fai stand in the way of that? Is that why you capture them and make them drudges?"

"Oh, yes. With the bliss, we developed the soulcatchers— the devices which steal a person's dominant soul. But let's not discuss all of that now. I brought you here so that you could pick out your jewels."

Disappointment squeezes my chest as we enter the vault. Lights on motion sensors blink to life when we walk down the aisles, and they create harsh shadows for Lyall and none for me. He chatters on about the treasure in the vault and all of the wonderful things they've reclaimed from all over the city. We pass row after row, the initial bank deposit boxes transitioning to more of a warehouse. It's full of junk from what I can see: furniture and artwork, frames, old computers, electrical equipment, parts of machines. So much stuff—these are the treasures he's so proud of?

The vault must take up most of this floor, because we just keep walking. Beyond the last shelf of crap, the cases are shorter and it's like we've entered a jewelry store. Reclaimed glass jewel cases surround me, all of them full to overflowing.

Necklaces and earrings and rings and items I can't even

name are laid out beneath the glass. Bliss floor lamps shine down on everything. I'm completely overwhelmed.

"Pick out a few things that you like," Lyall says, appearing pleased with my reaction.

I hesitate, still staring around me while he lifts the cover of the nearest case. It's full of chunky, gaudy baubles that look heavy and made for an old lady. I shake my head and move on to the next one, skimming my fingers across the glass. Toward the center of this section, I stop before a case with delicate silver necklaces bearing diamond and amethyst pendants. Purple is my favorite color and I admire the jewelry for long moments.

"Princesses wear rubies or garnets or topaz. We give pieces like these to those lower in rank. Gifts for attendants who please us or to the enemies of those we wish to push harder."

He leads me by the elbow to another case with items I like half as much. I suck in a breath, paste on a smile, then choose a few pieces at random. This is not for me. This is not my life. It's Celena's. I have no idea what she would like, but the choices please Lyall. He picks up the necklace I point at and drapes it around my neck. Helps me fasten the bracelets on my wrist.

There's no mirror, but I don't need to look at myself again anyway. I see the approval reflected in the face of my father— Celena's father—and I feel I've done well. But it leaves me brittle and empty.

"When you are queen, you will inherit your mother's jewels. I'm only sad that she will not be here to see it."

I struggle to picture her face. When I went to live with my father, I took nothing but the clothes on my back. I didn't even have a picture of her. Apparently, our landlord had thrown or given away all of our stuff while I was in the hospital.

Memories are fleeting and easily damaged. Perhaps even in my world the memory is somehow connected to the soul. I run a finger across the chunky jewels at my neck, still caught with one foot in the past. "How do you think I lost my memory soul? Unless a Nimali with one of those soulcatchers took it—"

"No Nimali would dare." He practically growls the words. "I control access to them personally."

"Of course. I just don't understand what could have happened."

He peers at me and then leads me to a mismatched set of armchairs against the wall. We sit and he reaches for my hands. "Your desire for a daimon was strong. Before you disappeared, you'd been very interested in the old legends. Ancient tales of early leashings. Long ago, dragon daimons were far more common, and some have theorized that the purity of the bliss is the reason."

I tilt my head in question.

"While we are not zealots like the Fai, some among the Nimali do believe that unmined bliss is more potent. That you have a better chance of leashing a powerful predator if you undergo the trial in an untouched bliss pool."

"So bliss is required for the trial."

"Yes, you must submerge yourself in liquid bliss to visit the spirit world and be chosen by a daimon. I believe that, driven by duty, you went outside the wall to find a source of untouched bliss. The Fai guard theirs stridently, and you must have believed you could avoid the Revokers somehow."

Chills run down my spine. I can recall exactly the terrifying sound of the Revoker. Those glowing red eyes. "That would have been very foolish of me."

"Very foolish indeed. But you are a deeply determined young woman, Celena. And, honestly, it is just the sort of thing I would have done at your age." His hands tighten on my own, still gentle, but firm.

"However, you must promise not to do it again. Your next trial will take place in the Citadel. Those old stories are nonsense—I leashed my daimon here and you will too. You *will* be queen, my dear."

The words are meant to be encouraging, but to my ears they sound ominous. Celena died in pursuit of a daimon, and our fates might not be that different.

Chapter Sixteen

RYIN

ONE OF THE first things you learn as a drudge is to avert your gaze. Never look at anyone in the eye, especially a Cardinal. They're the ones we have the most interaction with, and one of the aristocrats can get you sent to the locker or trammeled faster than an eye blink if they feel disrespected. The Azures aren't much better. On the occasions when they deal with a Fai drudge, it's like they want to assert what little power they have. They seem to think abusing us is a way to get fast tracked for an elevation in rank, so it's best to steer clear of them when possible. Umbers barely have higher status than we do and they're usually not a problem. So, much as it galls me, I keep my head down most of the time here. The upside is, you see a lot when you're looking at nothing.

Tonight, however, there's not much to report on in the ballroom. The place has started to fill up, though the royals have yet to make an appearance. A few soldiers on duty as guards are scattered across the large space, but I don't expect to be able to collect any intel.

I was ordered to report for duty here after leaving the princess—all hands were needed on deck for the celebratory dinner. It should be a welcome reprieve from having to follow Celena's every move. Though today's tour was a gold mine of information. Most of the Fai drudges work in the Citadel or one of the factories. We don't have free rein to traipse around the Nimali territory, so I took full advantage to memorize every detail I thought might be useful.

Von's new mission, to somehow prepare an attack on the Nimali from within the Citadel, is madness. I still believe our best option is to locate a weakness that the bulk of the Fai forces can exploit, and today's opportunity was a gift.

Memories of the afternoon in the shelter assault me unwillingly. Celena's scent, a light and citrusy aroma, has stayed with me all day. I can't recall ever noticing how the princess smelled before, but now I can't seem to forget it.

But these thoughts are dangerous and useless. I force myself to focus on the task at hand, carefully placing a tray of hors d'oeuvres on a table laden with fresh flowers. These state dinners, even with their excess and pretentious finery, are actually one of the only bright spots of my time here. Most Fai feel the same. On these occasions, the Nimali decorate the otherwise sterile ballroom not with reclaimed junk from before the Sorrows, but with a profusion of flowers.

Cascades of blooms from the hothouses adorn every surface. Clusters of chrysanthemums and cockscombs overflow their vases on the tables, while garlands made of yarrow and anemone are looped on the walls. They are reminders of our home, a green and fertile place that contrasts starkly with the unyielding urban wasteland in which the Nimali live. And even if these blossoms have been plucked from their roots and sit here dying, used as mere decoration, there are enough land daimons among the Fai to keep the plants alive.

After these events, all of the flowers are meant to be

thrown away, added to the compost used by the growhouses. But many are retained in secret, hidden out of sight of the Nimali in closets on Fai floors, kept alive by our daimons and bringing us small reminders of the home to which we long to return.

I'm admiring a delicate orchid set apart from the others when a hush falls across the room. I can feel her before I even turn toward the main doors. Celena has arrived.

She is escorted by the king and dressed in a blood-red, shimmering, backless gown with a plunging neckline. The architecture of the dress makes no sense to me, but she is stunning in it. For long moments I forget that I am supposed to be averting my gaze and stare openly at her.

She catches my eye and a pulse of awareness passes between us. It's like a live wire that shocks my senses and singes my skin. I break eye contact first to stare at the floor before someone notices. But that thing—whatever it was that shot from her to me—still buzzes through my blood, heating it.

Through my peripheral vision, I observe her taking in the ballroom and decorations for the first time. Witnessing her simple wonder as her life is revealed to her again lightens something within me. It's a sensation so disturbing that I need to physically turn away from her presence. I exit the ballroom to go back into the staging area where dozens of Fai toil to make this dinner happen.

Noomi hustles by with a covered platter in her hands. She takes one look at my face and stops, frowning.

"I'm fine," I whisper, but she knows me too well. It's hard to hide from her. Luckily her hands are full so she can't question me. "Really, I am." Then I turn like a coward and flee. Looks like I need to avoid more than one woman here this evening.

I take a position in a line of workers transferring the appetizers from the cooking trays brought up from the kitchens on other floors to the serving platters. It's mindless, repetitive work that keeps me away from my cousin's penetrating gaze.

The nearby door to the short hallway leading to the stairwell opens and closes constantly as food is delivered. I block it out until a change in the status quo makes me take notice. Beyond the door, I catch a glimpse of the back of Von's head and his distinctive copper-colored hair. Facing him is Enzo, wearing his perpetual glower. I can never quite tell what Enzo is feeling, as his expression rarely changes. But he finally shrugs and hands off something to Von before heading toward the staircase.

Von turns just as the door to the prep area is closing. He grabs the door and enters, passing right by me, clutching a small vial in his grip.

"What's that?" I sign.

He grins and puts a finger to his lips. A chill races across my skin.

I'm not aware of any missions going on tonight. A state dinner can be a good opportunity to reconnoiter targeted areas since virtually everyone in the Citadel will be in attendance, but most of those plans have been scrapped in favor of the new objectives. Whatever he's doing either wasn't planned or wasn't shared with the GenFi operatives. Both of those things make me nervous.

Everyone is busy working diligently, and though we're often left to ourselves, impromptu visits by the drudge supervisors happen at random. And if the food is late or improperly plated or found lacking in any way, someone will be punished. No one wants to be the cause of the trammeling of a brother or sister.

Von steps up to the table where the royals' dinners are being plated and warmed. He indicates he wants to join the line and the other workers shuffle around to make room. This leaves him in front of the tureen of synthetic beef soup awaiting the porcelain bowls that have been laid out.

With a mischievous smile on his face, Von uncorks the vial in his hand. I'm over to him in a flash, so fast my daimon must have helped without my conscious thought. I grip his wrist in my hand before he can tip the contents of the vial inside.

"What are you doing?" I demand. He opens his mouth and tries to pull away, but I tighten my hold and sniff. "*Blessed bliss*, are you insane?"

I wrench the vial from his hand and release him, stepping back. "Senna oil? Really?" I dump the liquid directly onto the floor and toss the tiny bottle into the nearest waste bin.

"You poison the royals and half a dozen of us get trammeled at random. Can you really be that stupid?"

His face contorts in anger as he signs. "You know very well it isn't deadly. It will just make them uncomfortable for a few hours. Perhaps clog up their sewage systems."

"We prepare the food here. Any *discomfort* will still fall on our heads. You would unthinkingly sentence the lives of your fellow Fai to a fate worse than death with something so juvenile?" Eyes narrowed, he sets his jaw stubbornly as I continue. "We all want them to suffer, brother. Those of us who have been here for years, who've witnessed countless atrocities. That's why we organize, and plan, and fight."

We've attracted attention. Fortunately, none of the supervisors have made one of their appearances.

"Besides, who do you think unclogs the sewers?" I shake my head, disgusted with him.

Noomi steps to my side, sniffing. The scent of the senna oil is already fading; in another few minutes, it will filter away completely, but she recognizes it too. Her elfin features draw down with her rage. "I hope you'll be at the ceremony tonight to see what your little trick might have cost us," she signs, seething. "You've never seen one, have you? A trammeling?"

Von crosses his arms and refuses to answer, but it's clear.

He's been here less than a full day and those kinds of horrors are unheard of in the Greenlands.

Without another word, he stalks off into the hallway. I for one am glad to see him gone.

"What could he have been thinking?" I ask Noomi.

"He wasn't. That's the problem." Her jaw is still tight and her eyes hard. "I can't believe the Crowns gave him so much responsibility. It should be you, Ryin. You should be leading GenFi."

I step back, not wanting to rehash this old argument again.

"Look what we're left with because you haven't stepped up," she continues.

I hold up my hands, hoping to stop her before she begins a tirade. Noomi is a sweet and gentle soul ninety percent of the time. The other ten percent, she's a harridan.

"Von just needs time to adjust. To learn how things work here. Adapting is difficult when you've been out there on the front lines skirmishing for years. I remember what it was like being new and full of anger. Maybe some of that energy will revitalize us. We'll just have to watch him closely."

Disappointment wafts from her. She purses her lips. "I'll talk to Xipporah. Tell her to keep an eye on him." Then she heads back to her duties just as one of the Nimali supervisors appears from the main ballroom.

The soup, sans laxative, has been ladled into bowls by another worker. I pick up a tray and head out to deliver it, my head warring with my heart the entire way. After my sister died and I was captured, the GenFi in the Citadel thought that I would pick up the mantle of my father and grandfather, both great and respected Fai warriors. But my heart was broken and so was my spirit. I was in no place to lead a rebellion. I could follow orders, take on the small missions, gather intel, help wherever possible, but responsibility? Having others depend on me? How could I do that when I couldn't even save the last member of my immediate family? The girl who had been relying on her big brother to protect her?

It was the right choice then and it's still the right one, no matter what Noomi says. But maybe the people I need to be watching aren't just my enemies, but my allies too.

Chapter Seventeen

TALIA

I sit at a long dining table on a raised dais taking shallow breaths in a gorgeous dress that doesn't leave me quite enough room to breathe deeply. I didn't realize there would be a formal dinner to celebrate my return, but apparently, the entire Citadel is here. The ballroom takes up most of the thirty-fifth floor. Music fills the air, bright and jaunty and strange. There are stringed instruments and drums and flutes played by a small orchestral group of musicians clad in blue—Azures—in the center of the room. Everyone here is dressed in the height of Nimali fashion, but only the Cardinals and a scattering of Azures are present.

I learned about the caste system from the library. It couldn't tell me why it was developed and if those particular colors represented something specifically, but Cardinals are aristocrats and usually have predator daimons. The Azures are the craftsmen, artisans, and innovators. While the Umbers are essentially peasants and their daimons are the "useless" animals like mice or bunnies or sparrows. They're the worker bees and just a few steps up from drudges.

Daimons aren't hereditary—apparently a child of parents with a predator is far more likely to leash a predator, but exceptions happen all the time. Family members end up in totally different castes and it's considered normal. The whole thing makes me vaguely sick to think about.

Lyall sits on my right; his portion of the table is populated by his Cabinet, a half dozen distinguished looking older people who I was introduced to when we sat down. But the names went by so fast I couldn't keep up with all of them. My half of the table is taken up by my courtiers. Elayne managed to sit next to me and seems very proud of herself about it—I wonder if there was some kind of power struggle involved there. Dominga is directly across from me, her back to the ballroom, kind of like she wants me within sight at all times—or am I being paranoid? Next to her sits a dark-skinned man, Sir Barrett, who favors her a great deal, even going so far as to wear a matching scowl. He's the minister of something or other—I wish I could remember.

Shad is seated at the far end of the table. I'd hoped he'd be closer and we'd get a chance to talk, though I guess this isn't really the time or place for any sort of meaningful conversation. I would like to get to know him better, though. His placement so far away, like he's a prince in name only, also makes me angry.

Lyall is deep in conversation with his Cabinet members and turned fully away from me, so I focus on my squad. "How often do you have dinners like these?" I ask.

"Every two or three months. There is much to celebrate here," Elayne responds happily. She goes into a long discourse on previous celebrations, filled with gossip about people who I don't know and couldn't care less about. But I listen politely and sip my water, taking appetizers when offered by passing Fai with platters.

Dominga stops me when I accept a brown sphere that

reminds me of a meatball. "You don't like those." Her simple words dig into me, and I smile.

"Thank—" I cut myself off when she narrows her eyes.

Lyall shifts in his seat next to me. It's strange that I can't hear anything of his conversation. Not that I'd understand much if I were to eavesdrop. But Elayne answers my unasked question. "They're using a dampener. Probably talking about state secrets at the dinner table. Always working." She shrugs.

I turn to Dominga. "Sir Barrett is your father?"

"Yes. He was an advisor of the king's for nearly twenty years before that."

"Are all of your parents in the Cabinet?" I ask the others.

Elayne chitters, shaking her head. "No. My father is merely one of his advisors. You were gracious enough to bring me in to your retinue two years ago."

Alaya pipes up. "I was in the Azure orphanage, where you do charity work. You invited me to become a courtier and I'm ever so grateful. It's quite an honor for someone like me to be elevated." Her gown is a pale rose and her quiet sincerity is so welcome. A caste can be changed, but only by a member of the royal family. I'm glad to know that Celena has done at least some good in her position.

Dominga, seated next to Alaya, gives the girl a look that is about ten degrees warmer than normal. Nice to see something can melt the ice.

Young Ofelia sits on Elayne's other side. She cranes her neck to speak softly. "My father was one of the king's valets. We were both elevated early last year." Her dress is even paler than Alaya's. She breathes a few more words that I don't catch before going back to her not-meatballs.

So, Celena chose to bring up two Azures to Cardinal status and add them to the two daughters of aristocrats as her crew. What does it mean? I wish I knew the politics of how this all works, but that kind of information isn't available in the library. Then another thought strikes me. I slide a gaze at Lyall, who is still ensconced in a silent-to-me conversation.

"What do you think of the Fai drudges? If they're prisoners of war, shouldn't they at some point be released? It seems cruel to keep them here and make them serve us."

Elayne opens her mouth, but Dominga speaks first. "The Fai are savages, Your Grace. They live in grass huts and chew on leaves and weeds. When they attack, they don't leave prisoners—they kill everyone in their path. And they hoard the lifeblood of our civilization, the bliss, like the religious zealots they are. We give them purpose, try to tame their barbarity. They should count themselves lucky to serve us."

Next to her, Sir Barrett glances over, and I wonder if they can hear us even though we can't hear them. Dominga doesn't acknowledge her father; she keeps her icy gaze on me.

I lower my voice and lean forward. "We steal their souls."

Dominga leans forward too, matching my movement. "It is expedient and protects our soldiers from their retribution." Elayne's mouth hangs open, and Alaya has ducked her head. I realize I've probably gone too far, so I swallow and sit back.

Chuckles rise from the other half of the table. They must have turned off their dampener, indicating the private conversation is over.

Lyall turns to me, grinning. "Enjoying the festivities?"

"Immensely. We've just been chatting. My courtiers are working to fill in the gaps in my knowledge."

"Yes, I know you all haven't spent much time together since you've returned. Rely on your retinue to get you back into the swing of things. You will need to recommence your normal duties so that there is no further break in your activities. Routines and predictable leadership keep us strong." He squeezes my hand for emphasis.

I smile and nod as if this makes total sense, but fear grips me. Dominga's hackles are up; she's suspicious of me, I just know it.

Lyall turns and barks at the nearest Fai. "Serve the dinner, enough with all these finger foods."

The woman hastens to do his bidding, practically running through the swinging door. Within seconds, the Fai in the ballroom all melt away and the lights lower. The music changes and covered platters begin to be delivered by light-footed Fai servants.

Ryin arrives with a tray full of soup bowls. He servers Lyall first, then me. When he leans over my shoulder to place the bowl, I inhale deeply. His scent had imprinted on me in the emergency shelter earlier, sort of a smoky jasmine spiciness that reminds me of incense and sitting in front of the fire on a cold, winter night. It will forever be associated with comfort in my mind...along with the weight of his hand on my back calming me and the rich baritone of his voice helping me lose myself in his words and distract me from my anxiety. And that brief brush of his fingertips on my exposed shoulder blades...the warmth of his skin and gentle scrape of his callouses...I close my eyes as I remember the moment.

Is it just my teenage crush on Victor made manifest on someone who shares his face? Or is it Ryin himself, his caution, his seriousness? The way he's been so real with me even when it puts him at risk?

A hole opens up in my stomach and I blink my eyes open to find Dominga staring. "Soup smells great," I say brightly. I don't dare look at Ryin now, much as I want to.

As the courses progress, others come to serve our table. Arrows of disappointment pierce me when he doesn't return.

Over the scrape of knives and forks, Sir Barrett's low voice resonates. "Have you given thought to when you will undergo the next daimon trial, Your Grace?"

I snap to attention. It seems that everyone along the entire table is staring at me. My mouth opens, but no words come out.

"She will do so very soon," Lyall says with confidence. "We have spoken of it."

"But if my memory soul is gone...if I fail again—"

"You will not." He says it in a way that removes all doubt and firmly puts an end to the conversation. Then, seeing my startled reaction, he adds, "You are the daughter of a dragon. You are destined to have a mighty daimon. You will not fail again."

I swallow thickly, completely unconvinced. He is willing to risk his daughter's life on this. Does he think the daimons care whether he's king and will leap to respond to his commands like everyone else does? What would happen to me if I tried to undergo the trial? I *think* I have a memory soul, but then again I should have a shadow soul as well. What if I really don't and however I was brought here stripped me of it somehow? Maybe I was supposed to die in that hospital and I'm destined to do so here, no matter what.

For once, I'm grateful for Elayne's chatter. She turns the conversation to mundane matters: weather, fashion, and entertainment. The troupe of actors we met today on the tour is putting on a play in a few weeks that she's excited about.

Finally, dessert arrives, and I startle when Ryin sets a small plate down in front of me. His jaw is tense and he doesn't meet my eyes. It would probably be unwise for him to do so, maybe even forbidden, but my chest clenches. He executes the duty quickly, then walks off. I can't help but watch him leave.

When I face forward, Dominga is eyeing me carefully. I can never read her expressions as she's cold as a block of marble, but she's watching. I just have no idea what she sees. If she suspects I have any sort of feelings for him, what would happen? What would she do?

I can't give her any more fuel for that particular fire, so I focus on the gelatinous purple and orange striped creation in front of me.

"This one is your favorite," Dominga says softly.

I take a bite and the flavors assault my tongue. It's awful, sour and bitter and difficult to swallow a single bite of. She watches my reaction so carefully, noticing everything I try to hide. Under her narrowed gaze, I eat the entire disgusting thing.

Chapter Eighteen

TALIA

THE PING COMES to my comm just as I'm getting ready for bed. No three-dimensional face extrudes from the device, just a voice. Shad's voice. "Celena, I'm sorry we did not get a chance to talk during dinner."

"That would have been kind of hard to do seeing as you were seated in a whole different zip code."

He pauses, and I'm not sure he gets the joke. "I've had a gift left for you; it's in your dressing room. When you open it, please ping me back."

The glowing device dims and he's gone without so much as a goodbye. But that just may be Nimali culture at play.

Dinner was stressful, and afterward I didn't have anything to do. Whatever camaraderie Ryin and I shared in the bunker seems to have dissolved, and though he followed me back to my suite dutifully, he didn't say a word to me. Mindful of Shad's warning about speaking indoors, I tried to treat him the way the princess would, much as it breaks me apart.

And on top of getting the silent treatment from Ryin, I have no idea how Celena spent her time. There are no books, no television or movies here as far as I can tell. No internet, of course. She must have had some kind of hobby, but I haven't discovered anything in her room—deciding to go to sleep relatively early was really my only option.

I pad over to the giant walk-in closet in my pajamas to investigate Shad's gift. A rectangular box decorated with a fabric ribbon sits on the white chaise lounge in the center of the room. Inside is a small, colorless cube that I recognize—a dampener. It sits nestled on top of a bundle of gray fabric, which turns out to be a Fai drudge uniform.

I tap the dampener to engage it and then ping Shad. "I'm using your gift," I say when he answers. "Thank you."

"You're welcome. They work best either with a great deal of ambient noise around or in an already muffled environment, like a large closet."

That's definitely good to know. "And the clothes?"

"There's something happening tonight that you should see. But it's best if you're disguised—the real Celena would not have attended, and when I asked the king about bringing you, he declined."

"So you think dressing as a drudge will hide me?"

"If you keep to the back, in the shadows, you won't be noticed."

"Wait, where is it, and what's happening?"

"Make your way to the thirty-sixth floor at midnight. There will be a...ceremony. Something that I think will be of interest to you, though it won't be easy to witness. Blend in with the drudges and stay quiet. I will try to find a way for us to speak tomorrow." He pauses and there's a muffled sound on his end. "I need to go."

"Wait, Shad—" But he's gone again.

Midnight on the thirty-sixty floor. That seems like a lot of cloak and dagger to me, which is a little scary and a little exciting. I replace the lid on the box and take it back to my bedroom. I slip it into the bottom of one of the wardrobes, behind a long robe. Then I look around the room. No alarm clock.

No clocks at all. I have no way of knowing when midnight even is. If the comm devices tell the time, no one's shown me how it works yet. I wonder if I ping Elayne or one of the other girls if they'd tell me. But is it too late for a call? They'd accept the princess's call for sure, but for something so stupid as to tell me how to tell time?

I head back into the main room, which is empty, but Ryin appears from the servant's door almost immediately.

"Hey, hi, umm...Are there any clocks anywhere?"

He stares at me blankly.

"So I can wake up...at some point."

He tilts his head. "Noomi will wake you when you ask. It's a part of her duties."

"And you all can just *feel* what time it is in your bones, right?"

"Our daimons are attuned to nature. So, in a way, yes."

I let out a weary sigh. If I don't let Noomi carry out her duties, she could get in trouble, but forcing her to cater to me just feels wrong. Especially when it involves doing something in the middle of the night.

Ryin must see the war on my face, because his expression gentles. "It is no trouble," he says, voice low.

"It is to me," I whisper. I'm not sure if he hears me, but his eyes turn soft and sympathetic.

"She will awaken you whenever you like and assist you in whatever way you need."

I blow out a frustrated breath then straighten, trying to practice looking regal. "Very well. I'm going to retire early. It's been quite an exhausting day. Please send her in to see me." Ryin's curving lips indicate I'm laying it on too thick. Scowling, I sweep out of the room and down the hall to my bedroom.

Noomi arrives moments later with a cup of something

vaguely tea-like, which she sets on the nightstand. Then she begins turning down my bed.

"I need to request the wake-up service. About a quarter to midnight. I know it's late, I'm sorry."

She tilts her head in a move that mimics Ryin's and I wonder if that's a Fai thing. Then she nods.

"Thank you." I glide between soft sheets that are still somehow suffocating. They attach themselves to my skin like cling wrap.

Noomi taps her palm against her heart twice and lowers her hand. *Thank you.* She's been repeating words to me in their signing language at my request. When she leaves, she dims the bliss lighting to a low glow on the way out. I don't think I'll sleep at all as curious and unsettled as I am, but soon enough something shakes me awake. Noomi's face is illuminated by a single candle, real flame, making her skin glow with the orange light.

I tap my chest twice in thanks and sit up, blearily. She points overhead, then to me, then to the candle, trying to explain something.

"The lights?"

She nods and points to me again.

"I have to turn them on?"

She mimics sleeping and I guess her meaning. "At night? I have to turn them on at night?"

She smiles and waits for me to adjust the lighting before leaving, candle in hand. It could be some kind of conservation method, or just a way to keep the Fai subjugated. One more thing I don't understand.

I dress quickly in the Fai uniform, which includes a pair of matching soft slippers. Now I just need to get to the thirty-sixth floor. Fortunately, Fai don't take the elevators unless, like Ryin, they've been assigned to. I don't mind at all ten flights of stairs if it keeps me out of that plummeting metal box.

The main room is dark and I pick my way through carefully, trying not to bump into anything on my way to the servant's room. That must be where the stairs are since there isn't anywhere else in the suite I haven't seen.

My handprint makes the door slide open and then I'm in a small kitchen. It's more like a narrow butler's pantry, with cabinets lining one side and a small sink. A meager cot sits against the wall. Is this where Noomi sleeps? It looks even thinner and harder than the one in the bunker that turned my butt cheeks numb.

Another door leads to a dim corridor and a stairwell, where I get my first shock. A Nimali guard dressed in black stands at attention there. I duck my head for a moment, hoping I haven't been spotted when I recognize Zanna.

"Shad sent you?" I whisper. She presses a finger against her lips and nods.

Relief drenches me. It would be awful to get caught before I even begin. We start climbing down in silence. The stairwells are fairly full of Fai heading in the same direction we are. They don't raise their eyes, so there's little chance of them recognizing me. I wonder how common a guard is here—it must not be noteworthy.

The walking tour earlier today was done at a very measured pace, but ten flights down makes my heart pump. I'm winded when we stop at the door with the number thirty-six stenciled on it. I follow the others into a gloomy hallway, just as sterile as the others in the building with blue light barely brightening cream-colored walls. The floor is polished concrete, not carpeted like on the other levels. The slippered feet of the Fai are nearly silent as we walk, passing double doors every dozen feet or so.

Zanna breaks off without a word and heads through a set of doors that the other Fai pass, so I go with them. We enter a vast and heavily shadowed room, with thick cement columns dividing a space that must take up the majority of this floor. The murmur of low voices hits me as I follow a pair of women around the edge of the room, staying cloaked in darkness. Only the center is brightly lit, as if by spotlights coming from the ceiling. A pretty large crowd, about a hundred people or so, stand around a raised platform that reminds me of a boxing ring, with only three sides bordered by light-colored ropes. Wide steps lead up to it like it's a stage. On it sits a large, rectangular object covered in black fabric.

Mindful of Shad's advice, I stop beside one of the huge pillars. The other Fai are spread out, many staying close to these beams in small clusters. From here I have a clear view of the platform, though I'm still a significant distance away. Too far to be easily seen by anyone. The people close to the platform wear mostly reds and blues with a smattering of browns thrown in.

I'm trying to see if I recognize anyone when the hairs on the back of my neck stand up in warning.

"Your Grace?" a voice murmurs in my ear, causing me to jump about a foot. Fortunately, I don't scream. I clutch my chest and spin around to find Ryin and Noomi standing there, frowns on their faces.

I blink rapidly. They're obviously surprised at my presence and my choice of clothes. I look down then up, then square my shoulders. "I don't want anyone to know I'm here. I need you both to promise to tell no one."

They look at each other for a moment, then back to me. "All right," Ryin says. Noomi nods. "Do you know what you're here to see?" His voice is low, directed into my ear.

"Not exactly."

He steps up to my left and Noomi stands on my right like they're trying to protect me. I guess if something happens to me and anyone finds out they knew I was here, they could get in trouble. But Shad wouldn't have sent me if it was dangerous, right? And Zanna is here somewhere.

Ryin leans in toward me. His presence creates a blast of heat on that side of my body. "The ceremony is about to begin," he whispers. His breath kisses the shell of my ear and I shiver. His eagle eyes take note. "Are you cold?"

"No. Just nervous." It's not entirely a lie. He eyes me dubiously and is more tense than usual. A dizzying fear unfurls within me, but the source of the fear has changed. It's not about being discovered—it's about how crazy I feel with him this close to me.

The already low hum of voices quiets, and a door opens on the far end of the room letting in a shard of light. Steady, insistent drumbeats vibrate through the floor, rattling my bones. A stream of people enter, heading for the stage. There are two lines of drummers beating wide bass drums strapped to their chests. Then six people follow: two in red, two in blue, and two in brown. They're in their early twenties or so and march with solemn steps onto the stage.

They're followed by a white-haired woman in a royal blue robe. Sequins or glittering embroidery winks from the edges and hem. She rests her slight weight on a walking stick and slowly climbs the steps to stand before the rest.

The drummers make up the front row of the audience, their thundering cadence ending in a crescendo of sound. When the vibrations fade away, the entire space is left so quiet you could hear an eyelash fall.

The old woman's reedy voice rises. "Tonight begins the journey of these chosen ones. They will reach beyond the borders of our world, into the realm of spirits, and undergo the trials to leash a daimon. By entering into a covenant with their spiritual familiar, they will prove themselves worthy to take their place in Nimali society. Let the trials begin."

A sudden coldness invades my body. These are the daimon trials. My already rapt attention ratchets up a little.

The older woman steps back a few paces and the first guy, a wiry, ebony-skinned young man, steps into the center of the platform. He removes his red pants and shirt with a flourish, revealing a bird chest and skinny legs. Dressed only in a pair of long shorts that look like swimming trunks, he moves to the side while the others step to the back of the stage.

The old woman removes the cloth covering the large box, revealing it to be a water tank. It's maybe ten feet long and waist high, with clear sides showing the liquid bliss inside.

The woman motions to the man, who sits on the side of the tank and then swings his legs in. He lies on his back in the liquid bliss and then the woman replaces the black shroud, covering it completely.

My breathing grows shallow. Bones turn to stone. This is the trial? I'm panting now, imagining myself entombed in that tiny box, my body sinking to the bottom. Ryin grips my hand and leans in to brush his words against my ear. "Once inside, your body becomes weightless and you are transported to the spirit world to meet your daimon. You don't feel closed in— you feel free."

I hold onto his hand, squeezing it so hard it must be painful, but he doesn't complain. The physical contact helps me slow my breathing.

"Now the spirits will weigh your souls to determine if you are worthy." The old woman's voice echoes around the cavernous space. When it ebbs, only silence is left. No one makes a sound and nothing happens for a long time. It's like we're all waiting with bated breath for whatever is next.

Finally, I turn to Ryin, a question in my gaze. His jasmine smoke scent fills my nostrils as he leans into me once again. "You meet many daimons on the other side. Their consciousnesses reach out to yours until you connect with a like-minded spirit. Then you agree to the covenant."

I try to control my reaction to his nearness, but shiver involuntarily. I try to pass it off as a nod and can only hope that he doesn't notice what his whispering in my ear is doing to my body. My stomach is tight; I press my legs together. No matter how much I try, I can't stop imagining his lips just a little lower, grazing the side of my neck.

Not the time, Talia! Or the place or even the right person. If Ryin doesn't hate me—which he has every right to do—at the very least he must resent me.

He retreats from my personal space and I can think again. Nothing has changed yet on the stage, and everyone is still waiting breathlessly.

Finally, there's movement—a welcome distraction. The covering of the tank ripples and the old woman pulls the cloth back. The guy shoots out of the liquid, standing up, though none of the precious bliss spills onto the ground.

He clambers out of the tank, somehow perfectly dry. His legs wobble and then his mouth falls open. It looks like he's about to scream when a brilliant flash of light explodes out of him, blinding us for a few seconds.

When it fades, a large red fox stands where he had been. Gasps rise from the audience and then raucous applause. Especially loud cheers and whoops come from a group of dark-skinned people near the front who might be his family.

The fox leaps from the stage and races around the crowd, pausing to sniff every few paces. He seems playful and happy and finally ends up with the group of hooting people. They bend down and pet and fuss over the little animal, obviously delighted.

Slowly, calm comes to the audience. The white-haired woman stands in the center of the stage again, beckoning the next young woman forward. The scene is repeated for all of them. One girl becomes an owl. One turns into a jaguar. Another transforms into an alligator or a crocodile, I'm not sure which. The second to last guy doesn't make it out of the tank before the bright light flashes out of him.

"A shark?" I whisper, amazed. It's a small shark, maybe six feet long, but the dorsal fin is clear.

A pair of soldiers run up the steps and lift the animal out of the tank. They carry it off to the side of the stage where another tank I hadn't noticed before, one actually filled with water, sits. The shark sinks into the water with a splash and the guy's family rushes over to coo at it.

I lean into Ryin, my chest brushing against his arm. "That seems inconvenient."

"The water Nimali patrol the Bay and ocean. They are fairly rare so it's an honor, especially for an Umber."

The final young woman, the other Umber, takes the longest. I stifle a yawn; it must be after one in the morning at this point, but no one is moving and they don't appear impatient. When the black fabric ripples and the older woman removes it, the girl is visibly shaken. Her dark hair pulled back in a messy ponytail, she climbs out of the tank before standing there for a moment and shaking her head quickly.

I gasp.

"No daimon," Ryin whispers sadly.

The girl descends the steps and falls into her family's waiting arms. I wonder which soul she lost. Tears prick my eyes and Ryin releases my hand. I'd forgotten he was holding it, but I flex my empty fingers then swipe at my face.

The stage clears, but no one leaves. The people who shifted remain in their animal forms in the audience, but soon the joyous atmosphere drains away. Then the drummers start up again, beating a low and ominous rhythm as a palpable tension rises from the crowd.

"What happens now?" I ask. But Ryin has turned to granite beside me. Noomi too, and her eyes fill with tears.

The far door opens and soldiers stream in, marching in lockstep. In their midst, head high and regal, strides King Lyall.

Chapter Nineteen

TALIA

SHAD ENTERS WITH THE SOLDIERS, towering over most of them. He's not in black tonight but wears a deep crimson version of his armor. This must be what he wanted me to see. The drumming continues as the prince climbs the stage; soldiers form two lines stretching from the doors to the steps. They create a sort of tunnel for Lyall to march through. The king is shorter than many of his guards and much shorter than Shad, but his presence is enormous and oppressive. The kindly father who had smiled so lovingly at me is nowhere to be found. My knees feel like they're about to give out.

Lyall climbs the steps and a retinue of advisors, all in red, bleed from the crowd and make their way up as well to stand in a line behind the king and prince. Most of the Cabinet members are present. Any lingering joy from the successful transformations has faded away.

Ryin's hands have turned into fists and I reach for him—I don't know why I do, it's obvious he's angry but also in pain.

I don't ask him what to expect or if he's okay, since it's

obvious that neither he nor Noomi are, so I just take his hand. Hold his balled-up fist in mine, trying to offer comfort.

He turns to me, his expression perplexed. It's like he's never seen me before and wonders what species of creature I am. And then his fist uncurls and he grips my hand. The same position as before, but me offering comfort this time. I give him a gentle squeeze.

Movement at the door catches my attention. Pairs of guards drag in two bound men, one in blue and one in Fai gray. Both are shackled at their wrists and ankles. They're hauled up onto the stage and pressed down until they're kneeling, side by side.

The Fai man is pale and blonde. Early forties, I'd guess, and thin. The Nimali man is of a similar age, broad-shouldered with Asian ancestry and hair that keeps flopping into his eyes. Their body language screams pure terror, but the Nimali leans into the Fai man and they both settle a bit. My throat thickens and tears fall freely.

Lyall steps forward and the silence grows even heavier, if possible, like an invisible blanket pressing down on everyone, stealing our breath and leeching all warmth and happiness from us.

"By proclamation, this sixth day of the Weed month, I, Lyall Lyonson, rightful ruler and king of Aurum, do pass judgment on those brought before me. Joowon Shiwooson, you are accused of conspiracy, consorting with an enemy combatant, and theft of covenant-ordained property." Joowon scowls up at Lyall.

"Silas Minusson, you stand accused of dereliction of duty, conspiring to assault a Nimali, and gross insolence." The blonde man doesn't look up. He continues staring down at the ground beneath his knees, his breaths becoming heavier, chest rising and falling as he sucks in air.

"Before I enact the sentences for your crimes, I want to remind you and everyone gathered that we all live and die by the covenant. No one is immune from its strictures." He gazes down at the men.

"I do not live by your covenant, beast!" Silas roars. The action seems to drain him and he sags against Joowon.

"But you will." Lyall's voice is low and sends chills through me. "The privileges of autonomous indenture previously afforded you have been rescinded. You are sentenced to trammeling. Bring his soul!" The last is a command and one of the aides on stage steps forward, a small box in his outstretched hand.

From the box, Lyall picks up a small dark sphere that looks like a marble, which he holds between his fingertips.

Silas turns to Joowon and the men kiss desperately, as if it will be their last. *Consorting with an enemy combatant.* My breathing hitches and I stifle the sob that wants to escape from my chest.

A guard lifts Silas to his feet then steps away. "No!" screams Joowon, the only sound in the room. In the aftermath of his shout, it's so quiet you could hear a tear drop. Mine plinks on the concrete below as Lyall lifts his arm like he's about to pitch a baseball. Then he throws the tiny dark marble right at Silas's chest.

It bursts open on his sternum, leaving a dark stain on the gray, like a tiny paintball. But the stain grows and spreads, extending across his whole body until he's being covered in a thick, black liquid, like molten latex. Its surface has an oily shimmer to it.

"Always remember, I love you," Silas says before his mouth and face are covered by the substance.

I squeeze Ryin's hand, certain I'm witnessing a death— that stuff will surely suffocate him. Joowon sobs helplessly, held back by the two guards with firm grips on his shoulders.

But the strange covering begins to dissolve, absorbed into Silas's skin. It fades away and, on the ground, a shadow spreads out from him. I hadn't even noticed that Silas didn't cast a shadow. But now he does. When his face is clear again, he looks amazed. I'm far away but can still see how much brighter he is. Even in this terrifying situation, his entire manner has changed.

Of course, that was his shadow soul being returned to him.

Silas's shoulders square and his head lifts. He looks around in wonder. Joowon stops his struggling and stares up at his love with amazement.

Then Lyall rears his hand back again and throws something else. It acts much like the first ball—the soul—but with significant differences. A black webbing crawls across Silas's body this time, wiping the bright sheen of completeness from his expression, as material like a net wraps him in what appears to be a body suit made out of fishnet stockings. Thin lines crisscross his skin and clothes and then, in moments, are absorbed into him as well.

The change is immediate. His affect flattens. His shoulders slump and his head shoots forward, gaze empty. He's perfectly still, motionless except for his breathing.

Joowon is silent, breaths heaving as he gazes up at him. "Silas?"

But I think that Silas is gone. I'm not sure how I can tell from a hundred feet away, but the change was so sudden and obvious. The man is now an empty shell. Whatever that net thing was removed the light from his eyes.

The same attendant who held the box with Silas's soul steps forward and clips something to the Fai's ear. It's an earpiece that attaches around the outer shell, like an old Bluetooth headset.

"Test it," Lyall orders. The attendant produces one of those data tablets and begins tapping away. Silas jerks, but his overall expression doesn't change.

"Ready, Your Majesty," the attendant says, looking expectantly at the king.

"Arms up," Lyall commands, and Silas's chained arms shoot up over his head and stay there.

"Down." They fly back down in front of him.

"Turn in a circle." Silas responds immediately, shuffling around clockwise until he's facing front again. It's like he's a puppet and Lyall the puppeteer. I want to vomit.

Lyall nods, appearing pleased. "Unchain him. We don't need those any longer." The guards rush to comply, freeing the man. He doesn't move or respond in any way. Still on his knees, Joowon whimpers quietly, watching it all unfold.

"Get him out of here. Put him on mining duty," Lyall commands. The guards march Silas away and he disappears through the open doors. The audience remains silent.

My tears flow freely, as do Noomi's. Ryin stares straight ahead, his grip on my hand loose. I have a feeling he's taken himself away, far away to a place in his mind where he can better deal with things. Could his daimon help him with this?

Back on the stage, the guards have hauled Joowon up to his feet.

"Trammeled drudges are at least useful," Lyall says, voice like steel. "But a traitorous Nimali does not deserve to share our resources. We will not waste food on you, nor clothing, nor housing, nor light. Not an ounce of bliss will go to support your existence. You are cast out into the wilds of the city to survive as best you can among the mundane humans. And if you are caught in our territory or pilfering any of our resources, you will be killed on sight. You are Nimali no more. You have forsaken the covenant and all that it entails. Bring the choker!"

A different attendant steps forward carrying another box, this one about the size of a shoebox. He reaches into it and pulls out a circle of glowing, blue rope. It must be made of, or powered with, bliss.

Joowon begins struggling again and screaming wordless noises of protest, anger, and despair. The king places the circle around the man's neck and it instantly begins tightening, strangling him until his shouts turn into gurgles of pain. Then the choker, too, is absorbed into his skin and he calms. It only lasts a second before he begins screaming again, his eyes, nose, and mouth glowing blue. Light pours from him, and very painfully, it seems.

I've seen this before, with the woman who had been feeding the exiled man. After she slit the man's throat, light poured from her face like this. What I didn't understand then was that was her daimon abandoning her.

Joowon's suffering stops soon enough along with his screaming. Then he's crying again and rubbing his chest.

"Toss him outside," Lyall says. The guards drag the sputtering man away.

My shoulders heave with suppressed sobs of my own. Noomi puts an arm around me and we lean into each other, crying silently, both devastated but trying to stay quiet.

Some of the Nimali in the crowd near the stage are similarly affected. They keep quiet too, but shoulders shake and sniffs ring out.

"The loss of a daimon is the harshest punishment we have," Lyall says, face grave. "I do not come to these decisions lightly. It is always painful when one of our own abandons our ways and betrays us." He drops his head as if he is truly saddened. "But we do what we must. For the covenant."

"For the covenant!" The response is hearty, but not, I think, as loud as it could be. Lyall steps from the stage and retreats through the line of soldiers, his retinue on his heels.

Shad remains, standing rigidly. While on the outside he is the stoic soldier and prince, I know what's happened here has affected him. And I understand why he wanted me to witness it. He's stiff when he leaves, exiting in a different direction than Lyall did and disappearing into darkness that swallows him whole.

The groups of Fai that watched the events all comfort

each other. Many lean on others as they grieve. They must have known Silas, and his fate now is awful.

"That is the punishment you told me about?" I whisper.

Ryin's eyes are downcast; he speaks through clenched teeth. "You asked why we do not just run away. Even the death of being out of proximity with our soul would be preferable to slavery. But we stay and withstand and act with *obedience* because of the threat of trammeling. If I were to run tonight and perish, three of the Fai I leave behind would be trammeled."

He blinks and shivers. "A trammeled shadow drudge becomes a puppet, their every action controlled by the puppet master with no free will of their own. They are often sent to the bliss mines to work. Forced to participate in that abomination." His eyes flash. "For voice drudges, they lose the ability to communicate entirely. No signing or even writing and they, too, are bound to follow all commands given. Memory drudges lose not only their past, but the ability to create new memories. They wake up every day with no knowledge of who they are or of how to do all but the most basic tasks. They're often used as factory workers, instructed in the same monotonous tasks every day, over and over again."

I'm speechless, unable to move, barely able to think.

"Trammeling us is the way they keep power over us. For none would knowingly sentence another to that fate. And so we comply."

My head begins shaking involuntarily, but he continues. "Silas had the misfortune to fall in love with a Nimali. They were planning to leave, to live among the covenant-free humans in the city." Ryin's face twists before all emotion leeches out. "Now he'll spend the rest of his days enslaved and enslaving the bliss."

It takes a few tries, but my voice comes to me. "And his partner? His daimon was stripped away."

"A forced covenant break. The Nimali are cruel to their own as well." He lifts a shoulder.

We're quiet for long moments. I just want to curl up somewhere and hide.

Ryin takes a deep breath and finally looks up. "Make sure she gets back to her suite."

Noomi frowns at him but he's already gone, masked by the shadows that surround us. She grabs my hand and tugs, leading me back to the door we entered through. Other Fai exit this way as well and fill the dingy hallway. I don't see Zanna again—I'm surrounded by grieving people trying to hold themselves together. We all file to the various stairwells, and all of us are silent.

I barely feel the ten-flight climb back to Celena's apartment. This world I've been brought to, this woman I'm impersonating—she must know all that happens, all that her father is responsible for. There is cruelty here like I've never experienced before. A bitter taste coats my tongue.

We move through the tiny space allotted for servants and back into the sitting room. When Noomi moves to follow me farther, I turn to her. "Please don't. Go...go wherever you want. I can't stand it if you do something nice for me right now or help me in any way."

Her red-rimmed eyes take me in and she nods slowly, then backs away. The door slides shut behind her and I crumple into a ball on the floor.

For the first time since I arrived in this place, I truly wish I was home.

Chapter Twenty

RYIN

MY FOOTSTEPS THUNDER in my ears as I pound down the stairwell. I race ahead of the other Fai leaving the meeting hall, not wanting to be swamped by their grief over the loss of another of our own. I did not know Silas Minusson well, but he was still a brother. I also need to escape the tears of the Nimali. They weep for their own, not caring about the fate of the Fai.

But the memory of the devastated expression on Celena's face almost makes me stumble. Her soft gasps and barely withheld sobs. She was truly moved by the plight of both victims tonight. Her presence was a shock—I wouldn't have expected her to even know about the ceremony. And how she got her hands on a Fai uniform is a mystery. But her reaction to the horrors on display convinces me that Noomi is right. The princess might be able to be turned to our cause.

Anger at the Nimali—and at myself—burns in my veins as I burst through the doors onto the sixteenth floor. Most of the Fai gather on floor thirty-two for prayer and meditation on trammeling nights. Usually I take part, eager to give offerings and fellowship, to support my grieving brethren and give what reassurances I can as part of the GenFi. But not tonight.

Tonight, cold rage disguises the grief and anguish, buries the fear that one day Silas's fate may befall me. To be stripped of all free will and agency. A passenger in my body, only able to carry out the commands of others. Whatever they may be. I share my body regularly with my daimon, but it never requires obedience. Merely a respect for it and the covenant. But what happens to the daimons of the trammeled?

We don't know. No one has ever been untrammeled and asked.

Perhaps the daimons abandon the hosts. Perhaps they watch helpless through vacant eyes, unable to be called forward because the host has no will of its own. It is truly a fate worse than death and one I've witnessed enacted on my people too often.

The Nimali treat it as their right to capture, enslave, and demean us with the threat of trammeling. *Autonomous indenture*, the king had said. I halt in the middle of the hallway, seething, then turn and put my fist through the wall.

The pain is clarifying. It brings the world back into focus, organizing my spiraling thoughts.

I punch the wall again and again, my fist passing through the thin material, shredding my skin and leaving dust covering my arm. My daimon longs to rush forward and heal my wounds, but I hold it back. Not yet.

Footsteps marching in lockstep sound behind me. I give the wall a final blow before spinning around to meet the soldiers. Watches are often doubled on trammeling nights. I had not forgotten; I just didn't care.

"Damaging Nimali property is a punishable offense, drudge," the soldier on the right says. He's bland and blond, a contrast to his brown-skinned partner.

"My apologies," I seethe through clenched teeth, obviously not sorry in the least.

The blond beast narrows his eyes at me. "Do you need a night in the locker to cool off?"

I don't answer since it wasn't a real question.

"Where are you supposed to be?" the second soldier asks.

"I'm assigned to the princess. I'm headed back up there now."

"If you were assigned to her then you should be with her, not here defacing our walls." The blond prick has an air of superiority around him that I'm certain is unearned. I tighten my fist, unsure if I will be able to hold back from defacing *him*.

His partner doesn't miss the move and tenses. I sense that he's a second away from detonating into whatever beast form his daimon provides, and that thought excites me. It's been too long since I've sparred; my fists are itching to meet either of their faces.

Two against one doesn't scare me in the least. They think the Fai chose poorly, not shifting shape, but I would not mind showing him the truth of our power, personally.

However, the partner doesn't shift. Instead, he pulls a pair of handcuffs from his pocket and dangles them at me. They are bliss powered and freezing cold, designed to chill the wrists to the point of pain. The cold weakens our daimons, making them sluggish and nearly impossible to call forward. We hide much of our power from the beasts, but they are not stupid.

I will not be chained, not tonight. Nor will I be taken to the locker, a frigid room on the third floor where both Fai and Nimali are punished. I've spent nights there before, especially when I first arrived and was ungovernable—even the threat of trammeling was not enough to pierce my misery and pain at the loss of my sister and my freedom.

But it was the trammeling of a friend, an older soldier who had been a mentor, for some light infraction that did me in. Seeing him vacant and senseless. Knowing it could be me.

Sometimes they punish *you* for what you do, sometimes you take the penalty for the sins of others, and sometimes you're punished for no reason at all, just to reinforce the fact that they can. The plight of my people was more chilling than the frigid locker, and knowing how my deeds could affect others, I slowly began to fall in line.

But now that old defiance is back in such force that I cannot shove it back into its box. Why now? Why tonight?

Is it the princess's tears pushing me over the edge? The feel of her soft hand clinging to mine?

These thoughts of her are not only distracting, but pointless. Tonight was proof of what happens when a Fai and a Nimali fancy feelings for one another. Not as if the princess would ever have such feelings for a drudge. Relationships between Fai and Umbers have occasionally happened, as the lowest caste of Nimali are not treated all that much better than us, and even more rarely, an Azure. But a Cardinal? A royal?

The impossibility of it all is laughable. That my thoughts have even veered in this direction is preposterous. The absurdity strikes my funny bone and I cannot hold back the laughter—a bright, bursting guffaw splashes between us. The faces of the guards mottle with anger.

The blond one wrenches me around by my shoulder and pulls my hands behind my back. I call my daimon forward and pull out of his grasp, stronger now than these men in their human forms. Sensing the threat, they both shift with a blinding flash of light, leaving me facing a leopard and a coyote, both snarling and ready to pounce.

I sink into the fighting stance I learned so long ago and prepare for the feel of their teeth on my flesh. The fight I've been longing for is finally here, and consequences be damned, I will let out my rage and pain on these creatures.

But both animals freeze, eyes going glassy, growls fading into silence. Then in another pop of light, they shift back into humans and fall to the ground, unconscious.

I look up to find Von and Xipporah standing behind them

in the hallway, both with their daimons called. I straighten when they approach, a little disappointed.

Xipporah kneels by the prone men, picking up the discarded cuffs. "When they awaken, they won't remember this at all. Best not to leave any evidence."

I nod and shake out my limbs, which still feel buzzy from the adrenaline. "Thank you."

She shrugs and motions to Von. "It was mostly him."

Air daimons like Von can recharge others' power and also deplete them, which can include draining them of all energy until they pass out. It's one of the many talents we've kept hidden from the Nimali for so long. But even with the aid of an amplifier like Xi, what he did is remarkable.

"Are you all right?" I ask, noticing him breathing heavily and leaning against the wall for stability as he takes a moment to gather himself.

"Fine. Doing two at once is difficult." His hands shake as he signs. Then his breathing slows and his daimon recedes. I release mine and Xi does the same.

"Impressive, though. I've seen three Air Fai with three amplifiers struggle to handle two at once."

"I have been training with the Air Priest," he signs. "But these two will awaken shortly, so we must go." We slip away down the hall and back to the stairwell.

"Attacking guards? Now who's being stupid, brother?" A mocking sneer contorts his face. "What happened to organizing and planning?"

I breathe deeply, still grateful for the assist but not in need of his snark. "It's been a difficult night."

"Indeed it has. We all must channel our anger, though. We will be free soon enough. In the coming days, be ready for my signal." Von gives me a meaningful glance as we climb.

"Signal for what?"

"To subdue and kidnap the princess. Then we will see what the king is willing to sacrifice to get her back."

His words are a stone sinking into my gut. My lips snap shut and I focus on the stairs underfoot.

They bid me goodbye on the thirty-second floor. I share a glance with Xipporah, who looks both weary and wary. At least she seems to be keeping an eye on Von.

The man's words haunt my steps as I make my way up flight after flight. They burn away what's left of my excess rage, leaving it once again at the low simmer I've held it to for the past three years. If I tell him of Celena's reaction to the trammeling, her sincere sorrow and grief, would it matter? Could we convince the Crowns that the Nimali princess could possibly help us, that her heart has changed a great deal due to her memory loss and perhaps whatever she suffered across the wall?

Hope has sprung within me, though I'd prefer to temper it. Just because she mourns the devastation of her enemy doesn't mean she'll act on it. And though much about her has changed, she has the same steely determination I remember. Even with her new emotionality, she is not a shrinking violet. *Can* she be a meaningful ally and not just a victim and pawn?

I finally arrive at her level and let myself into the main suite. Then almost trip over the bundle on the floor in front of the servant's room. The princess sleeps there, curled into herself, her cheeks still puffy and streaked with dried tears. I kneel before her, unsure of what to do.

Asleep, Celena looks peaceful and young. Innocent, even. Thinking such of a Nimali no longer brings a pang of shame.

I gather her into my arms, sucking in a breath as she curls into me and slings her arm around my neck. In sleep, she trusts me. That trust is new and fragile, and completely unwarranted since I will soon be commanded to betray it.

I swallow that thought down and head into her bedroom, depositing her on the massive bed.

She'll need to remove the drudge uniform she still wears before anyone sees her, but I certainly will not be so bold as to do that. Instead, I tuck her into the covers and she turns, restless, before sinking deeper into sleep.

I find myself unable to leave her. So I sit in the chair next to her bed and watch over her. I tell myself that this is part of the king's instructions—it's what I should have been doing last night, but that's so far from the truth it almost makes me laugh again. Watching her sleep, being near her at all, brings me joy and calm.

If I must betray her, then I will allow myself this moment. And tomorrow will bring what it may.

Chapter Twenty-One

TALIA

I AWAKEN in my bed and find Ryin sitting next to me in the embroidered silver armchair. It's startling—did he bring me in here? It sure looks like he's been here for a while. Before I can even clear my throat to ask him about it, he stands, gives me a hasty bow, and then rushes out like someone's chasing him.

I must look a hot mess, so it's for the best even though I have so many questions. Leaving them for later, I go through my morning routine, taking a long, restorative shower and then investigating a few of the jars on Celena's vanity. Still nothing that seems like deodorant, and I keep forgetting to ask.

No stylists wait for me, so I pick my own outfit—one that covers me up more than others I've been wearing but is still uncomfortably snug—from the vast closet and lace my boots myself. Everything feels different this morning. The aloneness is actually comforting—at least it's familiar. There's no one to pretend for, just me. Like always.

I was often alone in my father's house, retreating to my room on the top floor in the converted attic. My stepmother claimed it was so I'd have my own space and not be bothered by the twins, but it left me feeling more remote, never a part of things.

I should have moved out long ago but stayed, at first to help with the girls, and then because it was expensive to live on my own. I never asked my father for anything, including for help paying for college, so I worked my way through, taking a handful of classes at a time. Waitressing, bartending, walking dogs, babysitting for neighbors. No real skills, no real goals. I hadn't even picked a major after nearly five years of part-time classes. It always felt like I was waiting for something, hoping something would change. And change it did.

Be careful what you wish for.

I enter the main room to find Ryin seated in the ornate chair. As soon as I settle at the dining table, Noomi appears with the breakfast tray.

"You can switch the chair back if you want," I say while she sets out plates and fusses over their placement.

He doesn't respond, and I'm too tired and worn out to even try parsing his unreadable expression. The weight of last night's ceremony hangs heavily over me. I slept better than I expected, probably because I was so emotionally drained.

Noomi disappears, and I gaze at the food before me with no appetite. I stare for so long that I almost don't hear Ryin break the silence.

"Are you well?"

"How could I be well?" Sudden tears blur my eyes, and I fight them off. I cried too much last night. "How can I eat food prepared by Fai hands? It's so cruel. How can he do that to you all?" The last question is barely a whisper.

Ryin's voice is equally low when he responds, "Perhaps you should ask him."

I sit up straight, my head snapping over to him and wonder inflating me like a balloon. "You're right. I should." His brows lift in surprise.

Shad wanted me to pretend to be Celena not just to save my life, but also because of what Celena can do. Lyall loves her. He dotes on her and more, he's *proud* of her. He *respects* her. Maybe the old Celena didn't blink an eye at trammeling and slavery, but *this* Celena is going to try to exert some influence. Hopefully this will help whatever Shad is working on as well.

Other Nimali must hate the practice of trammeling as well, but it's just too dangerous for them to go against the king. As long as he believes I'm his daughter, especially with no memory, there's no way Lyall will harm me, even if I speak out.

My appetite returns in a rush of hunger. I want to be well-nourished for what I'm about to do. I finish my breakfast as quickly as I can, then I find my comm and ping the king.

HARSHAL, Callum, and Zanna, along with Ryin, accompany me out of the Citadel using a door I haven't seen before. It leads out the other side of the building from the plaza and onto Montgomery Street. Harshal leads the way down a narrow alley between two tall buildings, eventually approaching another place I recognize.

"Portsmouth Square?" A pang of homesickness thrums through me as we approach the swatch of concrete-covered ground that sits atop a parking garage, though the entrance underground is blocked with crumbling debris and chunks of concrete. The park itself is bordered by trees. Gone are the Chinese-inspired gazebos offering shade to the older residents who used to gather there—at least in my world. A few of the buildings lining the square still display the Chinese writing that marked this as part of the city's Chinatown. One of my favorite restaurants was just a few blocks away—I'd forgotten, and the reminder is bittersweet.

"The healer must stay here," Harshal says, pointing to the staircase leading up to the square. Three other glum-looking Fai stand there and Ryin silently joins them.

The guards lead me up the steps and onto the main level of the park. Instead of the elderly residents and tourists that used to crowd the place, the space is filled with dozens of shifted Nimali. They're grouped in loose rings with two animals in the center of each, fighting.

In the one closest to me, a lioness and a panther tussle. While over the heads of the next circle, a vulture and an eagle face off. Shrieks and roars and cries of pain form a chorus—blood drips from more than one mouth. I don't think they're fighting to death—God, I hope not—but they are really injuring each other.

A zebra in the last circle bleeds from a wound on its rump. Its opponent: a dark chestnut-colored horse. Those square herbivore teeth are enough to still cause damage. We reach a raised platform on the side of the courtyard where the king sits watching it all unfold.

Lyall greets me with a big hug, as always, and inquires about my breakfast and sleep. It's difficult to be enfolded in his arms, accepting the warmth offered, while images of Silas and Joowon run through my head. Recollections of the cold way this man had sent them to their fates play on repeat.

I return his hug without lingering and sit beside him in a padded chair. Thankfully, the bone throne is nowhere in sight.

"Are they sparring?" I ask as the lioness savages the panther's shoulder.

"Soldiers must train to stay sharp, my dear."

"But shouldn't they train against people in human form? Like the Fai?" Even as the words leave my mouth, I shiver at the thought.

"Ah, a very good question. But you see, the Fai daimons give them all the power, strength, and resilience of their animal aspect. So it is best to act as if you will be facing the animal even though it will be disguised as a human."

The red-haired man with glowing eyes, rising into the air with no wings, comes to mind. What other bird powers did he possess? Shaking off that thought, I press forward with my purpose for coming without revealing that I witnessed the horrors of last night.

"I had some questions about the Fai."

"Yes, dear." He turns to me with his whole attention, the training ground forgotten for the moment. That simple action makes my throat close up. When had I ever been the sole focus of my father's attention?

I push forward. "The Fai have been captured as prisoners of war. Do you plan to negotiate with their leaders to give them back at some point—perhaps as a strategy to gain access to some of the disputed bliss matrices?"

"I love that your mind is working toward the benefit of our people," he says with a smile. "It is something that we have considered; however, the Fai are extremists. There have been peace treaties over the years, but further negotiations always eventually sour. Their beliefs are too strongly held, too fundamental to who they are. They resist all reason and rationality and would never give up a matrix voluntarily. Even for the return of their own people."

Roars rise from the training ground. An enormous blue dragon has appeared—Shad. He's facing off against a dozen other large animals, including a rhino. Instead of three rings of sparring, everyone has become a giant circle, focused on this match.

"Shad is your stepson, right?" The curiosity over their relationship distracts me as he swats a brown bear away.

"Yes. After your beloved mother returned to the Origin, I vowed to never marry again. But when a young man emerged from the trials as a dragon, well, custom dictated that I take him under wing. Dragons are the rarest of all, aside from phoenixes. The best way to give him legitimacy was to marry his mother."

I sit back, unable to tear my eyes from Shad. He doesn't breathe fire and he's not really trying to hurt his own soldiers, but he still fights fiercely. And he's so large that even against twelve soldiers he appears evenly matched.

"Of course, his father had something to say about that."

"What?" I turn back to Lyall, who seems lost in the memory.

"The man was a good solider. A rare daimon. A yeti, if I'm not mistaken. Shame to lose him. I had to use the ancient law of honorable combat to challenge him, of course."

"Like a duel?"

"To the death. Nimali challenged with honorable combat cannot deny it, even if he knows he will lose. It was a great credit to him to be beaten by his king and give his wife and child over to my care. Shadrach's mother lived only a few months longer. An unpleasant woman, but sacrifices must be made for our people, and young men need their mothers for as long as possible."

I swallow. I'm unable to look at Lyall at the moment, so I turn back to Shad with my heart in my throat. No wonder there isn't much familial affection between them. The king killed his father, married his mother, and adopted him. Shock chokes me for long moments considering that Shakespearean tragedy.

"Does our culture have many such practices?" I croak.

"We are beasts, dear girl. The daimons who come to us, who we leash, are vicious brutes." He spreads his arm across the plaza as if showing his proof. "He who rules a society of savagery must do so with the same force the people display, otherwise all would be chaos.

"Every generation does not have a dragon to govern it, but when we rise, we reign with honor and strength. A lion or even a wolf may hold things together for a time, but only a dragon can truly bring the kind of leadership our people need in order to thrive. We would tear each other apart with gentleness or the type of open forums the Fai prefer."

His hazel eyes drill into me, his mood sharpening. "That is why you must undergo the trials again soon. Once you leash a dragon daimon, your memory will be restored along with your shadow soul and you will take your place as my heir. That is your legacy. You and Shad will rule together, a pair of dragons that no one, especially not the Fai, will be able to defeat."

"But if you're right, and I lost my memory soul in a second trial, then I would risk death trying again." My voice wavers slightly. "You would have me try a third time even if it kills me?"

Lyall leans against his armrest, thoughtful for a moment. "Thousands of years ago, the ancient Spartans sent their sons into the wilderness armed with only a spear and a blanket. At twelve years of age, they were given this test to see if they could survive for an entire month. Many failed; those who did not die of starvation and the elements came home early in shame. Only those who succeeded were allowed to become citizens. The Spartans were a mighty force for a millennia because their warriors, their citizens, had proved their value."

He reaches over to grip my hands in his. "You, my daughter, are worthy. You will prove your value and you will lead as queen. Your death would mean you were weak, and I know you are not."

Snarls and growls cleave the air as a wolf falls in the training ground, blood gushing from its wounds. Soldiers in human form rush forward with a gurney and load the animal onto it, then jog toward the edge of the park where one of the Fai waits, eyes glowing, her hands outstretched. At least they heal their injured. My chest numb, I pull my hands from Lyall's hold and rub at the ache uselessly.

"And when you are queen," he says, "if it is still your desire to attempt to negotiate with the Fai, you may do so.

Although I suspect once your memory returns, you will recall that the best thing we can do is wipe them off the face of the Earth. They are a scourge, and while I admire your compassion, it must be balanced with practicality. The Nimali require a ruthless hand, a leader who they fear as well as love. It is the only thing holding back the beasts from the door."

Shad's battle is done. All his opponents are down and several more limp toward the waiting Fai healers. The prince transforms back into his human shape and stalks off, disappearing around a corner heading away from the Citadel.

I sit rigidly, staring toward the scene before me with unseeing eyes. Another sparring session begins, but it's all white noise to me. I vaguely register Lyall's hand on my shoulder. A gesture designed to give solace. He squeezes lightly then releases me.

It brings no comfort at all, and a realization arises. Shad's secrecy and his need for a proxy princess make even more sense. I know what he's doing...the only thing he possibly could be, what I would do if I were in his shoes and left with no other options.

The prince is planning a coup.

Chapter Twenty-Two

RYIN

CELENA'S JAW is rigid as she stalks back from the training ground. She stares vacantly before her, lips quivering like the wings of a hummingbird. Her conversation with the king has left her holding on by a thread, and a new rage swells with me toward the beast. What did he say to her to make her react like this? And more importantly, why do I care?

The desire to rip his throat from his body is stronger than ever, but I tamp it down, gripping my hands into tight fists. The princess stops in the center of the narrow lane leading to the Citadel and looks back over her shoulder to where we came from, eyes filling with tears.

"Are you well, Your Grace?" I ask.

She shakes her head in three sharp movements. "I need... a moment."

The guards spring into action. The lead man, the eagle shifter, pivots and heads into a two-story building to the right. The interior is a wide room shrouded in shadow, the only light coming in through the large picture window. Empty clothing racks line the walls and the scarred floors have discolored, rectangular indentations indicating large display cases once sat there. No bliss lighting means this structure is currently unused by the Nimali. They must have stripped it of anything they found valuable.

The female guard remains outside as we file in. Celena's breathing is shaky. She crosses the space, moving toward a closed door in the back.

"I just, I need a minute alone," she says.

I follow and call my daimon forth; its concern for her matches my own. "If you're not well, Your Grace, I will need to examine you."

She swallows, her jaw trembling. "Fine." She grabs my arm and practically drags me through the door before slamming it shut.

We're in a lavatory. Two stall doors are still intact, but in the gap beneath them, holes in the floor reveal that the toilets were reclaimed. A long counter where a single sink was once embedded now features a gaping hole. The only light is from a small, dirty window near the ceiling.

Once we are inside alone, she releases me and slides down the wall into a crouch, covering her mouth with her hands. My daimon and I scan her body for ailments and find none— at least not the physical kind. Emotional distress is beyond the purview of my power.

Celena kneads her forehead and steadies her breathing. "I'm sorry about that," she says. "I know I can't just fall apart like this but it's been...a lot."

I lean against the wall next to her. My ire at the king is still fever-pitched, but expressing it will do neither of us any good. This narrow room is not even as large as the library's panic shelter, and my concern for her cools my rage. "Is this place too small for you to be comfortable in?"

She looks up. "The mirrors help. They give the illusion of space."

The mirror above the sink has large cracks running along

it but is still intact. It faces another large, cracked mirror on the opposite wall, reflecting the weak light along with the repeating image of the broken countertop.

I slide down the wall to sit next to her, maintaining a healthy distance between us in case one of the guards come in. Yesterday, it helped her anxiety for me to talk, so I do so now.

"We don't have mirrors in the Greenlands. The first time I saw one, I was about twelve, on my first salvage run. The Fai scout for materials in the Independent Zone that we can repurpose and reclaim. This was when it was safer. Before the Nimali raiding parties became so common. I came across a double mirror such as this in an apartment building. I thought the image reflecting into eternity was a glimpse into the Origin."

"That's where people go when they die?"

"It's also the home of the daimons and the bliss. The spirit plane. It seemed to my child's eyes like a vision of eternity. When I stood between those mirrors and found myself reflected so many times, I became a part of forever. Every move I made was captured in those two pieces of glass and saved. I thought it was recording me in some way."

I smile at the memory. I'd brought Dove to that place years later to share it with her. The smile drops from my face as pain intrudes.

Celena reaches out to grip my hand, shocking me into stillness. The memory of her touch from last night, her comfort then and now, is enough to rip me in two. The right thing to do is pull away—the guards could come in at any moment to check on their princess. But I didn't do it last night and I don't today. Instead, I turn my palm up to hold her hand for a few long moments. Enjoying the softness of her skin, breathing in her fragrance.

Then self-preservation returns and I disengage, resting my palm against my stomach.

"I asked Lyall," she says.

"It didn't go well, I take it?"

"I don't know how to reconcile the father with the tyrant. I don't know how to be the princess…am I supposed to be okay with this? How could she accept the way things are?" The last part is said in a whisper almost too soft to hear.

I've never heard someone without a memory soul disassociate from themselves like this, as if they were a totally different person before losing their memory. But Celena is obviously struggling.

"It is all you've known," I tell her. "But now you know nothing and find the things that were once normal to be…shocking."

Her eyes are wide when she turns to me. "Shocking is one way to put it. But I don't know how I can help."

I have the strong urge to take her into my confidence, trust her with the existence of the GenFi and enlist her aid. If it were just me at risk I might, but I cannot put all of the others into the crosshairs of the Nimali like that. If I'm wrong and we can't truly trust her, then it would be a disaster. So I keep my mouth shut.

"I wonder if what's inside him is inside of me too?" She stares forward, contemplative, seeming to be talking more to herself than to me now. "I knew my father was cold and difficult, but…" She blows out a frustrated breath.

This I know something about. "We are our parents' legacies," I tell her. "But we are not our parents. You were never much like him, and now you have the chance to start over. To differentiate yourself, if you choose to." Every word out of my mouth is a death sentence for me if another Nimali were to hear, but years of caution are brushed aside because as insane as it seems, I do trust her. And I can see my words are landing. Her gaze on me is steady, urging me to continue.

"We are not born monsters. We learn cruelty. Perhaps all we need to break the cycle is to forget and start over."

She shakes her head. "But I'm not absolved of what I've done before just because I can't remember."

"No. But you can work to make it right."

Tears fill her eyes. "I want to. I want to help. I just don't know how." She clutches her fist to her chest, the earnestness pouring from her.

Two swift raps hammer at the door. "Your Grace? Are you well?"

"Yes, Harshal, I'm coming out."

The bubble is broken and the moment ends. It's for the best, because seeing her like this is havoc on my defenses. I rise and offer my hand. More evidence that I've taken leave of my senses, but when she takes it and I help her stand, it feels right. She holds onto me when I try to let go, then takes a step closer.

"Thank you," she whispers. She squeezes my hand in both of hers and brings it to her lips. The kiss she places on the back of my hand is just a breath. A tiny press of her lips.

An earthquake rages inside me.

My daimon drops away and the princess releases me, then pushes through the door back into the empty storefront. When I emerge, seconds later, she's speaking to the guards. "...just overwhelmed. Nothing physical that he could heal, unfortunately."

The two soldiers don't even look at me, and that's for the best. I need time to wrangle my mask back into place. Time to re-armor myself for my life, once again prepared to exist among my enemy and not shatter or even show signs of cracking.

The hand she kissed stays pressed to my side. I must be imagining that it feels lighter than my other one.

The overcast day greets us and we head back to the Citadel. I maintain the distance of three steps behind the princess, walking without seeing. An entire squadron of Nimali troops could pass and I would miss it. King Lyall could parade my soul on a platter before me and I would have no idea. My entire focus is on the instant her lips touched my skin.

An uncontrollable shiver racks my body. A sinkhole has opened inside me, one that I suspect will be nearly impossible to close. Moreover, I don't want it gone.

The daughter of my greatest enemy has lodged herself within my heart. And what I'm starting to feel for her could get me killed by both her people and my own.

Chapter Twenty-Three

TALIA

THE CITADEL LOOMS before us like a giant standing watch over the city. I don't want to go back inside. If I could, I'd have stayed back in that bathroom with Ryin, crouched on the floor in the dark. No matter what cramped, dark space we're in, something about being alone with him can calm the worst of my unease. But the danger never eases.

Even though my guards know the truth about me, I have no idea how they feel about the Fai. And I won't risk being responsible for Ryin facing punishment in any way just because I consider him a friend. Because I wish he could be more.

Breaking down after talking to my not-father is *not* a princess move. If I'm going to pull this off—be Celena until I can find a way out of this place—then I need to get my shit together. Focus on helping these people, and it's obvious my influence on the king is not as great as I would have hoped.

"I'd like to speak with Shad," I tell Harshal. "Do you know where he might be?"

"I can ping him for you, Your Grace."

"I don't want to take him away from whatever he might be doing." Like strategizing for a coup? "Just, the next time you are in contact, please let him know."

Harshal winces a bit. "Of course, Your Grace."

I drop my voice to a whisper. "Too polite?"

His nod is quick. I take a deep breath and square my shoulders. Be Celena. *Be* Celena. Whoever she is.

"What are things that…I normally do?" I ask.

Harshal blinks and turns to Callum, who looks off in thought. "You are often seen among the orphanages. You spend time in the Umber and Azure infirmaries as well." Charity work, that makes sense. She's not a total monster.

"Your Grace is sometimes found in the Citadel's arcade, organizing some of the entertainments for the children," Zanna offers.

My ears perk up. "There's an arcade?"

"There are vids of you archived there leading the children in skits and plays."

Vids of Celena. That sounds like a gold mine! "Yes, let's head there."

THE NINETEENTH FLOOR is as loud and boisterous as any arcade I visited as a child. A woman in loose-fitting, dark brown clothing stands at a greeting station near the entrance. She bows low when I arrive and offers to lead me around the space.

Both old and young crowd the warren of rooms that take up the entire floor, but it's not the type of arcade I'd pictured. Instead of the weird, bliss-powered video games of my imagination, just about everything here is salvaged. Rows of people, old and young, play chess on water-damaged boards with pieces cannibalized from several different sets. A group of younger teens fold over one another playing Twister, while a handful of old men peer thoughtfully at a Monopoly board. Card games, dice, and dominoes are scattered across tables throughout the room, and some kids in the midst of what I'm pretty sure is a D&D campaign fill the cubby-like rooms on one side of the floor.

The other half of the large space is made up of what used to be small offices, but instead of doors, each has a thick, velvety black curtain covering the doorway.

"These are the theater and screening rooms, Your Grace," the woman says. "Groups come together to watch or record vids here." She pulls aside one of the curtains to reveal a group of teens acting out a scene. The glowing blue device affixed to one wall that looks like a supersized comm must be the camera. In another room, the same device serves as a projector—a three-dimensional holographic image of two lizard puppets fighting each other delights the pair of young boys seated on a bench, their attention rapt.

I smile at the obvious joy on their faces as they watch what is likely their own creation. They don't notice our observation and I back away before we intrude on their enjoyment. For all its faults, this world has some good parts too. Creativity seems to flourish. Necessity has pushed these kids into using their imaginations and making their own entertainment.

I'm surprised to find two of my courtiers, Ofelia and Alaya, in the last room. They *do* notice our presence and clamber to their feet to bow. I thank the attendant and let her go back to her duties. My three, ever-present guards, along with Ryin, wait outside when I join the girls.

"I hope I'm not bothering you," I tell them.

"Of course not, Your Grace, please come in." Alaya's smile is bright and she waves me forward. "In fact, I was going to give this to you the next time our paths crossed." She pulls a small box from the pocket of her dress.

"What is this?"

"It's a memory box. We made them a few weeks ago when

we were volunteering at the Umber school. We brought equipment there so the children could make their own vids and we recorded some of our own. Would you like to watch?"

"Yes, of course. I was hoping for something like this." I sit on one of the benches in the center of the room as she fiddles with the projector. My feet bounce with anticipation.

Just like the comm's video chat, the vids are all monochromatic, three-dimensional, and tinted blue. Like a hologram, they're projected out onto the ground at about one-quarter scale.

A grassy park dotted with spindly trees is the first thing that comes into view. Then children run through the frame, pretending to be animals. These kids are too young to have gone through the trials, and I laugh at their antics. Until I realize that they're playing at sparring and some of them lie on the ground, clutching imaginary wounds. I guess it's no different to how I'm used to seeing children play, but it's just more chilling knowing that many of these kids will grow up to be soldiers.

The scene changes, and I get my first glimpse of the real Celena. She sits straight backed and regal on a park bench. I've been trying to affect the same posture, but watching her makes me realize what a poor copy I am.

We are identical, though of course I must have about fifteen pounds on her. Staring at my face knowing it's not me is so strange. And then she opens her mouth and my voice comes out, but so different.

"Stop fidgeting with that and come sit down," she demands, but there's kindness in her tone. Dominga emerges from behind the camera and sits next to her, rolling her eyes. The woman is more relaxed than I've seen her. Still fierce, but the question I had upon meeting her is answered. She and the princess are best friends. Their closeness is obvious.

"This is for the memory box," Celena says.

"What in Origin's name is a memory box?"

"It's like a time capsule." Her bearing is of someone who has confidence dripping from her pores. Suddenly, I really *do* want to be her—not just pretend to be her, but have her life. Have the kind of life that makes you into this. I'm such a poor facsimile it's no wonder Dominga looks at me with barely concealed resentment. She lost her best friend and got me in return.

"A time capsule is a silly idea," Dominga gripes with no heat.

"The human ones we found are very elucidating. One day in the future someone will find ours, and I want them to know how we lived."

Dominga sighs. "Fine."

"And besides, when I am queen, I will want a record of my juvenilia."

"You are hardly a juvenile at twenty-three." It's the first time I've heard Dominga laugh, and it's shocking.

"You're right. At twenty-three, I should have a daimon." Celena drops her head and Doming grabs her hand to comfort her.

"You will. Your next trial will be successful."

Doubt clouds Celena's expression even as she nods in agreement. Doubt and pain…maybe even shame. I feel my own cheeks burning in sympathy.

Other courtiers come into view. I'm honestly surprised it took Elayne so long to push her way in. Her jealousy is apparent and her behavior now makes even more sense. If the princess doesn't remember her best friend, then Elayne has a chance to fill the spot.

The five of them arrange themselves on the bench and then pose and preen for the camera. Then the vid ends.

"This reel was discarded," Alaya says. "I think that you kept the final version in your suite, Your Grace."

"Thank you so much for showing this to me. I…I think I'd like to watch it again."

Alaya looks at Ofelia and the girls stand. "We will leave you to it."

"Oh, I didn't mean to kick you out of here."

"No, we have elocution lessons starting shortly."

"For promoted Cardinals," Ofelia says nearly inaudibly.

"Before you go, will you show me how to work this?"

Alaya complies, and after another round of bows, they're gone. I watch the vid again, inspecting everything about Celena from how she tilts her head, to her smile, to the glimpse of wistfulness on her face when she talks about having a daimon.

I don't think I'll ever truly know her, but hearing her thoughts in her own words, getting a chance to "meet" her—it means a lot. And shines a spotlight on all of my deficits in impersonating her.

I'm starting the projector for the third time when Ryin peeks his head in. "Sir Harshal bid me to come in to ensure you weren't lying on the ground in a pool of your own vomit."

My brows rise. "He said that?"

Ryin's lips purse. "Not in so many words. But after the incident earlier today, he seems concerned."

"Fair enough. I'm fine, just learning about...myself."

He looks at the frozen image and nods. "I will leave you to it."

"No, wait—" I stand and grab his arm. His skin burns hot under my hand.

"Sorry," I say, releasing him. He tilts his head to the side, waiting for me. "It's just...What was she like?" I motion to the woman on the screen.

Ryin scrutinizes the image for a moment. "*She* was a princess through and through. Haughty and superior, but not cruel. She spent time with the orphans, gave aid to the Umbers, distributed food during the Month of Wildness when the rains flooded some of the residences on the outskirts of the territory."

His gaze settles on me. "She did not thank those who were kind to her. She did not learn Fai sign language nor care what a drudge thought of her."

I blink, chastened. But his voice is gentle. "When people lose their memory souls, they generally do not undergo massive personality shifts. But in this case..."

I hang on his words. "In this case?"

Dark eyes glitter, piercing me. "I am glad of it."

He is standing quite close. I would only have to lift my hand to stroke his cheek if I wanted. The urge is strong.

But I push it back.

If I can somehow manage to play this role to completion and survive, I could give him his freedom. Only if I am queen.

The idea seems impossible and fantastical, but I cling to it as his eyes roam over me, warming me in places that have not felt heat in a long time. The intensity of his gaze stirs feelings that have nothing to do with my crush on a boy who looked like him years ago. I almost do reach for him, graze his skin with my fingertips just to know what it feels like.

"You know that I would never cause you any harm, don't you?" I ask.

He nods. Is he closer now somehow? I think his lips are. They're full and the bow of the top lip is mesmerizing me. I can't tear my gaze away. I want to trace it with my finger. With my tongue.

Yes, he's definitely closer, or maybe I am—I'm breathing in his airspace now. His breath is warm and smells of melons. Sweet. He must have had the same dark red mash for breakfast that reminds me of cantaloupes.

I swallow, visually tracing a path through the freckles on his face that stand out against his cinnamon skin. I want to feel the scrape of the stubble on his jaw.

His eyes flash, reflecting the same forbidden desire that is coursing within me.

I reach for him, blind to all the reasons why this is a terrible idea.

And then movement from the corner of my eye has us breaking apart.

The thick curtain slides aside, revealing Dominga, glaring. Her nostrils flare and her eyes are diamond chips. She's just as different from the laughing woman on the vid as I am.

"Wait outside, healer. I need a word with our princess."

He bows to her, doesn't look at me, and retreats without a word.

I force myself not to watch him leave as Dominga stalks closer.

She glances at the projection then back to me, her expression hardening. "I've been trying to figure it out for days. When I heard you'd returned, my heart was so...full." A melancholy expression crosses her face before anger and hurt swamps her features again. "But this person who came back to us..." She shakes her head.

Celena in the vid is confident and cool, steeped in the knowledge of her place in the world. Surrounded by people who loved her. None of which I've had in a very long time.

"A whole life gone," I say, still shaken by her sudden arrival. "It changes things."

"We've all known those who lost memory souls before. None have ever acted as you do. And the worst thing is, I begged you not to do it." She spits the words out and then her face falls. Grief blends with the anger.

"Not do what?"

"The second trial. That's where you went." She steps closer to me, forcing me back a pace. "Off to do it alone. To find an unblemished source of bliss."

"The king was right," I whisper.

"He suspected as much, though he didn't want to believe you'd ever disobey him like that."

I swallow as she sits next to me, leaning into my space.

"What happened to you out there? Did the bliss across the wall change you? You had a plan. You were so certain it was going to work." Her jaw clenches as tears well in her eyes.

Misery drowns me. "I'm sorry, Dominga. I'm so sorry that your best friend didn't come back to you. I'm sorry to be such a bad substitute. But I'm doing the best I can."

She snorts. Then stares at me in the dim light coming from the projector. A frown mars the rigid perfection of her skin. She leans closer, like she's about to whisper in my ear.

I incline my head away. Is she trying to smell me?

Her eyes narrow even further. Then she jerks back. "Who are you?"

My eyes widen as fear nearly chokes my response. "C-Celena."

She tilts her head, looking me up and down. Scrutinizing me again. Then she stands suddenly. "No. You can't be."

She spins on her heel and leaves. And my heart clenches.

She knows.

Chapter Twenty-Four

RYIN

LADY DOMINGA RUSHES out from behind the curtain, her face a thunderstorm. The guards share a look, unease passing between them.

Sir Harshal takes a step toward the entry, then pauses. "Healer, perhaps you should check on the princess again."

"I can do nothing for emotional distress, sir."

"I'm not certain that's true."

I keep my expression rigid and his belies no suspicion, but his words put me on alert. The urge to rush in and protect her from any harm, physical or emotional, real or imagined, is strong, but it wars with the desire to keep more space between us. To not give into the doomed pull I feel for her.

I slowly enter the screening room to find it empty. I spin around, then head for the partially hidden doorway leading to the servant's hall. It runs along the outer wall of the arcade level to allow for delivery of food and such without disturbing the entertainments.

Sure enough, Celena is walking away from me, her steps hurried. "Your Grace!" I call out. She looks over her shoulder but doesn't stop. The passageway is too dim for me to parse her expression, but panic grips me and I jog to meet her.

"Your Grace, what's wrong?"

Celena slows and puts a hand to her neck. Her breathing is rapid, eyes frantic. "She knows. I need to get out of here."

"She knows what?"

"Please." There is true fear in her eyes. Obviously she and Lady Dominga had words and now it seems Celena isn't thinking clearly. She didn't want to face the guards or the people in the arcade. Maybe all she needs is another quiet few minutes to gather her thoughts.

"I don't want to be there if she comes back."

A thousand questions come to my mind, but apparently my thought process is taking too long, because the princess turns on her heel and heads away toward the stairwell. My feet unstick themselves from the floor and I follow.

"The guards, Your Grace," I call out, but she ignores me and bursts through the door.

Footsteps sound above us. She looks up in a panic and then heads down. I keep pace with her, unsure of where she's going.

"What's the next Fai floor?" she asks.

My answer is automatic. "Sixteen."

She races down the three flights to the sixteenth floor and pushes through. I'm quite certain no royal has ever stepped foot on a Fai floor before. No one is around, but if we come across a patrol of guards, they will definitely escort her away.

The princess looks left and right in the nondescript hall-way, unsure of where to go.

"Where are you—" But footsteps pounding in unison rise from around the corner, and I tense. "Guards are coming."

Her eyes grow wide and she takes off in the opposite direction. I race past her, looking for a place to hide. This floor is larger than the upper Fai floors where I spend more time so I'm not as familiar with the layout, but it's obvious Celena has no desire to cross paths with any guards. I try the first door we encounter, hoping for a supply or maintenance closet, but it has a biometric sensor, not a handle, and won't open. I've never seen a sensor on a Fai floor before. I try it again but it won't budge.

The footsteps are drawing nearer and Celena's face is a mask of horror. She places her hand against the sensor and the door swishes open. We slide in just as the boots come into view from around the corner.

The door snicks shut. We're in a small, dark space, a vestibule of some kind that has no motion-activated bliss lights. I'm glad of it.

I call my daimon to give off its slight illumination. Celena sucks in a breath but doesn't move away. Another sensor-controlled door is behind us, but who knows where that leads? The narrow space is really only big enough for us to stand very close together like this.

"What happened?" I whisper. "What made you so upset, and where were you going?"

"I need to get out of here. Dominga knows the truth." Her eyes are pools of fear, and I want to eliminate whatever has her looking like that.

"What truth?"

"That I'm not Celena."

My heart stutters.

"I tried to tell you and Shad that first day, remember? I didn't lose my memory soul. I'm from another place, like this one but different. I look like her, but I'm not her. Watching those videos, it's amazing how anyone could believe that I *am* her. We're so, so different."

The breath escapes from my lungs in a gush. Her sincerity is apparent, and it would explain so much. "Who are you, then?"

"Talia. My name is Talia."

Everything clicks into place, and I believe her. I do recall her making the claim before, but it made no sense then. The princess was missing but now returned. Simple. But really not so simple.

"How did you get here? What could have brought you here from...where? Another world?"

"I have no idea." She shakes her head. "I wish I knew the hows or whys of it all. I wish I knew how to get back. But I was dead in that world. I thought this was my afterlife, but...I don't think I deserve this hell."

The urge is too strong to resist. I wrap my arms around her and pull her close. She doesn't resist, but flows to me like the tide coming in. The tension in her limbs drains away immediately.

"In your world, you are not a princess, are you?"

A snort leaves her lips. "In my world, I'm more like a drudge."

Her compassion, Noomi's conviction. They all come into sharper focus, and I tighten my grip on her. "Talia," I whisper into her hair, testing her name on my tongue. Inhaling her scent. It's like sunshine and honey.

Her arms come across my back and she squeezes me to her. She is loose now, no longer the ball of tension that escaped the arcade in a panic.

"Talia," I say again. Not the princess.

"How do you do it?"

"What?"

"Make everything better."

She looks up at me, her gaze resting on my lips, and reason flees. I press my lips to hers. She pushes into me, responding in kind, eagerly tasting me. I groan into her mouth, enjoying her essence, the dance of lips and tongue.

Her body beneath my hands feels so good, I roam her figure, skating over her curves. She explores my back, hands slipping beneath my tunic to coast from hip to neck. I pick her up, pressing her against the wall. Her legs wrap around my waist, and a moan rumbles up from her.

It's all happening so fast, it's like I've lost control of myself. She's just as desperate as I am. The kisses are frenzied, unyielding, barely allowing us any air. She's more real to me than ever before—not a princess, not a Nimali at all, but someone completely new.

Her hands leave my back and she arches up into me, flinging her arms to the side and whimpering as I nibble on her neck and graze her earlobe.

Strong legs tighten around me, then the solid surface of the wall holding our weight disappears and we tumble through a suddenly open doorway. She must have accidentally activated the sensor. I catch her, turning at the last moment and taking the brunt of the fall with her on top of us.

She rises, hands planted on my chest, breath heaving, as motion-activated lights wink on in response to our presence.

When she shifts off of me, I groan, missing the weight of her and the grip of her thighs around mine. But then I begin to notice where we are. All lust drains from my mind and body as the room is revealed.

It's a laboratory. A counter runs along the wall full of scientific equipment. I have no name for any of these things; the Fai do not utilize them, and my time here has not educated me about them. The center of the room is filled with cages. Occupied cages.

We both stand in a rush. Talia presses herself to my side, her jaw dropping open.

Thick bars and a clear plastic barrier protect us from the occupants, but I take a protective step in front of her, holding my arms out as my daimon surges.

A dozen cells. A Revoker inside each one.

Those closest to us appear drugged. They lie on the ground, plated chests rising and falling slowly. But when I take note of the rest of their bodies, nausea cramps my stomach. They've been...experimented upon.

My breathing is shallow as I step closer to the nearest cage. Yes, the Revokers are our enemies, they are vicious beasts that kill without compunction. We must eliminate them for our own protection, but this? This is evidence of a cruelty that staggers belief.

Limbs and wings have been removed. Portions of jaws. Fresh wounds cover empty eye sockets. The creatures farther down the line are less injured...perhaps newly caught?

Disgust boils within. Even drugged and maimed, these things could get loose. Keeping them inside a building full of people? Women and children?

"The alarm from yesterday," I whisper.

Talia looks over at me, understanding dawning. "Lyall said a Revoker had made it into the territory. But that would be nearly impossible, right?"

"Even if one had crossed the wall, I can't imagine the soldiers would allow it to get all the way here."

"One of these must have gotten loose."

My throat is thick with disgust. I break away from her to walk down the aisle, peering at each cage. The locking mechanisms appear secure, recently updated—probably because of the incident. I'd heard that three drudges were attacked in the melee, but another Fire Fai had healed them, siphoning out the poison as I'd done for Talia when she first arrived on the wall.

It seems so long ago. I return to where she stands, shaking and blinking as if she still can't believe her eyes, and take her hand. Revokers can die just as any other creature does. They feel pain the same as everything else.

The Revoker in the cage closest to us stirs, opening its remaining red eye. The pupil is leached of color, muted, as it stares blearily at us.

The creature gives a half-hearted growl so weak it barely

resonates. Sorrow fills me. This is an enemy, but no living thing deserves to be treated this way. Defeat them honorably in battle, certainly. Protect your people and land, but this? I shake my head.

"Do you think the king will tell you what the purpose of this is?" I ask her. "What they're doing here?"

Talia turns away from the cage as if she can't bear to witness this any longer. "If he still believes I'm his daughter, he will."

I come around in front of her and lift her chin. "What exactly did Dominga say?"

"She stared at me and asked who I am. I don't know what she saw to make her suspect, but she's been suspicious ever since I arrived." Her lips quiver.

"She has no proof. Nothing that anyone would believe. What you describe has never occurred—there's no reason to believe you aren't the princess." I draw her into a hug, resting my head on top of hers.

"I have nowhere else to go anyway," she says into my chest. "And you're right, I know you are—I was just freaking out. I think it will take a lot to convince Lyall I'm a fake. Until then…"

She pulls away and smiles up at me sadly, then her worried gaze scans the room again. "I need to do what I can. Get answers from Lyall. Find out exactly what is going on and come up with a way to stop it. It's the least I can do for bene-fitting from her life."

The fear and uncertainty are still there, but her resolve is overpowering them. My respect for her grows.

"We should get back," I say. "The guards will worry." Talia nods.

I listen for footsteps outside the door. All is quiet, so we leave the lab. I lead Talia to the stairwell and back up to the arcade level, entering the screening room using the Fai passages without running into another soul. Her guards will hopefully never know she was gone.

But I must warn the Fai of the danger in our midst. The Nimali keep those creatures on a Fai floor for a reason, knowing we will be the first injured if one escapes. Just like yesterday.

Should I tell Von the truth about the princess, her true identity? I immediately discount the idea. His plans have never sat right with me, not even when I thought Talia was Celena. If he and the Crowns knew that the princess is an imposter, it would put Talia in even more danger.

As Celena, she is protected; no Nimali would see her harmed, and the Fai could not expect Lyall to negotiate if his precious daughter were injured in any way. As an imposter, though...All bets are off. They could maim or kill her just to gauge the king's reaction.

I squeeze her hand, then cup her face and give her a brief kiss. Dangerous, but necessary for my own well-being if not hers.

She tilts her head up to me, so trusting. Fragile and delicate, but still strong. Determination shines in her eyes when I pull away.

We share a silent communication, then I slip out of the screening room and rejoin the guards. The beasts have much to answer for, but for the first time in years, my priorities are in flux. Freedom is still top of mind, but can I take it at the risk of her safety?

I know the answer before the question has even fully formed in my mind. I could not protect my sister, but I will do whatever it takes to keep Talia safe. Not just because she doesn't deserve to be used as a pawn. But because I'm beginning to suspect that she is mine.

Chapter Twenty-Five

TALIA

An attendant summons me to dinner in Lyall's apartment, which takes up the whole of the thirty-seventh floor. I'm surprised it's not higher, but once I enter I understand why—this space feels huge. The floors of the pyramid get progressively smaller as they reach the top, so here he can spread his wings metaphorically and perhaps literally, since it's basically just one large open concept.

Instead of the mismatched salvaged furniture of Celena's suite, the king's chamber is minimalist. Not fashionable. Maybe that is a statement in and of itself. He has no need to follow the prevailing trends. It's not particularly comfortable-looking, either. There is a seating area in the center of the room with extremely modern couches with hard, thin cushions. An enormous dining table that could probably seat twenty stands against the wall, but only two table settings have been placed down at the end.

A pair of Fai stand at attention behind the table. Ryin crosses the space and disappears without a word behind a door to what I assume is the servants' room.

Lyall appears from a hidden door, talking to someone on his comm. He smiles at me kindly and pulls out my chair, helping me settle into the seat comfortably before sitting himself.

With a flick of his wrist, he orders one of the Fai to pour drinks and ends his call.

"I heard you went to the arcade," he says. He jerks his head at the pair of Fai men, who retreat to the same door Ryin used. "You used to so enjoy those entertainments as a child. You would want to spend all of your time there." He sighs, lost in a memory.

I take in the similarities and differences between him and my real father. Aren't we all a product of our own experiences? What made this man into who he is? Is he a monster or a loving father? Can he truly be both?

"Are you experimenting on Revokers in the Citadel, Father?" I ask.

If he's surprised by the question, he does a great job of masking it. He simply puts down his glass and pulls a dampener from his pocket, pressing the center to turn it on. It glows with a pulsing blue light. Then he leans his elbows on the table.

"Yes." His voice nearly echoes off the empty pale walls. "We developed this strategy about six months ago. The soldiers who patrol across the wall lure and capture them. It has been difficult, and costly, but worthwhile." He tilts his head. "How did you discover this?"

I swallow, trying to breathe through the knot constricting my throat. "To what end?"

"Understanding their physiology helps us hone our battle techniques." He clasps his hands together, studying me intently. "And we are studying their venom. It is the most powerful poisoning agent we've ever seen. Knowing how it works will allow us to create an antidote that doesn't require a Fai healer." He spread his hands apart. "A worthy goal, no?"

"Is that all?"

"Do you truly want to know?"

"Did I know before?"

He nods.

"Then yes. I would like to know."

His scrutiny ends and he breaks eye contact, looking down at his hands before giving a little shrug. "I doubt you will support the plan any more than you did before. But, you certainly have the right to know. We cannot allow the Fai to continue to hoard the bliss. Our survival depends on our access to it. Our remaining mines are producing less and less. Pockets of bliss within the matrices are becoming more difficult and dangerous to find. When an area is emptied, the voids left are delicate and prone to cave-ins. We've lost three trammeled drudges this week alone in mine collapses."

I gasp and try to tamp down my reaction, but he makes no mention of it.

"The Fai are difficult to fight in their home territory. The Greenlands are heavily forested and of course they have home field advantage. We have attempted various deforesting chemicals to kill their trees and ground cover, but too many of their daimons are skilled in growth. They just bring the plants back." He chuckles as if amused at the audacity of these people to repair the damage to their land.

"But synthesizing the Revoker poison," he continues, "well, it allows us to kill multiple birds with one stone, as it were. The poison is deadly both to Fai and vegetation, and with enough of it, we can overwhelm their ability to heal themselves and their greenery."

I blink. "You're trying to recreate Revoker poison?"

"We have been *trying* for months. We have finally succeeded." A broad grin breaks over his face, revealing sharp, white teeth.

My stomach seizes.

"We are now working on the distribution methods, developing a way for our air force to deliver the poison. Within the next week, our tests should be complete, and we will be ready to finally bring this conflict to an end."

He reaches out to take my hand, which lies cold and lifeless in his grip. "I know you do not approve, and I am certain you will make the same arguments as before, dear one. But we cannot allow these ambushes and skirmishes to continue. Our need is too great. Without bliss, life would be chaos once again as it was just after the Sorrows. Neither you nor I remember, but my father told me of the suffering. The brutality as we destroyed one another for resources, battled the remaining mundane humans and the Fai. It cannot be like that again. It is my duty to preserve our way of life and create a legacy for you and your children."

I pull my hand from his grip. "Please don't say you're going to wipe out an entire people for me." I shake my head in disbelief.

"Nimali lives will be at risk if we continue as we are, if we lose our advantage."

My head is still shaking rapidly. I don't know how to process this.

"You are disappointed in me, I see," he says, sorrow edging into his voice.

I steady my breathing before responding. "I think it should be possible to rule without cruelty."

"What you see as cruelty, I see as expedience. The Fai threaten the lives of every Nimali. We capture some of them, keep them bound to us with their souls locked away, but don't ever think that if they had the ability they would not do the same to us. I assure you that at this moment they are plotting ways to destroy each and every one of us."

I purse my lips. He gives me a rueful glance. "You still wish to negotiate?" he asks. His expression is all patience. His respect for my thoughts and opinions is clear on his face, but I can't answer. I drop my head, feeling twisted inside.

He leans forward. "Say we were to release a handful of drudges, pull their souls from the vault, restore them, and send the Fai on their way as an act of good faith. They would know too much about our organization, how we do things. We'd be sending back the perfect spies." He shakes his head. "No Fai that has lived in the Citadel can ever leave, my dear. You understand that is not possible at this point."

My brain is stuck. "Their souls are in the vault?"

He takes another sip of his drink and nods. "Of course. Safe from any threat of theft and near enough so that they cannot leave here. But you do see why they must stay, why bargaining for their freedom cannot work."

I nod mechanically. "Yes, Father, of course I do. I wasn't thinking clearly. My own...experience beyond the wall, whatever it was, must have colored my thoughts."

Something clarifies within me, coming into sharp focus. I cannot take part in this ruse much longer. I have to find a way to stop this genocide.

My stomach growls and it wipes the contemplative look from his face. He shuts off the dampener and pats my hand again.

A whistle appears in his hands and he blows it in sharp blasts that hurt my eardrums. The Fai appear immediately, trays in hand as if they've been standing waiting on the other side of the door listening for his call.

I'm not sure how I eat with my stomach in such turmoil, but I need the energy. I keep up the facade, chatting with Lyall about my day. Listening to him complain of some of the jealousy of his councilors—jealousy he himself instigated to keep them off balance. I nod and smile at all the right moments. I bide my time.

If it's a matter of days until the destruction of the Fai homeland and the genocide of an entire people, then what I must do becomes startlingly clear.

And I don't want Lyall to see it coming.

RYIN

I slip out of the king's apartment to the back staircase and race down to the thirty-second floor. The king often lingers with his meals, and I'm certain he and "Celena" have much to talk about. Still, I cannot tarry—I'll need to be there when I'm summoned. Talia will stall for time as much as possible to give me the opportunity to warn my people.

I wish I were a telepath, able to contact others at will, but that is not one of my daimon's gifts. I burst onto the Fai floor and nearly run into an older man.

"Von? Xipporah?" I ask, a bit wildly. He points me to the east kitchens, and I race in like something is chasing me.

Xipporah stands at the stove stirring a steaming pot. She looks odd there, her graceful form honed from years of training. She's a soldier, not a cook, and even though she was captured voluntarily, the sight of her wasting her gifts rankles.

"Emergency meeting," I sign. There are no guards visible, but we never speak about meetings aloud. "Where is Von?"

Xi immediately stops what she's doing. The woman who had been chopping cubes of cloned meat at the counter next to her smoothly steps up to take her place at the stove. Xi removes the apron covering her drudge uniform and motions with her head for me to follow.

We rush through the halls, keeping an eye out for patrols, and end up in the mechanical room, where Von sits at a small, folding table in front of a wall of bliss-powered equipment. Enzo and Nyana, two more GenFi members, are with him.

It's hot and noisy in here, with pipes and tubes running from floor to ceiling. Panels with gauges and switches line the opposite wall. On the table, sheets of crumpled schematics are laid out. They are pre-Sorrows plans for the building's machinery, the paper somehow having survived the destruction, but someone has drawn additions in the margins. The words "biometric security override" are scrawled in slanting script. Farther down the page is written, "blood, hair, dna???"

All three straighten at our arrival. Von stands, a frown on his face.

"Revokers on floor sixteen. They're in a lab. Being experimented on." The looks I receive in return are all horrified. Everyone exchanges glances and Von closes his eyes. Xi steps up and grabs his arm.

I'd forgotten that he has a direct line to our leaders back home. Even with an amplifier, no other telepath in the Citadel can manage communicating over such a distance.

When he opens his eyes, blue with the light of his daimon, his face is a hardened mask. His fingers fly as he signs. "We do this tonight. Where is the princess?"

Talia's secret burns a hole in my chest. Should I tell them or not? Indecision wars within me. What will keep her safer, being the princess or not?

"Where is she, brother?" Von signs again.

"Dining with the king," I say through clenched teeth.

"Tonight then, after she goes to bed. Wait for my signal and then grab her, subdue her by whatever means necessary. We will kidnap her tonight and make our demands of the king."

"We do not yet know what they're doing with those Revokers. The princess is asking the king as we speak. She will be able to give us more information."

"Do you think it is anything good?" Von scoffs. "Experimenting on them? Keeping them on one of *our* floors? Whatever else is going on, we will pay the price."

He's right. But I don't like the idea of using Talia as a pawn. Even less than I liked the idea of doing so with Celena.

Von steps toward me, eyes shining bright. "What is the cause of your hesitance, brother?"

"She is turning. She is the reason we have this information

in the first place. Noomi was right, the princess—the one who returned—has sympathy for our plight. Using her like this does not sit well with me when there may be other options."

He considers this. "Whatever change of heart she may be having will be too slow for us. Her influence over the king will not get us what we want now. We need our freedom, not tomorrow, not next year, but *today*. And we cannot wait for anyone else to give it to us. We must take it. If I've learned one thing from the Nimali way of doing things, it's that.

"The Crowns have need of you. Your people do. What does the fate of the princess of the beasts have to do with us? What care do they take with their prisoners, *us*? I intend to show our Nimali captive exactly the same care her people have shown to us." He grins, wide and feral.

I take a step back, the war within me raging. How can I agree to this? But how can I not? I swallow as misery tears my gut apart. "What are you all doing in here, anyway? What are these plans?" I motion to the schematics.

Xipporah speaks up. "Nyana here found these headed for the compost. They were hidden in a ceiling during a renovation of a Cardinal apartment."

"The bliss technology was added directly over the building's original electric and mechanical infrastructure," Nyana adds. "They modified some things but left other systems in place that no longer worked. If we can get them working again, we can override their tech and get into restricted areas. Cause some real trouble." The woman grins.

"Those are big ifs," Von signs. "And would have taken too long anyway. We have our new orders." He turns to me. "It all hinges on you getting the princess where we need her."

The others all stare at me. Xipporah looks worried. Enzo and Nyana, soldiers who I have shared this hell with and fought beside for years before, they are counting on me. Every Fai in this building is counting on me. I am the one best placed near the princess. The one with access to her.

I take a deep breath. "Yes. Fine. When you give the signal."

I tell myself I will keep her safe. It's better that I do it than anyone else. But apprehension prickles at me.

Von steps back, his daimon receding. There is a glint in his eye that I do not like. Noomi's reproach echoes in my ears. If I had stepped up to leadership in GenFi like she wanted me to, like others expected given my family history, I could have pushed us in another direction. Maybe she was right—is my cowardice to blame for whatever happens next?

Freedom is on the line. The lives of all of my brothers and sisters are at stake. And how can I possibly keep Talia safe and not betray my people?

The question haunts me as I return to the king's chambers and wait for dinner to end.

Chapter Twenty-Six

TALIA

RYIN'S EXPRESSION is particularly stony as we head back to my suite. I want to tell him what I learned from the king, but Shad is waiting for me outside my door. Two new guards stand at their positions looking especially fearsome, so as eager as I am to talk to the prince, I keep my expression neutral.

Once we're inside, Ryin bows stiffly before disappearing into the servants' room. He seems edgy and off, but maybe he's just trying to avoid any display of emotion toward me. I'm hoping it doesn't mean those emotions have already fizzled out. I'm not looking for any kind of PDA or anything else that would get him punished, but part of me is expecting him to come to his senses and realize that whatever attraction he had toward me is fleeting.

But I'll worry about that later. Now Shad has some explaining to do.

Silently, he leads me into the dressing room and engages a dampener. "Harsh said you wanted to talk to me."

I sit on the chaise lounge, back straight, and look him in the eye. "Do you know about the Revokers in the building?

The experiments? Lyall's plans for destroying the Fai homeland?"

Shad closes his eyes on a grimace and rubs a hand over his face, then squeezes his jaw. "That is exactly what I've been trying to stop."

He slides down to the ground to sit leaning against the large cabinet in the center of the room. "We've lost dozens of soldiers capturing those Revokers. Men and women who I command. And the danger to the Citadel…" He shakes his head. "Three Fai were killed just yesterday. I think it's madness. Genocide is madness. It would stain all of our souls and decimate our covenants. But the king will not be moved."

"And so he has to go."

Shad looks up at me, brows raised.

"You're planning a coup, right?" I say it sotto voce, but his eyes still widen and dart to the dampener between us.

He comes over to sit beside me on the chaise and whisper in my ear. "How did you know?"

"Educated guess. How is it going? Will you be able to stop this?"

His expression is grim. "I do not know. There are enough who oppose the king and are willing to stand beside me, but some of my most powerful allies are having second thoughts."

"Why?"

"They believe the king suspects me. He and his diehards have been showing greater interest in certain allies. No threats, just the opposite, rewarding them with promotions and greater responsibilities."

"Ensuring their loyalty?" I ask.

"Or keeping them close."

I draw my knees up and rest my chin on them, thinking. "So, no coup before the Greenlands are poisoned."

"I cannot guarantee it." His tone is solemn.

"Do you have any other way to stop it?"

He looks at me wearily. "I am making progress on sabotaging the poison delivery system."

Well, that's something. "Okay, you stay on that. I have a plan of my own."

"Care to share?" A corner of his mouth lifts, but I shake my head.

"Plausible deniability," I tell him. "But it's happening tonight. And if I pull it off, you'll know."

AFTER SHAD LEAVES, I call for Ryin—not using the stupid whistle that I've still refused to consider, but the old-fashioned way, using his name. He emerges from the servants' room, sharp cheekbones looking more severe than ever. I make the sign for "talk" that Noomi taught me and lead him into the dressing room. Seems like I'll be spending a lot of time in here.

The dampener Shad left me sits on the center cabinet. I push it until it pulses blue and Ryin tilts his head, studying me. Again, I settle onto the white chaise, this time perching on the edge. Ryin sits next to me, right next to me, warming my side. A knot of fear within me loosens. He's not keeping his distance. His unasked questions are probably the cause of the furrow in his brow.

I swallow, getting caught up in the clarity of his whisky dark eyes. I could use a shot of whisky and I hate the stuff. *Brown liquor is for the unevolved,* my stepmother used to say. I huff a humorless laugh at the memory, which turns into a choked sob. Then I suck in a breath.

"He's going to wipe you all out. They've been trying to recreate the Revoker poison to use on the Fai and the Greenlands, destroy the forest that protects your home and kill all the Fai to get to your matrices."

His jaw tightens, but other than that, his reaction is muted.

My fists clench on my lap. One of his hands covers both of mine, the red undertones in his skin a contrast to my darker tone. The back of his hand is covered in freckles. I wonder if his whole body is, too. The thought is so intrusive and out of place that I shove it away.

"I wonder where *other* people go when they die." My head drops, heavy from the weight of all my thoughts. "I always thought it would be a better place."

"How *did* you die, Talia?" he asks, squeezing my hands gently.

I sniff and look up at him. "It wasn't heroic or anything. I had this car—my father's old car, one he gave me. I guess our world is like this one before the Sorrows. We all had cars and drove everywhere. Anyway, mine was a piece of crap. And I'd told Dad about the weird sound it was making and the lights flashing on the dashboard, and he said that he'd take care of it. Promised, in fact." I roll my eyes thinking of how often he promised things that never happened.

"Of course, one day, when I was running late for one of my jobs, the thing refused to start. Neither of my stepsisters would let me use their cars, either—brand-new ones, I might add—so I had to take the bus. Except, since we lived in the suburbs, the nearest bus stop was about a mile and a half away."

I sigh. "Long story short, I was hit crossing the street. A truck came out of nowhere, ran the stop sign, crashed right into me." What I remember after that is a blur. And I'm not sure which car accident it is scrambling my thoughts: the one from a few weeks ago or the one from years ago. My head is a blur of sounds, glass crunching, my screams, my mother's screams. I was in that car with her for hours before someone found us.

Trapped in the dark. Pinned by my seat belt and the crunched-in metal of the door against my side. Walls closing in.

I shake it off. Blink hard.

"Then I was here. And there were growls and snarls and pain."

I'm still caught somewhere between the near past and the distant past when his hand once again tightens on mine. "And I opened my eyes and saw you."

"You thought I was someone else."

I nod, rueful. "If I'm Celena here, you're Victor there. But he died a long time ago. And I still have no idea how I got here. Or why." I figure Akeem hasn't found any answers or he would have reached out.

I want to think I was brought here so that I can save them. Save Ryin. Though I'm not sure it's within my power. However, if I can get into the vault and find the souls...

The Fai man who was trammeled—Silas—his face comes to mind. The look on it when his soul was restored. What would Ryin look like with his shadow back? Would he finally smile? Would he and the others then be able to find a way to stop Lyall or at least warn their people?

Ryin's palm, large and warm, cups my cheek. I lean into him.

"You seem lost," he says.

"You have no idea. I have no home. I'm not even supposed to be here." I unclench my fists and wrap my arms around him, sinking into his warmth.

"Me either," he whispers, pulling me tighter. He inhales a jagged breath, arms enclosing me in safety and acceptance.

The air leaves my lungs in a way that isn't painful—it feels complete, like a puzzle piece snapping into place. Then he pulls back, brown eyes shining, not from his daimon but from some inner light. And then he kisses me like I'm his last breath.

It is consuming. An inferno opens up within both of us, feeding one another. Teeth scrape, his stubble abrades my jaw, his tongue tangles in mine. We pulse with need and desperation. I grip his neck, pressing myself into him.

He pushes me against the chaise, straddles me, using his weight to keep me in place. I wrap my legs around him, the urgency pushing us forward. He palms my ass, grinding against me like he's trying to fuse our bodies together even though we're fully clothed.

As if reading my mind, he fumbles for the laces of my bodice as I pull up his shirt. We have to break apart to undress, fabric flying, and then we come together again, clothes tossed carelessly all over the giant closet, shoes gone, just us. I barely get a chance to look at him, to verify the freckles covering his body, before he's on me. Ravenous and famished. His heated flesh searing my own.

I cling to him as his lips feed on my ear, neck, collarbone, chest. Then he finally reaches my breasts and I'm lost. My head presses back against the smooth cushion as he feasts. The urgency hasn't lessened, but he slows down a fraction. Passion drives me forward; I don't need foreplay, I need him inside me. I tug on his head, pulling him back up, and then reach down to stroke his rigid length.

Greedy, starving, I bring him between my thighs. He freezes for one long moment before sinking into me, impossibly hot and hard. I cling to him tighter as his muscles bunch. His eyes squeeze shut, then open again, staring down at me as he takes me with deep, claiming strokes.

I kiss him, shivers rolling through me. Holding in the moan climbing up my throat. Stretched to an overflowing fullness by his invasion. I'm soon undone. Broken into a million pieces by the friction of him sliding out. Put back together when he glides back in.

It's an ebb and flow; a delicious pressure builds as we combine to invent a new creature of emotion and pleasure, of sweat and skin and sensation. He plunges inside me, deeper than before, and the veins in his neck pop in bold relief. I come a moment before he does, and then we're spilling over together. Crying out each other's names and then collapsing. I'm oversensitive and hot, my skin sticking to his.

I gasp as he pulls out of me, feeling suddenly hollow. His gaze is soft and he cups my face again with his palm, letting me know I'm not alone. "Talia," he says, then he just repeats my name over and over like a prayer.

At some point, we get up, take our clothes, and retreat to my bedroom. All in silence, the dampener having run out of power. I hope it lasted long enough to cover the sounds of our lovemaking. But maybe after tonight it won't matter.

We clean each other off in the bathroom and then tumble into bed, wordlessly. Ryin is asleep in seconds. He's seemed tired these past couple of days; I guess the life of a drudge doesn't offer much rest.

I watch him sleep, comforted by the rising and falling of his chest. Freckles everywhere.

Guilt threatens, but I know it's the right decision not to tell him what I have planned. This stolen moment of peace is precious; I wouldn't want to taint it with either false hope or my failure.

I also don't want to leave him now, but it's the perfect time. Late enough so that no one should be around. I can go up to the vault and try to locate the Fai souls. If I fail, he won't know I tried at all, and if I succeed...Well, I can't even think that far ahead. All I know is that I cannot allow the Fai to be destroyed without at least trying to do something about it.

So I leave the last place I want to, the warmth of being by Ryin's side. I slip from the bed and dress in silence, hoping that the next time I see him things will be different.

Chapter Twenty-Seven

RYIN

THE BED SHIFTS, pushing me out of slumber. Talia rises and I expect her to go into the bathroom, not to head toward the wardrobe in her room—as if there were not an entire closet full of clothes just down the hall—and dress quickly in the dark. The low illumination through the crack under the door shows me her movements. She slips on pants and a snug tunic. Soft slippers instead of her boots. This puts me on alert. What does she have planned?

She glides out the door and I'm on my feet in an instant. Locating my clothes and pulling them back on. I wait in the doorway as she disappears into the servants' room. After a few seconds, I follow her, rushing forward to stop the door to the stairwell from closing completely.

Her light footsteps creep one level up, and I follow. She hasn't noticed me, and I'm used to sneaking around the Citadel.

The door to the forty-seventh floor is operated by biometric sensor. No Fai are allowed, so I've never been up there, but this is her destination. She presses her hand to the sensor and the door snicks open. I wait as she disappears into the hallway, then race up the steps, skipping three at a time to catch the edge of the door once again before it shuts.

This is insanity. I try to talk myself out of following, but a quick check on the other side shows that I can still enter the stairwell from this level if I need to make a getaway. Of course, if there are guards here, then a lone Fai on a forbidden floor means guaranteed time in the locker, if not worse.

Talia pauses in the hallway, wringing her hands, apparently caught in indecision. My own choice crystallizes before me. Whatever she's contemplating, I want to know. The stairwell door closes behind me and I come to her side. She stiffens but doesn't turn around. However, her lack of fear and the defeated slump of her shoulders lets me know she knows it's me.

"You're a light sleeper," she whispers.

I match her volume. "We have to be. We can be called day or night." She winces visibly and I'm sorry for inflicting that slight dig, but I'm also hurt by her secrets. Of course I'm not exactly entitled to them, but still.

Finally, she spins to face me fully, her eyes blazing. "Go back. I didn't tell you I was coming here for a reason."

Hurt is a spiraling bloom within me, but then I see the fear lurking behind her expression. "What are you doing here?"

"Going to the vault."

"Why? In the middle of the night?"

She crosses her arms and seals her lips shut.

"I've been ordered to accompany you everywhere."

"You are not allowed in the vault." Her jaw is tense.

"So, I will stay outside."

She glares at me, an expression I'm not used to seeing on her. It mars the placid quality she usually possesses. I trace the crease in her forehead with my finger to smooth it, and her eyes widen.

Her nostrils flare but I see the acquiescence before she

speaks. "Fine." Though she worries her bottom lip with her teeth, as if nervous about my presence. I should go back, leave her to whatever it is she's doing. For all intents and purposes, she is the princess and not in any danger. And yet…

And yet, she is. Sometime tonight, Von will give the word and I will have to kidnap her. If I refuse, someone else will do it. The wrongness of it beats within me. Can I still go through with it? How can I not? I should warn her, should have done so earlier, but she starts marching forward before I can speak.

I straighten and remain the customary three steps behind her as she walks the empty hallway. The closed doors on the left are unlabeled and our path draws us nearer to the main elevators. Just beyond them, guards stand on either side of a door with three sensors embedded into the wall.

Talia nods at them, a grizzled, gray-haired soldier and a narrow-eyed younger man. They bow to their princess and eye me suspiciously.

"Fai are not allowed on this floor, Your Grace," the younger man says.

Talia tilts her chin. "This is my personal healer. He accompanies me everywhere. What if I fall ill suddenly? He must remain nearby."

The soldiers share a look that's almost comical. They have their orders, but they're also duty bound to obey the princess.

"He'll stay right here with you all here to watch him." She glances at me over her shoulder. "Stay. Be good," she says with both a smirk and an apologetic gleam in her eye.

I merely stand at military rest, arms clasped behind me. I ignore the scrutiny of the guards while Talia engages the sensors one at a time. The last one takes a drop of blood from her.

What could she possibly need from the vault at this hour that would have her sneaking away to retrieve? Why would she refuse to tell me? The questions beat at me until the door slides open and she steps through, disappearing inside. Then, I'm struggling not to lunge after her.

My daimon flares, desperately wanting to come to the surface. I clamp down on it, squeezing my eyes shut as it tries to break free. The guards would be spooked if I called it forward. They would certainly call theirs and then there would be a fight.

While the door was opened, as Talia was walking across the threshold, I felt something inside there calling to me. Tugging at me.

I need to get inside that vault.

Two on one are odds I'm willing to try, but I hold myself still with every bit of willpower I possess. It's harder and harder to do as the minutes tick by. My daimon is impatient with me; it sensed something when the door opened, something it desperately wants to feel again.

Finally, Talia returns, looking annoyed and somewhat defeated. She stands there blocking the closing of the doors, and that's when I feel it more fully.

My soul.

Is inside.

I meet her gaze, my eyes widening. Wonder overtakes her face. I cannot hold it back any longer. The daimon leaps forward, causing the guards to stiffen.

Before they can react or even shift, Talia screams and collapses in the doorway, forcing their attention to her. My daimon's power shoots out, instinctively checking her for injuries. But it finds nothing. She's perfectly healthy, and she's given me a distraction.

I spring at the guards, whose attention is on the crumpled form of their princess. With their inattention and my superior strength, it takes only a moment to knock them both unconscious.

I fish out their handcuffs and restrain them, leaving them sitting, backs against the wall. While I take care of them, Talia rises, keeping the door open. "What happened? Why did your daimon come out?"

I rise, the spirit within urging me forward. "I can feel my soul in there."

I brush past her and run into the space, past the little sitting area and into the warehouse. It's nothing but row after row of shelving. I am wild, frenetic. I rise into the air and fly down the first aisle.

"Wait!" Talia calls, but I can't slow down. My daimon can't bear to because it senses the one thing that would make me, us, whole again. Our souls connect our bodies to the spirit plane—it's like they exist in both places, just like bliss does. Somehow the walls of this vault must hide them from us— how could we have been living in the same building as our souls all this time, been this close, and not known?

The shelves race by as I soar toward the thing that's pulling me like a tether—one hooked straight into my remaining souls.

I pass boxes, baskets, buckets of objects overflowing some shelves. Many of the things here I don't recognize: Nimali treasures, salvaged from the old world. Electronics and gadgets that don't work any longer take up a great deal of space. Artwork, sculptures, paintings, furniture. So many useless objects and trinkets that they find valuable.

I draw to a stop suddenly, almost like I've hit a wall. I'm at the back corner of the vault and my daimon is practically seething with rage. I float to the ground and find myself standing before an oblong, black box that radiates...evil. That's the best way I can describe it. I'm tempted to open it, but another tug pulls me away.

On the other side of the row are trays marked with inden- tations, like smaller versions of the egg cartons used before the Sorrows. Inside each notch, a soul is nestled. The tiny spheres glow with inner light, an inky darkness tinged with purple for the shadow souls. A deep indigo for the voice souls and cerulean for the memory souls. Dozens and dozens of souls—one for every drudge in the Citadel.

I'm frozen in place, staring at the souls before me with tears in my eyes.

Talia comes up behind me, breathing hard. She takes a look at me and then at what I'm staring at. "Is that them?"

I nod, unable to form words.

"No wonder I couldn't find them all the way back here." Then she disappears around the corner.

She's back in moments, a large tote bag in her hands. With a glance at my immobile form, she begins grabbing handfuls of souls and dropping them into the tote bag. An inauspicious way to handle something so precious, but it won't actually harm them. When that's too slow, she upends an entire tray, dumping its contents.

My bones unstick and I begin helping her. Filling the bag with the souls of my people. A few drop and slide away on the ground, but I crouch to retrieve them. We will leave no one behind. Mine is here somewhere, but I don't have time to linger. Having it in my possession right now, being closer to my shadow soul than I have been in years…I blink away the tears and finish gathering all the souls.

Once we're done, Talia is ready to leave, but I stop her with a hand on her forearm. I turn back around to the box on the shelf behind us. I grab it and tuck it under my arm, hating the feel of the thing.

"What is that?" she asks as we head back toward the entrance.

"The trammels."

She misses a step and I steady her, then take the bag of souls from her grip and sling it on my shoulder. It's heavy; this is the most precious cargo I've ever been entrusted with.

Before we leave, I turn to her. "He'll know it was you."

Her lips part and her eyes shine with unshed tears. "Then I guess you'll have to take me with you."

I press a quick kiss to her lips and we cross the threshold back into the hallway. The guards are still out cold, thank the tors. One of them has slid down to the floor and lies on his side, eyes closed.

We've done it—Talia's plan, the one she wanted to keep secret for some reason—has worked. I'm only moments away from being whole again, to having my soul back and being able to leave this place once and for all.

That's when I feel the sharp pain in my head. An overwhelming presence in my brain, erasing all other thoughts. Von's voice blasts. "Now!" he says. "Take the princess now and bring her to the basement level. We escape tonight."

Chapter Twenty-Eight

TALIA

RYIN CLUTCHES his head and bends nearly in half. I grab his shoulder, alarmed. "What's wrong? Are you all right?"

He gasps for breath. I'm not sure what's happening to him —does being near his soul make him ill? But he rises quickly like the wave that just overtook him has passed. His eyes are a bit wild when he looks at me. "We need to go back to your rooms and restore the souls. We should be able to free everyone before the guards awaken."

He takes off running and I'm on his heels, heading back to the stairwell and down one flight to the door leading to Celena's suite. We stop in the servants' room and Ryin gently sets the bag with souls on the ground. He places the box with the trammels several feet away, which I find odd.

Just then, Noomi bursts through the door. Another woman —a slightly taller, slightly thicker version of Noomi—is with her. I recognize her from the ambush the night I was brought to the Citadel. She must have been captured soon after that.

"Why aren't you headed to the basement level?" the woman spits, glaring at Ryin.

Ryin kneels next to the bag. "You wouldn't have felt it as strongly, Xipporah, since it's only been a couple of days since yours was taken, but this is why." He opens the bag, revealing the souls.

Noomi's jaw drops open, her eyes so round they take over most of her face. Xipporah's reaction is more muted, but she's obviously shocked. "How did you…Where did you…"

"They've been in the vault this whole time. All we needed was one of the two people with access to open the door." He looks toward me meaningfully, and I fidget under three pairs of eyes.

Both women stare at me with equal parts awe and surprise. Tears stream down Noomi's face. She kneels and hovers her hands over the souls in the bag, not seeming to know what to do.

"We have to hurry. I had to subdue the two guards on the vault level and they'll be awake soon."

Noomi rises to her feet and holds out her hands. Xipporah takes one and Ryin takes the other.

"What do you have to do?" I ask.

"Our daimons will do it for us," Ryin says. "They will send each soul to its rightful owner. Xipporah's Land daimon can amplify me and Noomi so it happens quickly."

I take a step back, not wanting to intrude. The three of them connect with their daimons and close their eyes. Then the bag with the souls in it begins to shake.

It's gentle at first, just a low vibration. But soon, souls begin shooting up out of it, tiny globes of soft light that swirl in the air before disappearing through the walls.

I gasp and duck as one whizzes by my head.

Tiny balls of purple, and deep blue, and aquamarine rise and fly around me. One smashes into Noomi's chest. Just like before with poor Silas, her soul expands in an indigo coating, covering her completely like she was dipped in paint before fading away.

She jerks in place then opens her eyes, swaying a bit on her feet. A brilliant smile overtakes her face, transforming her. She was always beautiful, but now she's radiant. It's like she went from black and white to full Technicolor—she shines.

The same thing happens to Xipporah when her soul is reinstated. My mind understands that I'm looking at the same person. She looks the same—her features haven't changed at all—but the difference between incomplete and complete is truly night and day.

Ryin's soul is among the last to be returned to him. The dark purple globe hovers in front of his chest for long moments before crashing into him. He jerks backward and doubles over, releasing his grip on Noomi's hand.

He stays in that position for several seconds until I'm starting to get worried for him. His change is happening in slow motion, much slower than for the other two. But finally he straightens and the color is absorbed into his skin. He opens his eyes, daimon free, and stares at me.

It's like I'm seeing him for the first time. All of the materials that made him up have been polished to a high gloss. He's positively incandescent. The same cinnamon skin and rust-colored hair. The same freckles dust his face and arms, but the man is different. His shadow spreads out across the wall behind him.

I'm a little apprehensive as I approach, carried on legs that have a mind of their own. Until this moment, I haven't considered if a restored soul could change his personality at all. Will he really be the same man I made love to just hours ago?

I stand toe to toe with him, searching his eyes. Hoping that the man I care for hasn't been irretrievably lost by becoming whole again.

And then he smiles at me. My arms go around him, squeezing him tightly. Laughter bubbles up inside of me, impossible to contain.

I cup his cheeks with my hands and stare, almost in disbelief. *He's smiling*. At me. And it's glorious.

His breath is warm and sweet against my lips. He's far too beautiful to look at this close, so I shut my eyes. But he's burned on the backs of my eyelids: the sharp cheekbones, the stubbled jaw. His lips press against me and I melt, sugar over a flame.

We've kissed before, but this one is different. It makes me see stars in the dark. My knees turn to molten lava. I'm slick and loose and ready to fall to the floor, but he's there to catch me.

Finally, I pull back and recall we have an audience. Xipporah is glaring at us. Her well-muscled arms are crossed defensively and her expression is all the more fierce with her souls intact. Noomi appears worried, her brow lowered and gaze darting between me and Ryin.

It's Ryin who speaks. "Princess Celena never returned. This is Talia. She was brought here somehow from another version of this world and has been pretending to be Celena since she was found across the wall."

His words register. Xipporah still seems suspicious, but a smile spreads across Noomi's face. "Of course," she says, and it's my first time hearing her voice. She laughs and spreads her arms wide, rushing over to embrace me. "Of course you're not her." She's quite strong to be such a small person, but I hug her back, happy to do so. Her voice is pure music, rich and strong and melodious.

I'm still in her embrace, laughing along with her, when the door to the stairwell slams open. I don't even have time to react when I'm pulled out of her arms. Whatever has taken a hold of me doesn't feel like hands—it's like the air hardens against my body and drags me away.

"No!" Ryin calls out, rushing toward me.

Now I do feel hands, strong hands wrenching my arms behind me. Placing icy cold handcuffs around my wrists. I twist to find the copper-haired Fai man from the ambush behind me, gripping me roughly.

But Ryin leaps forward with a growl and pulls me away and over to him. "Von, no! She's the reason we have our souls back. She's not who you think." He rubs my forearms, just above the handcuffs, soothing the burn from Von's grip.

"What I *think* is that your commitment to our cause is shaky, brother." The man's voice is sharp, his words cutting.

"Give me the key to the cuffs." Ryin holds out his hand.

Von narrows his amber eyes. "Did you really free our souls?" he asks me.

"Yes," I grit out, still chilled to the bone by the ice around my wrists.

"And you think we should thank you? When your people never should have had our souls in the first place?"

"You're right. We shouldn't. I'm not asking for thanks."

He pauses. I think I caught him off guard.

"Give. Me. The key." Ryin is seething. "We do this another way."

Von snorts. "We won't harm your precious princess, but we do need her. And I'm not sure you're reliable enough to—"

Xipporah walks up to him and plunges her hand into the pocket of his pants, retrieving the key and tossing it to Ryin. She crosses her arms, staring Von down. "Be smart enough to distinguish an ally from an enemy."

Von rounds on her, but she's half a head taller and scowling savagely. "And so she's absolved now?" he asks. "Of all her people have done?" He turns back to me with pure hatred in his gaze, and honestly I can't blame him. If I *were* Nimali, I would deserve it.

Once Ryin removes the cuffs, I rub my freezing wrists. Actual frost has developed on my skin from them.

Noomi steps up next to Xipporah, crossing her arms in the same way. Though she's not as physically intimidating, her anger is palpable and I wouldn't put it past her to be able to back it up. "She is not Celena," Noomi says.

"What do you mean?" Von asks, incredulous.

An alarm begins to sound, blaring through hidden speakers in the walls. "We don't have time for this, we have to go." Ryin grabs my hand and heads for the door, but Von blocks it.

"I can't trust you with our hostage." His razor-edged gaze is like a thousand needles perforating my flesh.

"She is not a hostage!"

Von's eyes glow blue and my heart contracts in my chest. Ryin's grip on me is solid; he calls his daimon as well. Then my whole body lifts and we rise into the air. I let out a screech. Von lifts off the ground too, hovering just below the ceiling, but there's really nowhere to go.

Ryin wraps his arms around me. I trust him to keep hold of me, though I wish I'd had some warning. He rushes forward, making a break for the doorway at the same time a heaviness settles inside me. My eyelids droop like they have weights attached. They grow heavier until I can't keep them open anymore. It's like I've been shot full of anesthesia. I know the feeling well and I only have a few seconds of consciousness left. I try to warn Ryin, but speech has already left me.

The last thing I know of reality is Von's triumphant smile and Ryin's echoing roar, following me into blackness.

Chapter Twenty-Nine

RYIN

WHEN VON KNOCKS Talia out with his power, her body grows limp in my arms. My vision whites out with rage and my skin begins to heat. I must control my powers while holding her, but the desire to do physical harm to Von is strong.

His crow daimon easily allows him to dart and dip through the air; he races out into the stairwell with great speed, disappearing from view. I want to strangle him, but we don't have time. The alarm means the Citadel is locking down. They must have found the guards I knocked out or witnessed us receiving our souls—maybe both. Either way, no Fai in this place is safe.

The oblong box still sits on the floor. "Get that box!" I shout to Xi as I heft Talia onto my shoulder. "It contains the trammels. We need to destroy them." I don't see either sister's reaction to my statement since I'm already on my way out the door.

I race down the stairwell to the next Fai floor, where I hear pounding. I pull at the door handle, but it's locked.

"We can't get out!" someone screams. "We're trapped!"

"Let's go out a window. We can reopen one of them," another voice calls out.

"Air daimons can carry the ones who can't fly or climb down."

"No," I yell through the door. "They'll pick us off easily that way. Take the smoke tower. Make a hole in the wall to the right of the stairwell."

More voices shout; they search for someone with a large, powerful daimon such as a hippo or rhino. Xipporah comes up behind me and starts punching at the wall as well with fists backed by her tiger daimon's power. In a few moments, she's made an opening large enough for us to pass through. I heal her bloodied fists with a thought.

The smoke tower is an empty shaft as wide as the stairwell that runs the full height of the building. Inside, vents are located every dozen feet—an exhaust so that, in the case of a fire, the stairwells don't fill with smoke. Most of those who can't fly or crawl down should be able to grab hold of the slats of the vents and use the enhanced agility their daimons provide to make their way down.

I fly through the hole, careful with Talia's immobile form, and begin floating down. Above me, Xipporah helps Noomi, whose dolphin daimon would otherwise have trouble. The Fai trapped on this floor have begun emerging as well. Amphibian and reptile hosts simply climb down the walls, their human arms and legs imbued with animal ability. Cats leap with amazing dexterity. Birds carry those with water daimons. Others with fire daimons—scorpions, salamanders, and the like—make short work of the many flights down.

Talia is still out cold. I don't know how long she will stay unconscious. At the bottom of the shaft, the blades of a giant air supply fan spin slowly. The wall vent on this level has already been smashed through and my brethren rush into the abandoned underground garage.

These lower levels were sealed off after the Sorrows when

the foundation of the building was shored up and the garage deemed unsafe for continued usage. However, there is a hidden entrance somewhere down here to the old tunnels that run underground throughout the city. Subterranean trains once traversed this peninsula, and between those and the other pre-Sorrows maintenance tunnels and sewers, plus the more recent passageways dug out by the Fai, there is a network that runs far beneath the notice of the Nimali.

My feet touch the ground carefully, and I tuck Talia closer to me as I move through the ragged opening and into the garage. Piles of rubble and broken concrete along with the husks of old, abandoned vehicles form barriers all around. The others pick their way through the maze gingerly.

"Which way to the tunnels?" someone asks.

"Follow me!" Von's voice is confident and clear. The voice of a leader—but a ruthless one. "Step carefully, and beware of the boobytraps."

I don't get more than a few steps toward his voice before the crashing dissonance of an explosion rings out. The ground rumbles beneath my feet, knocking me off balance. My first thought is someone triggered one of the traps—though the Nimali have little knowledge of our tunnel system, the Fai have taken great care to protect them.

But as I steady myself, bliss light filters in through a haze of smoke and dust. The blocked off entrance to the garage, covered long ago by the grass of the plaza above, has caved in and lamplight spears the gloom. An acrid scent fills the air, exceptionally harsh to my enhanced senses. I know that scent: it's a Nimali explosive. The blast wasn't one of our people triggering a boobytrap, it was the beasts. They've figured out our exit plan and are here to reclaim their slaves.

I shift Talia's unconscious form in my arms and carefully hand her to Noomi. "Get her out of here. Take the other civilians."

My cousin and I share a look before her gaze hardens and

she nods, then turns and hurries off with the princess. A hippo host has moved an enormous chunk of concrete out of the way, revealing a tunnel access point, and those who aren't trained to fight begin disappearing through the opening.

I turn to face our threat along with the other Fai warriors.

At the garage entrance, two giant black bears lift debris out of the way to enlarge the ingress. Bliss light and fresh air streams in, helping to dissipate the smoke from the blast. Roars and bellows resound as predator soldiers face us, filling up the opening as quickly as fragments of concrete and rebar and hunks of dirt are removed.

They stand just above us, at the top of an incline. Nimali have transformed into their beast forms: wolves, coyotes, big cats of every stripe and spot, warrior birds, crocodiles, and more. The Fai predators don't look as impressive in our human forms, but each of us have our daimons in the fore-front, and we are every bit as deadly.

I take a breath, feeling every iota of strength, speed, and agility my daimon has gifted me with, and step forward so I am in front of the other Fai. Then I exhale, a breath of pure fire that fills the space between our two people.

The blaze enlarges, expanding and growing hotter, orange flames changing to blue as they eat up the distance. Yelps and mewls of pain sound, and the scents of sizzling fur and flesh meet my nose. I need a moment before I can call the fire again, but the other warriors are there, rushing forward to leap into the fray, battling the beasts, claws and fangs against human fingers and teeth. Enhanced with our daimons' powers, our blunt nails hold the strength and danger of talons.

A woman screams and leaps high into the air, taking flight then diving down to meet a hawk as it fights her in a well-matched battle. A jaguar rushes me, its roar beating against my eardrums, mouth outstretched for a bite. My fist smashes against the side of its head and it flies into what remains of a thick support beam, crumbling the concrete into dust and leaving an indentation.

Screams ring from human and animal throats alike. I rise into the air to hover near the low ceiling as an eagle targets the wolf host beside me. I prepare another fire breath, hoping to pick off the back of the Nimali line, when the light coming in from the plaza dims, obscured by the silhouette of an enormous creature filling the entryway. The blue and gold dragon can barely fit inside the opening but squeezes its bulk through nonetheless.

"Fall back!" I scream to my people as I take my stance at the front of the line once again. Dragon fire can melt diamonds, so it would decimate even the heartiest Fai…except for those with fire daimons. My fire is not quite as powerful as that of a dragon; it can inflict damage if given enough time, but dragon hides are tough. Of all my people, I'm the only one who can stand against this threat.

The other Nimali move aside, giving their prince the space he needs to move. They don't want to be caught in the crossfire, either.

Prince Shad's golden, slitted eyes regard me. They're cold and alien, almost hypnotizing in their variation and depth. Was this what Dove saw as she looked up into the sky during her last moments? Before her small body was incinerated so badly all that was left was a charred husk? Were these the same eyes?

The enormous beast opens his mouth, revealing row after row of jagged teeth. I brace myself for impact and he lets loose a stream of white-hot flames. Only, instead of hitting me directly, they arc over my head, creating a wall of heat that only a Fire Fai could withstand. Sweat beads my brow, but the attack I feared does not come. It's akin to him pulling his punch.

I release my own fire again, opting for a direct hit. He moves much faster than a creature of his size should be able to, so the fire only grazes his side and doesn't reach his wings as I'd hoped.

The retreating footsteps behind me continue. I need to buy enough time for at least the civilians to get away, but Shad and I both need a few moments to regenerate our flames.

The dragon snorts, smoke rising from nostrils the size of my head. Three Nimali draw closer to him, a bear, a lion, and an eagle. These are the soldiers who guarded the princess. Handpicked by the prince, as I recall, now here to stand beside him.

Fighting continues on either side of me, in the shadows and corners, but Shad takes up so much space that he's effectively cut the battle in half. Then Xipporah is beside me, scratched and bleeding, her face a mask of anger.

"The tunnel is a dead end. They must have found it and blocked it off before it meets the main branch we'd hoped to use."

I spit out a curse and eye the dragon warily as another figure steps into my peripheral vision. It's Von, and he's carrying Talia like a ragdoll.

A frenzied inferno ignites inside me.

His expression is triumphant. "You will stand down, beasts, or your princess will pay the price." My jaw clenches along with my fists, only this time, it's Von I want to punch.

"My people will leave here today unharmed, along with your princess, and we will contact you about negotiating for her release," Von shouts.

I scan Talia's limp form again to ensure that she's still just knocked out from his power—she is. There is no other damage to heal. A war rages within me. I want to grab her from him, but if the Nimali sense any dissension among our ranks, it would be like blood in the water.

Bellows and howls of animal anguish assault my ears, but the fighting ceases instantly. The dragon shimmers and transforms back into the prince, whose eyes blaze with anger.

"There is only one way out of this garage, Fai." He spreads an arm to indicate the gaping hole he stands in.

Von and Shad stand off for a long moment. Then Von shifts Talia in his grasp so that a hand is around her neck. "If all of my people do not make it out of here safely, I will snap her neck."

I lunge forward, vibrating with rage at the way he manhandles her, but a strong grip holds me back. Enzo, who hosts a gorilla daimon, and Nyana, who has a hippo daimon, each clutch one of my arms. Struggling against their powerful holds is useless, so I still.

Shad's gaze flicks to me, then back to Von. His jaw tightens and he orders his troops to fall back. They form two lines, borders on the path out of the garage and into the night.

We file onto the plaza where Nimali soldiers await, both shifted and in human form. They funnel us into the center of the lawn, surrounded on all sides by them. I'm still sandwiched between two of our strongest warriors who have yet to release me. It's the only thing holding me back from taking Von's head off.

Noomi and the other civilians are clustered together in the center of our group. Trained soldiers are on the outside, a layer of protection for them. I don't know every Fai in the Citadel, but I recognize them by sight. I hope everyone is accounted for.

Xipporah comes to my side, eying my captors belligerently. "What are you doing?" she grits out.

"Von told us to keep this one in line," Enzo says, squeezing my biceps.

I unclench my jaw to reassure Xi. "It's all right. But Von will feel my wrath when this is done. What of the trammels?"

"Smashed in the tunnel."

I exhale in relief. At least they're destroyed, and I don't think the Nimali had any more than the stock in the vault, so that's one threat no longer at issue. But Talia's fate is still at risk and I rage inside, needing to protect her.

However, an even bigger threat marches our way as the thunderous footsteps of a dozen Nimali approach. King Lyall steps onto the plaza, his gaze colder than I've ever seen.

He stares at Von holding the woman he believes is his daughter, and I don't need the locker to feel the chill. I think Von has deeply miscalculated, and I wonder if any of us will get out of this alive.

Chapter Thirty

TALIA

I come to with a pounding headache and little blue lights dancing behind my closed eyelids.

"On your feet now," a menacing voice growls in my ear. The soles of my feet are on the ground, grass crunching under the thin slippers. But a hand rests around my throat.

With great difficulty and through the beating of a thousand drums inside my skull, I open my eyes. It's nighttime and I'm on the plaza, surrounded by Fai. Who are in turn surrounded by Nimali. Most are shifted into animal forms, and I shiver at so many vicious predators so close. Of course they always have been—they were just in disguise. How did everything go so wrong?

When I try to turn my head, I'm stopped by that grip around my neck. I get a glimpse of my captor, though—Von. His other arm is a band around my waist, holding me as close as a lover but cruelly.

I search for Ryin and find him only a few feet away. An empty perimeter surrounds Von and I amidst the crowd, like no one wants to get too close, but whether to me or him, I'm not sure. Ryin's jaw is clenched so tightly, it's like he's going to crack a tooth. His eyes are blazing, not just with his daimon but with pure rage. The gaze is directed at Von, and Ryin seems like he's a split second away from launching himself at the man.

But I realize why he doesn't. A Fai man and a woman stand on either side of him, gripping his arms. They are holding him back from charging at us.

If me being a hostage can help the Fai out of this, then I can understand why they wouldn't want Ryin to intervene. Though I can't move my neck much, I shake my head as much as I can. His eyes narrow and his lips press together.

In my peripheral vision, the light from Von's glowing eyes shines. The added strength his daimon provides is clear from the iron bands around my waist and neck. It would be so easy for him to kill me, but then how would he negotiate?

"What is the meaning of this?" an enraged voice roars somewhere out of the range of my vision. Lyall.

Von turns us so that I can see the edge of the plaza where the king stands surrounded by guards.

"Tell your people to stand down," Von shouts. "Release the Fai to return to our homeland. Once we arrive safely, you will receive word on what is necessary for us to return our hostage...unharmed. However, if you make any false moves, if a single Fai comes to harm..." His grip around my neck tightens, and I whimper involuntarily. "You will receive your daughter back in pieces."

I thought Lyall looked angry before, but it's nothing compared to his expression now. His chest heaves. The glare he sends Von would turn my hair white if it were settled on me. He must know that I released the Fai souls, but he doesn't know why. He hasn't completely written me off yet, it seems.

My captor's grip on me doesn't loosen. Thankfully, it doesn't tighten either.

Then Lyall turns away. I think he's going to do it, order

the soldiers to retreat and let the Fai go in order to get me back. These men and women who have been toiling under duress for so long will have their freedom—I can't be mad at that, even if it means I get carted around the city as a hostage.

Shad is at Lyall's side now, speaking urgently with him in tones too low to hear. He looks like he's trying to convince him of something, but Lyall brushes him aside and stomps away a short distance. Neither the prince nor his guards follow.

Then he spins around, his caramel complexion darkening almost to purple. "You would threaten my daughter!" Spittle flies from his mouth as he screams, his booming voice taking over the plaza, echoing off the buildings.

"You would *dare* touch one hair on her head and expect to live to see the morning?" Lyall's eyes seem to almost glow with pure fury.

"Nimali!" he shouts, his entire body shaking with something much like madness. "I want one Fai life taken for every *second* the princess is in their clutches. Destroy them all until she is in my arms again."

I stiffen, dread and terror turning me to stone. Von's fingers are bruising, cutting off my air as his hand tightens. "If even one of my brothers or sisters dies this night, you will too," he snarls in my ear.

His nails cut into me and a trickle of warm blood snakes down my neck. Ryin is hissing, struggling against the two people holding him. Xipporah cries out in protest and launches herself at the woman restraining Ryin.

And while I expect the Nimali soldiers to immediately leap to their king's command, they hesitate.

"Nimali!" Shad yells. He stands several feet from Lyall, his arms spread apart. Ryin calms and so does Xipporah and her opponent. "Your king would have you break your covenant. We do not kill innocents. Not every Fai before you is a soldier, and those that are were captured as prisoners of war—

covenant sanctioned. We must fight with honor as our daimons demand or risk losing them."

All around us Nimali, both in human and animal form, seem torn. They look to one another and then to their king and their prince.

"I am your king." Lyall's voice is more controlled but still manages to carry. "I am your law." He rounds on Shad, who straightens to stand even taller. "*Prince Shad,*" Lyall's voice drips with condescension. "The Umber who was gifted a dragon daimon. You have never had the necessary strength to rule our people. Even now you work against me, scurrying behind my back, trying to bring others to your cause. I had hoped your machinations indicated the proper ruthlessness necessary to rule, which is why I allowed it. Prove it to me now. Demonstrate that you deserve the throne. Do your duty. Shift and destroy the enemy who would threaten us. Do. Your. Duty!"

Shad's jaw is set and his arms cross. "I will *never* purposefully kill an innocent. I will not betray my covenant."

"*I* am your covenant," Lyall says. "And you will obey me or you will die." Then he takes two steps back, and with a flash of blinding light, the red dragon is before us.

There almost isn't time to blink before a gush of flames pours from Lyall's mouth. It hits the burst of light that explodes out of Shad as he transforms, but it also hits the Nimali soldiers who had stood near the king, Lyall's own honor guard.

No blue dragon emerges from the flames. The flashing light of Shad's shift still shines—is he caught in the space between human and dragon? The fire Lyall produces seems endless. I don't even know how long it lasts. A half-dozen of his own men lay in a charred heap when it's over, but Shad is still caught in that brightness of the shift.

Then the light dies and his human form is visible. Smoke rises from him. He falls to the ground, motionless, a blackened husk of scorched flesh. I can hardly bear to look at him, but I force myself to, wanting to bear witness. He stood up to Lyall, finally, and this is the consequence. I can barely make out the rise and fall of his chest. Somehow, he's still alive, but the burns are horrific—I don't think he'll live for long.

Tears flow freely down my cheeks and Von is shocked into loosening his grip. His focus is on the drama unfolding between the king and prince, so even the arm around my waist has loosened. I contemplate trying to break free, but it would be pointless, surrounded as we are.

Lyall is back in his human form, breathing heavily as if he's just run a race. His gaze travels around the square at all of the people gathered here. He raises an arm and points at me. "Ice them all down and bring the soulcatchers. This rebellion ends tonight."

The distraction is apparently all that Ryin needed. I feel a burst of air at my side and then Von is on the ground, beneath an enraged Ryin, who grapples with him to keep him down. Xipporah is there as well, facing off against the two other Fai. A growl rumbles from her throat and I wonder what her animal is.

"Think long and hard about what you do next," Xipporah says, her voice dripping in menace. "That is Ryin Arinson, and you would do well to remember." The man and woman share a glance, then step back, shame and regret obvious in their expressions.

I don't know what just happened, but I'm glad not to be in Von's crushing grip anymore. Noomi comes to my side and holds my hand. On the ground, Von is out cold and Ryin rises just as heavy footfalls announce the arrival of something large.

I turn to find the sea of Nimali has shifted to allow two large, white furry creatures to pass through. Walking on all fours, they're several heads above the tallest humans. Then they rise. I don't know exactly what I'm looking at, some kind of cross between a polar bear and a silverback gorilla. On two legs they're at least two stories high. Long fangs protrude from their mouths.

One opens its mouth, and I expect a roar, but it just sucks in a deep breath. When it breathes out, the air around us turns frigid. White, cloudy breath flows from its mouth and expands, settling over the Fai. *Ice them down.*

I begin shivering uncontrollably as a layer of frost covers my skin. My hand detaches from Noomi's and I cross my arms. The Fai surrounding me, those with their daimons shining in their eyes, slacken, the blue glow fading. Even a few Nimali standing too close to the Fai are thrown out of their shifted form by the sudden cold. The voice of the librarian repeats in my head: *Daimons cannot emerge in temperatures below freezing.*

Ryin is in front of me, reaching for me. Only a few steps separate us, but it hurts to move. My limbs are sluggish. Before I can even take a full step, rough hands pull me back. Nimali soldiers in human form stand on either side of me, each gripping one of my arms and firmly but gently towing me away.

Their hands bring warmth, but my gaze returns to Ryin, who's trying to follow. Only this time, Noomi and Xipporah halt him with a gentle touch and whispered words.

"I'm all right," I call out before I'm pulled away. The soldiers turn me around before I can catch more of his expression.

My breathing is jagged. As soon as I leave the circle of Fai, the temperature warms and the frost covering me starts to melt. I'm enveloped in a sea of black clad soldiers who all produce pairs of handcuffs from their belts.

As I'm frog marched over to Lyall, Nimali start shackling the frozen Fai, who are unable to fight back without their daimons. Their shouts and wails fill my ears and tears form, spilling onto my cold cheeks.

Images assault me: Shad's burnt form lying on the grass.

The madness in the king's gaze. His calm expression as he ordered the re-enslavement of the Fai.

I don't see him at first, but I spot the patch of burnt grass where Shad fell. He's gone now, taken away. I don't know what the Nimali do with their dead.

And then a group of them part, revealing their leader. My guards slow to a halt and the king approaches, gaze intent on me.

"Are you hurt?" His voice is clipped, nothing of the warmth I've come to expect. More like my real father.

"No."

"Were you forced to remove the Fai souls from the vault? Did someone compel you?"

A sob racks my chest. Even now he wants to believe in me, that I would only betray him because of duress. I swallow, unable to look away. His eyes are penetrating, drilling deep inside me, but not seeing enough. I don't answer. He already knows.

My guards take a step back and Lyall moves forward, no rage evident, but I stiffen anyway. I've seen him turn on a dime before.

"My darling girl," he whispers, reaching out a hand to stroke my cheek, some of the old warmth returning. "What have you done?"

I gasp and choke, weeping now uncontrollably. There is so much disappointment in his voice, and it tears at me. But what right does he have to be disappointed in *me*? The only father who has ever loved me is a murdering tyrant. And still it hurts to face his dissatisfaction.

"Your Majesty," a voice calls out from behind me. One I recognize. Dominga steps up to my side and bows at the king. "I think I can shed some light on this woman's actions."

My heart seizes. She doesn't even look at me.

"This is not Princess Celena. And I can prove it."

Chapter Thirty-One

RYIN

I'M ENTIRELY NUMB, not just from the cold at my wrists, penetrating my entire body, but from every emotion draining out of me. How to endure this again? Having my soul taken again, which is what the Nimali are planning. While murder doesn't fit into their covenant, slavery apparently does, a fact which makes absolutely no sense to me. My daimon balks at the very idea.

Xipporah's expression is fierce—it's like she's shooting nails from her eyeballs. She stands next to her sister, stoic and strong. They told me it was suicide to try and follow Talia when the soldiers took her away. I must live to fight for her.

Ice forms in my chest where my heart used to be. I focus on my anger to keep me grounded in the here and now. Anger at the Nimali, at Von, at Enzo and Nyana for holding me back when Von had Talia in his grip.

Talia. The frost within me cracks into slivers when I catch a glimpse of her.

She stands with the king and Lady Dominga, who just arrived. The Nimali soldiers do not guard us as closely now that we are of little threat, iced and shackled as we are. The cold breath of the yeti shifters has faded, but my frozen wrists ensure I can mount no defense.

So I make my way closer to the king unhindered, even as others shy away. I need to be near to Talia. The fear in her expression is beginning to thaw every numb place within me.

Lady Dominga has a comm in her hand and waves it around as she speaks. I'm finally close enough to hear. Talia doesn't notice my presence; she's too busy staring at Dominga.

"Your Majesty, the proof is right here. I've been searching for it all night. If you will?"

King Lyall frowns at her but gives a tiny nod. Dominga opens the comm and swipes at it, engaging the projector functionality. An image of Celena hovers just off the ground. Dominga fiddles with the device and the princess's face grows larger, the image zooming in on her features.

"Do you see it, my king? The month before she disappeared, Princess Celena and I were volunteering with the flood victims. We were entertaining some of the children when a young girl fell down in the midst of a seizure. Her arms and legs flailed about and she accidentally hit Celena in the face, scratching her upper lip deeply.

"Celena didn't want the child to get into trouble, so she told no one. No Fai healer attended to her. She used a liquid bandage and hid the mark with makeup. It left a scar, which you can see in this vid on a day she'd forgotten to hide it."

Dominga pointed to the princess's frozen face, a deep crescent moon-shaped scar lay just above her top lip. Aside from that, she was identical to Talia, except for the frost present in the gleam of her eye.

"We talked about that scar all the time," Dominga continues. "I told her she should have it looked at by a healer before it was too late to remove, but she refused. She liked the way it looked. Said it made her appear formidable, like a warrior queen, and one day she would no longer hide it."

Dominga turned to Talia, her eyes flashing. "This woman wears no makeup and has no scar. The time has passed for a Fai healer to be able to heal the mark. How could it be gone, then? Who are you?"

Lyall's gaze moves between Dominga and Talia. His face is impassive, but Talia shrinks under it. Then she firms her mouth and squares her shoulders, tilting her chin up.

"She's right." Her voice is almost too low for me to hear, and I tense as she makes her admission. "My name is Talia Dubroca. I am not your daughter."

If my wrists weren't bound and my daimon subdued, I would leap to her side to protect her. Lyall blinks, still staring at her. His jaw is tight, and I'm afraid he's going to order her killed right now. Or taken to the locker to be jailed. And something within me cannot let that happen. I have to distract him.

"Lyall Lyonson!" I shout, and now everyone on the plaza is focused on me.

Talia's eyes widen with fear. I wish I could reassure her, but I want to draw attention away from her. And also, get my revenge.

"You have broken your covenant and killed innocents. Children, even." My voice cracks at the end and I swallow, steadying my breathing. "I call you out by the ancient law of honorable combat. I demand a duel to avenge the death of my sister, Dove Malinasdaughter, who you cut down with no mercy three years ago."

Lyall peers at me as he would a bug under his shoe, but I don't back down. There will be no other time for me to settle this score. I recognized the truth in Shad's voice when he talked of his covenant preventing the murder of innocents and finally knew who to blame for my sister's death. Dove deserves justice, and while the king of the Nimali is powerful, so is my grief and rage. So am I.

"By custom and law, I cannot refuse," Lyall says after a

moment of consideration, "even if the challenge comes from one as unworthy as you. Let us be done with this quickly."

He motions to a guard, who approaches and detaches my handcuffs. Warmth fills me, though the night is cool. The bliss cuffs create an unnatural chilling effect that does not last after their removal. The other Fai present slowly back away, making a large space on the grass—large enough for a dragon to fight a man.

"Ryin, no!" Talia calls out, her voice desperate. She shakes her head either in disbelief or warning.

I want to tell her to run. While the king is distracted, she should get away from here. I wish my gift was telepathy so I could show her every thought in my head. Every wish I had for things to be different.

I would tell her I dream of a world where we could be free. Could we have been so in her world? I would share my desire to show her my homeland and climb to the tops of one of the great trees with her. High enough for us to see the ocean and the bay, the lands to the north and the south. To watch the fog roll across the water. To take her to visit my parents' graves. Our bliss shrine. The home I built with my hands and planned to live out my days in.

But a flash of light replaces the king, and before the dragon emerges, I call forth my daimon and focus on the fight ahead.

The first blast of flame catches my feet as I dodge it, shooting upward. The stench of burning grass makes my nose crinkle; my daimon heals my injury effortlessly. I take a deep breath and send a stream of fire from my throat, singing his scales and wings. His tough hide is incredibly difficult to break through. He is largely fire resistant, though a Fire Fai can still harm him. And while his flames will take longer to penetrate my daimon-toughened skin, I, too, will burn as I did before.

For all Lyall's bulk, he is light and nimble on his feet, but I can maneuver more nimbly simply due to being smaller.

However, there is nowhere to hide here on the plaza, and a flurry of flame hits my side, igniting me with pain. I am in agony, but already beginning to heal. Still, the wound slows me down. I cannot both heal and be on the offense at the same time; my daimon must focus to accomplish complex tasks. Flying and healing at once, perhaps, but as I do those things, no flame will come.

I circle around him, hovering at his back in order to catch my breath. But he spins faster than I'd anticipated, impossibly graceful. He releases his flame and it meets mine in the middle, fire against fire, our spirit-fueled blazes battling each other in a way natural flames could not.

My head reverberates with echoes of my sister's screams. Her shuddering body beneath me taking its final breaths. I draw deeply from the well of pain and grief within me and assault him with all the fire I can muster.

It hits him, searing his scales. Burning through his wings. Smoke rises from his sinuous neck. He yowls in pain, and while I long to hit him again immediately, I need a few moments for the flames to come. His tail flicks out, swatting me. It connects with my rib cage, pushing me to the side.

I correct in mid-air and he backs away as I fly toward him. I'm intent on his eyes, the pain in them. It satisfies a vicious part of me that needs his suffering. But another cry rings out, this time Talia shouting in agony.

I shouldn't split my focus, but I can't help it. The dragon's tail has swatted her, throwing her across the lawn. She crashes into one of the metal lamp posts and lies motionless. Rage subsumes me and I turn back to the king.

However, he has effectively used my distraction against me. He launches a fire assault that consumes me. I fall from the air to the ground in a thud, every inch of me aflame and suffering. Clothes, grass, dirt, skin…they all burn, the mingling scent all I can focus on aside from the pain.

I peel my eyes open to stare at the sky, starless tonight. I'm unable to move. My muscles are burnt, the fire licking through them all the way to my bones, scorching me, roasting me.

I am done, this much I know. And I cannot move even so much as to find Talia. To see if she's all right. To tell her not to worry. I want my daimon to heal her, but my vision blacks out before I can do more than think it.

The king's voice is the last thing I hear. "Well met, healer. A worthy challenge."

And then all goes dark.

Chapter Thirty-Two

TALIA

EVERYTHING HURTS. I groan and roll over, then sit up as my head spins. Someone has draped a coat over me...no, it's a large, black shirt. One of the soldier's. It still smells of sweat and body odor. Whoever it was must have just taken it off.

I peel it off even though I'm still chilly and look around as my vision clears. At my back is one of the faux gas lamps leaving me in a pool of bluish bliss light. It props me up as I gather my wits. Someone hurries over and crouches at my side. I turn my face away when I see it's Lyall. Beyond him, the Fai gather together looking wretched. The pain in my limbs fades to a dull roar. I wipe at my head and my fingers come away coated in blood.

"What happened?"

"The healer, you care for him?" Lyall asks. It's such a strange question. What is even happening right now? But then I remember the fight. Ryin versus the dragon. The dragon is next to me, so where is Ryin?

I crane my neck, searching, and then freeze when I find him—Ryin's body, what's left of him, is a charred ruin.

He's gone.

I clutch my throat and start screaming. "Ryin!"

My palms hit the grass. I try to crawl forward to get to him, but Lyall pulls me back into his arms. My fists thump against him as I wail like a banshee. "You killed him! You killed him!"

His grip is iron, but gentle. "He fought bravely and died well."

My body stills and I look over at Ryin again, lying so still. Only patches of unburnt skin are visible. None of the Fai can help him, either—all the other healers are shackled, unable to access their daimons. If there's even anything left to heal.

Why did he have to challenge Lyall to that duel? My chest shakes as I crumple, sinking further into this nightmare.

"I'm sorry for hurting you, dear girl. But you were his weakness. Just like you are mine."

I turn my head until we're eye to eye. "You hit me on purpose to distract him."

He looks truly remorseful about it. A sob rises to my throat —I don't know if it's for what Lyall did, for Ryin, for being trapped here, or all of the above. I don't want this man touching me and try to get away, but he's so much stronger than me. And he refuses to let me go. Eventually, I stop fighting, not really having any energy left. I'm as slack as a noodle, and he's the only thing holding me up.

"You are truly not Celena."

It's a statement, not a question, but I answer anyway. "No. I'm not." I sniff and close my eyes.

"But you recognized me. When you first arrived here on the plaza. I saw the recognition in your eyes."

"You are identical to my real father." My voice is robotic. My emotions drained. Everything is numb now. I'm going to turn to stone right here so I don't have to feel anything ever again.

"Ah." He finally releases me, sitting back on his haunches. "And my daughter, do you know where she is?"

I scoot away, leaning against the light post again, and shake my head. "I promise you I don't. I wish I did."

He sits, right there on the ground next to me. "Where do you come from?"

The automaton that I've turned into is the one who answers. "A world like this one. Well, like this one used to be, but without any shifters."

Lyall blocks my view of Ryin's body, which is for the best. The king stares off into space, face downcast. "You aren't even much like her. Not anymore. You remind me of Celena when she was young. I thought…" He chuckles. "I thought I had my little girl back. It was foolish."

This man is such a study in contradictions. Real emotions pour from him, and yet he's got to be a sociopath.

"In this other world you come from, is Rada there? Celena's mother?" I vaguely recognize the wistfulness in his voice.

"She died a long time ago."

He sighs. "Then she is at peace with the Origin in your world, too. As it should be, I suppose."

I feel so heavy that I'm surprised I'm not sinking into the earth beneath me. "Why aren't you more angry? I thought you would kill me when you found out the truth."

He turns back to me, searching my face. "You look too much like my daughter for me to kill. I could snap your neck now, but it would be like snapping hers."

I should be afraid of these cruel words, but I still feel nothing. Everything has drained out of me.

"Though you have caused quite a ruckus, I must say. Releasing the souls. Rada always told me I spoiled you too much." He shakes his head ruefully.

"Not me," I whisper.

"Of course. Not you." He clears his throat. "I spoiled my daughter. She is very precious to me."

Something pierces the granite that's encased me. It's hot and molten like lava—jealousy. "I'm sure she must love you very much." My voice wavers.

Lyall notices and his gaze sharpens. "Your real father, he does not spoil you?" He makes it sound like this is an unbelievable notion. This conversation is what's unbelievable, but the stone around me makes it seem like someone else is talking.

"We don't get along," I whisper hoarsely. "He never wanted me. He had another family." A splash of that lava burns all the way through, melting enough of the rock to allow a shard of pain to reach me.

"Oh, dear girl," Lyall says with so much love it makes my throat tighten.

"He let me down over and over." Something wet drips down my cheeks. It takes long moments for me to understand that these are tears. My tears. The beast who looks like my father reaches over to stroke my hair and makes gentle noises meant to soothe me.

"He chose them over me again and again," I continue, my own mouth out of my control. "And even when I was injured and in the hospital, he didn't come to see me."

My nose runs and my throat is clogged. My skin is on fire with rogue emotion. I'd rather stay numb, but I can't quite achieve it anymore.

There is tenderness in his gaze as he pulls his hand away. "I am truly sorry he made you feel unworthy. But how could anyone not love you?"

The words tear my chest apart, destroying the last of the mask meant to protect me. I scoot away from him and rise, standing on wobbly legs, every part of me still one big ache, inside and out.

The Fai still stand wretchedly, clustered together comforting themselves. They were free for a few moments, but ultimately I failed. I made things worse. Noomi and Xipporah are side by side holding their bound hands together. They stand over Ryin's body.

My breath hitches. Did his position change? Did someone move him? He looks different than he had a few minutes ago.

I search around for Dominga and find her near the doors of the Citadel, scowling at me. Lyall has risen too; I need to keep him in my sights. Part of me is still convinced he's going to fly into a rage and burn me to death as well.

"Where are the soulcatchers I ordered?" the king barks, turning once again from loving father to brutal dictator.

I continue to move away from him, my legs finding their strength. It's true, I failed, Ryin is gone, Shad is gone, everything is worse now. But I couldn't have done nothing. I had to try.

I call out to Lyall, capturing his attention immediately. "You say that you rule beasts and must be one to control them, but I think there has to be another way. If you showed your people something different, then your city, your world, could be different."

He shakes his head sadly and reaches an arm toward me, but I cringe, staying out of reach. "Celena," he begins, then shakes his head with a little laugh. "Talia, is it?"

I nod.

"Talia—"

But whatever else he was going to say is swallowed by a screeching roar and the sound of breaking glass. Debris falls from above, from one of the high floors of the Citadel.

I move out of the way as concrete, plaster, and glass rain down in chunks. Around me, men and women shift into their animal forms, ready to face this threat. Lyall pushes me away, and I stumble backward, craning my neck as a monstrous head forces its way through an opening in the outer wall of the tower. Even from here I can see its red eyes.

The Revokers are free.

Chapter Thirty-Three

TALIA

"GET OUT OF HERE, get to safety!" Lyall shouts before shifting into the red dragon.

The smell of sulfur and the brightness of flashing lights as Nimali change forms all around briefly paralyze me. Then Callum and Zanna appear, pulling me off the plaza and to the opposite side of the yard. The other Nimali complete their shifts and the Revoker pushes the bulk of its body through the opening.

As it falls, its wings flap, not giving it lift, but slowing its descent. According to the library, the creatures can't truly fly —they're like chickens in that way. Their wings will get them a few feet off the ground, but no more. However, they're enough to allow them to glide down from the sixteenth floor.

Nimali birds of prey rise to meet the monster as another launches itself out the hole in the side of the building. Then another.

Revoker roars send chills through my bones. The hands of my guards fall away and I'm left standing behind the protective forms of Zanna's massive bear and Callum's ferocious lion. They nudge me back even farther, away from the fray. Why are they still protecting me even though the ruse is up? I'm grateful—I have no other means of defense—but it doesn't make sense.

At least a dozen Revokers tumble from the building. Some, whose wings were removed during the experiments, plummet directly to the ground but amazingly aren't killed by the descent. They rise with rage-filled cries and attack. Even the hawks and eagles and other war birds can't stop the assaulting creatures. All of the Revokers make it to the ground. And all are enraged and ready for battle.

The Fai scatter, running, trying to flee. But they're still hemmed in by the Nimali surrounding them and can't defend themselves since they're shackled, their daimons suppressed. The screaming Fai, the snarling animals, the sounds of flesh tearing, creatures in pain. It brings me back to my first moments in this world. Locked in fear and soon attacked, cut down, bleeding. Even injured and maimed, these Revokers are deadly.

I'm happy to see a Nimali man, one of the few in human form, has had the presence of mind to begin unshackling the Fai. It's Harshal.

"Zanna, Callum, help Harshal free the Fai. They'll be slaughtered without their daimons."

Callum's lion turns his intelligent eyes to me and takes off, shifting back to man in mid-run. Zanna stays, still in bear form, and motions with her enormous head behind me.

"Talia!" a deep voice calls out. I turn to find Akeem standing in the library doorway, his trunk curled, motioning me toward him. When I look over my shoulder, Zanna is already loping away.

I race to the library and slip around Akeem to enter. He closes and bolts the main doors, but I suspect that will do little to stop a Revoker when it's raging.

I'm bent over in the entry, breaths heaving. "Thank you.

Should I head down to the shelter?" The thought of it gives me goosebumps even as the words leave my lips.

"No, you will be safe here. The Revokers have many more targets at the moment."

Here, in the quiet, echoing emptiness of the library, I fall to my knees, the weight of all that's happened crashing down on me. Ryin gone. Shad as well. The hope of something better for these people taken with the prince. And now this.

"The soldiers have battled Revokers many times," Akeem says. "There are enough of us to prevail."

I swallow and stand.

"I have discovered something," he says. "I thought I would get the chance to speak with you tomorrow."

A tiny spark of hope punctures my gloom. "You figured out how to send me back?"

Dark eyes regard me from his gray face. "No, not exactly. But I believe I know how you arrived."

My heart starts to pound. "How?"

"The answers lie in the Origin. There is a spirit there who can tell you more."

"Why can't you tell me?"

"You want to know why you were brought here. I believe it is best to consult the source."

Shock makes my head swim. "A daimon brought me?"

His large head nods.

"How do I talk to it?"

He paces over to the far wall and taps at a sensor embedded there with his trunk. Several feet away, one of the floor tiles retracts. "You must travel to the Origin."

I walk over, curiosity mixing with suspicion. Beneath the floor of the library lies a pool of bliss. It makes sense—the stuff shoots up in the stream of data and disappears back into the ground. It had to be stored here somewhere. But I look at Akeem, confused. "This is like the daimon trials."

"It is exactly like the daimon trials. That is the only way

you may speak with the spirit who brought you here and find the answers you seek."

Apprehension makes it hard to breathe. The floor tile is about six feet by six feet. It's like a square bathtub, the blue water dark beneath me.

"I would have to climb in and...submerge myself." I'm unwillingly drawn back fifteen years to the hours I spent encased in metal, my mother's screams echoing in my ears. The dashboard pressed against my knees. Door caved in at my side. Gasping for shallow breaths. Pain, nothing but pain.

I blink and I'm back in the library, somewhat dizzy. I didn't realize an elephant could look concerned, but this one does. He's crossed back over to me, so light on his feet, and sits on his back legs.

"I don't think I can do that," I say, shaking my head. "What makes you so sure a daimon brought me here?"

His trunk sways left and right. "It told me."

I can no long hear the sounds of battle outside, but I know they're happening. I'm useless, fully human, no way to defend myself or protect others. No way to help and nowhere left to go. What if I fail at this, too? Was my memory soul taken with my shadow soul when I arrived? Is this pool just a shortcut to my death?

I close my eyes and push away the old memories that try to creep in again. There are better memories that I can draw on to buoy me. Ryin holding me. The feel of lying in his arms. He told me about the Origin, how safe he felt there. Like he was a part of eternity.

Is he there now? Could I find him there?

I have nothing left to lose, nothing here to keep me tethered and nowhere else to go. No one left who cares for me.

How could anyone not love you? Lyall's words reverberate in my head, unbidden. The sincerity behind them was clear. Vicious and cruel as he is, he believes it.

I open my eyes and stare at the pool of bliss before me. "I do want answers."

I imagine soothing circles rubbed into my back, calming me as I face my fears. A daimon brought me here. I need to know why.

I take a deep, stabilizing breath and dip my legs into the bliss, then slide all the way in. The liquid is warm; I hadn't considered that. Warm and thick and viscous like it's mixed with oil. I float on my back and am surprised at the sense of peace that invades me. Beyond the walls, a war rages, but here…it truly is bliss.

My breathing slows. My eyes grow heavy. I think I might fall asleep.

Then I'm not in the tank any longer. Heavy liquid no longer covers my clothes and skin. Somehow I'm standing up. And everything around me is blue.

It's like I'm on a soundstage or inside a giant empty warehouse with no visible walls, just soft blue light surrounding me like a cocoon. The air is muggy and the ground beneath my slippers is firm, but sort of springy.

"Hello?" I expect an echo, but there isn't any. My voice doesn't travel far and the answering voice causes a jolt of surprise.

"Talia, you have found your way here."

I swallow and turn around in a circle, but I can see nothing, no glimpse of the spirit I'm speaking with. "You're a daimon?"

"I am." The voice sounds amused. "I am *your* daimon." It's actually not a voice at all, but I don't know how else to describe it. Words and thoughts come into my head, voice-like, but inhuman. Neither male nor female, and I'm not even sure it's speaking in a language, exactly. But it's perfectly understandable. Its emotions are also somehow clear to me. Hope pours into me.

"How can I have a daimon? I'm not from Aurum."

"No, but I searched long and far for you. I combed the multiverse, in fact, and brought you here so that we could join." The daimon seems proud of this, but it leaves me dizzy.

"I don't understand. Why?"

"Because my parallel formed a covenant, and we were supposed to experience the mortal realm together. But I lost the host I was meant to join. I needed a new one, and you are the only one in all the worlds who fit."

I'm processing this and a tiny burst of pride sprouts within me, making me feel special. But this is all still so deeply weird.

"I had to wait for your death in your world," the daimon continues, "before I could bring you here. It is not exactly sanctioned, though not unprecedented." The spirit shows no remorse.

"Wait, what is a parallel?"

"Sit, please, you are tired."

I comply and sit on the springy ground, which is somehow the most comfortable thing I've ever sat on. But do I even have a body here in the spirit plane? I don't bother to ask, for the daimon is already speaking again.

"A parallel is like the human notion of a soulmate. We, of course, do not have souls as you do, and not every daimon has a parallel, but those who do treasure them. Often we enter the material world with them and live alongside them for a time. Sometimes as mother and child, or brother and sister, or husband and wife. We are not beings of romance as humans —still, the connection with our parallel is deep and we are lost without them."

"So your parallel found a human host?"

The daimon's energy vibrates in agreement. "My parallel joined its host earlier than I did—though time here is not as you know it. But the host I had chosen died, and I needed another."

"Who was your host?"

"Her name was Dove. She was Ryin's sister."

I jolt.

"My parallel and I had planned to enter the world as siblings. But the dragon king broke his covenant and killed her. His daimon is corrupted and allows such atrocities. Most would have abandoned their hosts." A heavy sadness comes from the spirit.

"But…" Questions swirl in my mind as I try to wrap it around this knowledge. "How did you know Ryin would let me close to him once I arrived? That we would even be friends much less…more."

"That is why I searched."

"But what were you looking for?"

"You."

The daimon's logic is making my head spin. There is something like a shrug that comes from my sense of the spirit. "I cannot give you answers that would satisfy you. There is nothing in your logical mind that can understand the things of spirit. For a daimon parallel, even if our hosts are separated for periods, they will always find their way back to one another. You are the one who will always find your way back to him."

The notion warms my heart, even if it makes no sense. The daimon seems to read my hesitancy. "Is it not enough to know that you are special? That you have another out in the worlds who you are meant for?"

I'm quiet for a long time, pondering. "But he's gone." My voice doesn't carry far. Saying it aloud cools the warm sensation that had started to spread.

"Have a little faith, Talia. Do you not know what his daimon is?"

"He would never tell me," I whisper. "He must be a dragon, though. He's a Fire Fai."

"You will see for yourself soon enough. Are you ready to join me now?"

I find it hard to believe the daimon's words about Ryin. I

saw his charred form. But the notion of having a daimon would at least let me find a place in this world. "What will it be like?"

Joy pours from the spirit. "Human and daimon work together for our mutual benefit. I will experience touch and taste. Walk across the ground and breath in air. And you will share my gifts to enhance and hopefully heal your world."

A deep longing fills me. At least I'll never be alone again. "What do I have to do?"

"Simply agree. Pledge yourself to the covenant that we strike together. To kill no creature that is not seeking to kill you. To take from none who has less than you. To love with all your heart when love finds you. And to be grateful for every day you are granted."

I'm surprised that this covenant they all speak of is so simple. But I like it.

"Yes, I agree."

"Then open your heart and find wholeness and peace. When you rise from the bliss, I will be with you."

The feeling of liquid bliss covering my skin comes on suddenly, and my eyes are heavy again. When I open them, the gray of the ceiling far overhead comes into focus. Everything is silent, and I take stock of my body. I sense the spirit there, the daimon waiting inside me. It's a strange feeling, like a second heart in my chest. A consciousness who I can sense via emotions and desires more than thoughts. I try to speak to it again, but can't anymore. That must only be possible in the Origin. However, I sense its heart and know it can sense mine.

There is a wholeness now to me that I haven't experienced before. I'm deeply grateful.

A realization hits me—I didn't even ask it what type of animal it is. I'm sure I didn't ask a lot of things that I should have if that is the only time I'll be able to talk to it directly. I suppose I'll find out soon enough.

I'm also aware that being inside this dark, coffin-like tank isn't sparking any terror. I take another second to be sure—but it's gone. The pressure that would close in on me, the fear of tight, dim spaces. Have I truly overcome it?

I climb out of the tank to find Akeem waiting a few steps away.

His trunk rises and the corners of his mouth rise in an odd elephant smile. "You found the answers you seek?"

"Yes, thank you, Akeem. I owe you so much."

He gives a soft trumpet. "You owe me nothing."

A faint shadow stretches across the ground, barely visible because of the low lighting, but still attached to me. I wobble a bit then find my footing.

"My shadow is back," I say, grinning. "But I still don't know what I am."

"Well, now is a good time to find out."

The possibilities run through my mind. I don't really care if I'm a bunny rabbit or a squirrel...I'm just happy my daimon is here.

All right. Come forward. You never told me what we'd become.

The daimon is giddy within me, and a glow emanates from my eyes. But it doesn't stop there. The light surrounds me completely, blocking my vision, numbing my body for long seconds. When the light recedes, everything about me is different.

Where my hands once were, sharp claws emerge from digits of brilliant emerald green. Behind me swishes a long, thick tail of darker green with spiky things poking out of it.

I assumed since Ryin is Fai and our daimons are parallels that I would be also, but that is not the case. I've transformed, shifted into something bigger and greener and—

A feeling sizzles in my chest like heartburn seeking escape. I turn away from Akeem and point my mouth toward the ceiling, so far away. Fire flies from my throat, shooting into the air in long streams.

When it dies, smoke rises from my lips, and I'm frozen in

place for a moment. Then I focus on the ceiling, which is already starting to retract. Akeem must have known what I would want as soon as he saw me shift. Sounds of the battle on the plaza filter through the open roof.

I don't have to sit back and allow others to fight for me anymore.

I am a dragon. Hear me roar.

Chapter Thirty-Four

RYIN

THE SPIRIT PLANE stretches out around me, comforting me and holding me tightly in a blue womb made of light. Its hold is firm and warm and healing.

"Do you want to return?" the voice of my daimon sounds within my mind. I have not heard it in years, but it, too, is comforting.

"You always have a choice," it says.

The time I was asked before, I almost said no. That day I knew the last of my family was gone. The daimon did not pressure me then—it did not share its opinion as to whether or not I should use its power to return to my life.

If I did not, in time it would find another host, form another covenant. It would be fine. It is, after all, an infinite spirit, not bound by things like love and revenge. Or so I thought.

Now, it stays quiet, allowing me the time to make my choice, but I sense its anxiousness. Its desire to get back to the world.

That desire matches my own.

"Yes," I say. "I want to return."

I have never seen it, for there is nothing to see, and yet I have the sense that if it had a mouth, it would be smiling.

Swirling arcs of light and magic enfold me and the true power of my daimon engages. There is a brief brush of feathers, and I lift into the air. We Fai do not take on the physical aspects of our daimons, true, but sometimes, we see images of the animals in our minds. Wings and plumes of feathers made of light ghost against my shriveled, charred skin, restoring it. The image of a bird partially made of smoke and flame brushes my consciousness before retreating. And then I am back.

I hover a foot off the ground, body mended, clothing too through some ancillary magic. On the plaza, two dragons are locked in battle with two Revokers. *There are Revokers loose in the city?* The unexpected sight stops me short. But here they are, though one is missing an eye and the other has no wings.

These are the creatures from the lab, then, somehow escaped again and wreaking havoc. And the dragons—one is red and the other…green? There is no green dragon in Aurum, but my daimon practically coos in response to seeing the beast. My stomach drops away as recognition hits.

"Talia?"

The dragon turns its head, and that moment of distraction is all the Revoker needs. It swipes a claw out at her, glancing off her viridescent scales. Dragon Talia growls in response and shoots a blaze of flame its way. She is not trained, but she is fierce all the same. So many questions swarm my mind, but they will keep, because a third monster approaches. I add my skills to the fight, breathing fire at it.

I fight alongside the king's red dragon, which is something I cannot stop to contemplate at the moment. It is life or death and we will deal with all the rest later.

Other Fai are in the fight, defending the retreat of our brothers and sisters, though they stay out of the reach of the dragons' and my flames. All across the plaza, over a half-dozen of the Revokers are already down.

Another enemy a dozen feet away breaks free of its fight with two large cats and three swooping war birds and begins heading my way. I shoot flames at it, making it bound off in the opposite direction.

The remaining Revokers are locked in battle, while the bulk of the Fai are escaping, running down the streets bordering the plaza and disappearing between buildings. I move to cover their retreat, breathing fire at any red-eyed brute that comes this way.

"Get to safety. Head for the tunnels beyond the territory!" I shout.

Xipporah joins me and we clash with a creature, still fierce notwithstanding both its front claws are missing.

"Noomi?" I ask, dodging teeth.

"Already gone."

"Good."

We take down the Revoker together and then Xipporah, too, gets ready to make her escape. There are only three Revokers left, and the Nimali can handle them.

"Have you seen Von?" I ask before she heads away.

"No, I lost him. He's probably on his way back home."

"When I see him again, he'll have much to answer for."

"More than you know," Xi says mysteriously. "We'll speak more at home. You're right behind me, *right?*"

I nod but don't give voice to what might be a lie.

She looks back with some alarm at the new green dragon. She likely doesn't know who it is but asks no more questions before taking off at tiger speeds down the asphalt drive.

Leaving me with the pair of dragons.

Talia has so much heart, but she doesn't know how to use her powerful body yet and is being overwhelmed. I rush forward as she falls under the force of blows of two of the three remaining Revokers. She's on the ground, kicking out and snarling.

The king's dragon roars and releases a catastrophic conflagration of flames. He leaps to Talia's side and moves in front of her, taking the rips and slashes meant for her. The two Revokers claw at him as he pummels them with flame.

I fly to Talia's side, next to her massive head. She's the smallest of the dragons, but still enormous. Razor sharp claws have managed to pierce her scaly hide. Black poison drips out of her wounds once again, pooling on the charred grass.

A dazzling flash of light emerges from her and she's human again, torn and bleeding, but Talia. I cradle her head in my lap and direct my daimon to heal her wounds. The poison is ejected from her flesh and the slices in her skin heal before my eyes.

She gazes up at me, gasping for breath, unable to tear herself away from my face. "Ryin," she whispers, voice weak. "I thought you were dead. How…?"

"I'm a phoenix, love. I'll always come back to you."

She smiles brilliantly, just as a terrifying yell rends the air.

Talia scrambles to a seated position and we both witness the red dragon searing the last Revoker until it stops charging and eventually stops moving at all.

The king has won, but it's clear the victory has come at a great cost.

With a flash of light, he transforms back to human, deep slashes gouging him all over. He stumbles then falls to a knee, bracing himself on the ground.

He groans and sinks down, rolling onto his back. Talia covers her gasp with a hand, holding it there with her eyes wide.

She slowly rises and approaches him with me on her heels.

The king is dying, this much is clear. He's been pierced in a dozen places by Revoker claws and the poison must be going deep.

Even if I had the mind to heal him, I suspect it is already too late. Talia's cheeks are covered in tears. She wraps an arm around her middle; her chest convulses in a sob.

I swallow. Does she truly care for him?

I look down into the face of the man who has caused so much suffering, the man who murdered my sister. My daimon is quiet inside me. It always urges mercy, but even it knows that this would be too much.

"I'm sorry, Talia. I cannot—"

She quiets me with a hand on my arm. "I would never ask you to."

Still, she kneels beside him and takes a bloody hand in her own. "I would give you peace before you pass to the Origin," she says.

"You already have, my dear girl." And then the king of the Nimali closes his eyes and he's gone.

Chapter Thirty-Five

TALIA

RYIN HELPS me to my feet. I hold his hand and look down upon the face of my father. Upon a man so flawed and brutal and yet so loving. How can the human heart be capable of such extremes?

I swipe at my tears and look up. Ryin is the only Fai who remains, and the Nimali around us all appear exhausted. Some have not yet shifted back to their human forms. Many lie bleeding, poisoned from the Revokers.

I spot Harshal, Callum, and Zanna. They all limp over, a bit battered and bruised, but whole. Ryin stiffens beside me.

"The king is dead," Harshal says, dark eyes grim but not with grief.

I nod.

He glances at Ryin and then back at me. "The Fai will not be safe unless the Nimali have a strong leader."

Too much has happened for me to be able to follow his words. "You know I'm not Celena. What is the line of succession?" I'm not even sure why he's brought this to me.

"Prince Shad lives. Barely." Now he stares at Ryin.

My chest feels like it's going to cave in. Shad is alive. The ground tilts and Ryin shoots out a hand to stabilize me.

He and Harshal share a whole conversation in one protracted gaze. Finally, Ryin speaks. "Will he be a good king?"

"If they let him, he will be the best." The soldier's words are simple, but achingly honest.

Ryin nods and steps back. "Lead the way."

"You'll heal him?" I ask, somewhat surprised.

"He may be our best chance of lasting peace," Ryin says. "A Nimali king who respects the covenant and pledges not to kill innocents? It is a chance worth taking."

The three of them lead us into the building to a large room on the first floor. It's a military barracks with dormitories filled with bunk beds. At the end of one row, a motionless figure lies on top of the covers. I shudder, looking at the burnt form of the prince of the Nimali.

Someone has placed an IV bag of fluids next to him with a tube snaking into his arm, but I can't imagine it's doing anything.

"How is he even still alive?" I murmur.

"He was in mid-shift when the fire hit him," Zanna says, crouching beside him.

"Those with fire daimons are able to withstand more fire than most," Ryin adds. Callum and Harshal stand solemnly at the foot of the bed.

Ryin perches gingerly at Shad's side and takes a deep breath before closing his eyes. The glow begins behind his eyelids as his daimon comes forward.

It feels like it takes a lifetime, but it must only be a few minutes before Shad's blackened, crisped skin begins to transform. It smooths and fades back to his deep brown complexion. That awful smell of scorched flesh that clung in the air fades away. The barely detectable rise and fall of his chest becomes more pronounced and finally, finally, he opens his eyes.

Zanna, the stoic bear shifter, lets out a sob then slams her fist against her lips.

Shad smiles weakly. "I couldn't take it if you fall apart, Zan."

She chuckles through watery eyes, visibly pulls herself together, then stands.

"Harsh. Callum," he calls to his other two friends. Both nod at him, choked with emotion as well. Then Shad peers up at Ryin and me.

The daimon is still in Ryin's eyes, making him look other-worldly. It finally recedes and he rises.

"Your Majesty," Ryin says with a slight bow. His voice is cautious.

Shad's brows rise. He looks to his friends, who nod, confirming the title. Then he looks to me, blinking, a question in his gaze.

I smile down at him. "You missed a lot."

———

RYIN and I leave the Citadel a short while later with Harshal, Callum, and Zanna as guides. Shad hasn't been officially crowned yet and wanted to make sure we didn't have any issues getting out of the territory now that the dust is beginning to settle.

But the plaza is empty when we emerge into the early morning sunshine.

"Would you like a vehicle?" Harshal asks.

"Thank you, but there's no need," Ryin replies. I think it's about five miles from here to Golden Gate Park, which is where the Greenlands are in my world. Not a terrible walk. And the morning is crisp, the air fresh.

The soldiers accompany us to the edge of the reclaimed

part of their territory. Then we say our goodbyes and head down the crumbling streets.

"Did you want to walk and enjoy all of this?" I ask him with a laugh, motioning at the dystopic display around us.

"No, I want to fly." He grabs me around the waist with an arm under my knees in a bridal carry and his eyes begin to glow just before we shoot into the air.

A startled cry escapes me; I grip him tightly around the neck. "You could give me some warning, you know!"

"It's more fun this way."

I should have known we wouldn't be walking. It will probably take some time for me to settle into this whole shifter thing and the fact that Ryin can not only heal, but breathe flames and take to the air at will. The benefits of having a phoenix inside him.

My hold on him loosens, and I try to enjoy the flight. My own flying is still clumsy. I made it out of the library and into the fray of battle all right, but I wouldn't trust my own wings to make it all the way to the Greenlands. That will take some practice. So I watch the city stretching out below us, the city I grew up in, so similar but so different. The morning fog still clings to the streets and buildings—what's left of them anyway —but the sunlight is burning it away.

I wonder what my reception will be in the Fai homeland, me who wears the face of the princess of their enemy? And especially since my daimon—Ryin's parallel—apparently made the executive decision to shift forms when I call it. Does that make me a Nimali? Will I even be accepted by the Fai?

Questions and fears swirl in my head as I face the unknown.

"Why are you frowning?" Ryin asks, looking down at me.

"I didn't realize I was." He is free now after so long in captivity and I should give him at least a little while to enjoy it before I assault him with all my misgivings and uncertainty.

"What will we do now?" I ask.

He smiles at me brilliantly. I've never seen a smile like this on his face, and it transforms him. The heavy gaze that always spoke of sorrow is gone, lifted like the mist fading away below us.

He lowers his lips to mine and kisses me, long and slow. I think for a moment that he should probably watch where he's going, but sink into the kiss all the same. Growing breathless with it.

"Whatever we want to," he replies and then laughs. The sound is a balm to all three of my souls.

I lean my head against him, secure in Ryin's arms as we race through the air. Free and safe and happy. And grateful I was brought to this savage city.

Epilogue

SHAD

I exit the plaza to the sound of raucous applause. It follows me through the lobby, thankfully ending when the elevator doors swoosh closed. I am alone with my thoughts for the time it takes to rise to the forty-eighth floor, the highest and smallest one in this tower, the throne room.

The bone throne awaits, though I have no desire to sit on it. For though I worked to overthrow Lyall, it was not out of a strident desire to accept what today's coronation has just solidified into being. A king who doesn't want to be king. I didn't want it when I was eighteen and went through my trial to be cursed with a dragon daimon, and now, over eight years later, I still wish I could change things.

But I cannot.

The elevator dings again and Harsh, Zanna, and Callum nearly walk right into me since I'm still standing in front of the doors.

"Excuse us, Your Majesty," Callum says wryly. He comes to stand in front of me, smirk firmly in place. These are my closest friends and the only people I trust now.

"That went well," Harshal says, stepping to my side.

"No one tried to murder you," Zanna adds from my other side.

"Not yet," I say.

But we all know that an assassination attempt is likely in the near future.

Though some of my people look to me with hope in their eyes, with the longing for something better after decades of tyranny, many others view me with suspicion and doubt.

"If they kill you, who will lead them?" Harsh asks. "There is no one else who could."

"That won't stop them from trying. There are many ambitious predators who think they could be king," I say under my breath and finally step toward the wretched throne.

It was built generations ago from dragon bones, supposedly the bones of the first dragon Nimali, but I doubt that very much.

I stare down at it, disgusted, then spin around and settle my weight onto its seat. The thing creaks ominously.

"They expected you to have the throne on the plaza for the coronation," Zanna says.

Lyall usually had the damned thing dragged downstairs for any gathering, just to show it off. Not many ever get to see the throne room, after all, small as it is.

"It's just more fuel for the fire," she adds.

Harsh regards her with hard eyes. "The fire will die down as soon as he has the opportunity to show them who he really is."

Zanna crosses her arms. "He did not defeat the old king in a duel, neither was he the chosen heir. Lyall defeated *him*"— she points her finger at me, jabbing the air—"Dishonorable though it was. Still, it's left the taint of weakness on him. They will oppose him at every turn and you know it."

Because of the strength of my daimon, none will challenge me outright in honorable combat. No, there will be no duels in my future. My enemies will come more subtly, trying to weaken my position from within.

There is only one thing that will help me retain order among the Nimali.

"We need to find Celena."

They all turn to me, shocked into silence.

"What makes you think she's alive?" Callum asks.

"I don't know. She could very well be dead, or she could have been magically taken to some other world the way Talia was." That one still has me scratching my head. "But I hope she is alive and out there somewhere. If the *preferred* heir returns and we marry as Lyall intended, that is the only way we will know true peace."

And we need peace, for the Fai are no doubt planning their revenge, and the bliss is still running low, and the Revokers will one day find a way over that wall, I'm convinced of it.

A voice pipes up from the shadowed corner behind the throne. Zanna immediately shifts into her bear and growls at the intruder. Callum turns into his lion, crouching menacingly. Harsh is the only one to keep his head—his eagle remains within him.

It didn't occur to me that I would need to use a dampener in my own throne room. Perhaps Lyall's paranoia was more justified than I thought.

I rise from the uncomfortable seat and turn to find Lady Dominga emerge from the darkness, back ramrod straight, expression icy as ever. The surprise of her appearance made me miss what she said.

"What was that?" I bark as she draws closer. She's dressed in a deep magenta dress that sweeps the floor, making it look like she's gliding more than walking.

"I said," her voice rising in irritation, "I know where Celena went."

My heart thumps a jagged rhythm. I fear I'm about to have to make a deal with a devil.

Acknowledgments

This book has been a very long time coming and has had quite a twisty birthing process. If you know anything about the history of my fantasy series, Earthsinger Chronicles, you may recall that I initially self-published the first two books. A year after I released *Song of Blood & Stone*, I received an email from an editor at St. Martin's Press, Monique Patterson, who eventually offered to republish that series. But before that, she asked me what I was working on next.

I pitched her the initial idea for this novel, a story which began as a spin-off of my paranormal romance series, The Eternal Flame Series. The original story revolved around a character from *Angelfall* who was going to disappear through a portal in the third planned book (a book that has not, as of this writing, been completed).

I tweaked the pitch, made the book a standalone, and gave the heroine a different name and backstory. This new iteration of the story was only connected to the world of *Angelborn* by the existence of portals to other dimensions. However, all three series (Earthsinger Chronicles, Eternal Flame, The Bliss Wars) exist in the same multiverse, and savvy readers familiar with my other books will see the connections that link these worlds together.

Of course, my editor did not end up purchasing *Savage City*, and the manuscript sat gathering dust while I worked on my contracted projects. I would pick it up again at various times over the years. My agent gave me feedback on it twice, in fact.

At one point, I was going to turn it into a YA novel. I briefly experimented with it being a Middle Grade book and aging everyone down quite a bit. However, once I completed Earthsinger Chronicles and had more time and space for this story to breathe, I realized my heroine needed to go back to her original age, and I would try to make her story work. I threw out the many, many other drafts from over the years and began writing from scratch. And Reader, I finally finished it, as you can see.

Many thanks, as ever, go to my accountability and sanity partners, Ines Johnson and Cerece Rennie Murphy.

To my agent, Sara Megibow, for her invaluable feedback over the years.

To the Humpback pod, with whom I workshopped many of the chapters. Special thanks to beta readers: Olivia Bedford, Jean McAuliffe, Elizabeth Ollo, and Erika Springer.

To my editor, Danielle Poiesz, who pushed me to dig deeper.

To my copy editor, Sidney Thompson, whose red pen is a mighty sword.

And finally, to my family: my brother and first reader, Paul, who I keep making read my kissing books. My mother, who always shares my kissing books with all of her friends. And my husband, who keeps inspiring me to write kissing books and always encourages me to roar.

About the Author

L. Penelope has been writing since she could hold a pen and loves getting lost in the worlds in her head. She is an award-winning fantasy and paranormal romance author. Her novel *Song of Blood & Stone* was chosen as one of *TIME* Magazine's 100 Best Fantasy Books of All Time. Equally left and right-brained, she studied filmmaking and computer science in college and sometimes dreams in HTML. She hosts the *My Imaginary Friends* podcast and lives in Maryland with her husband and furry dependents.

www.lpenelope.com
hello@lpenelope.com

CPSIA information can be obtained
at www.ICGtesting.com
Printed in the USA
LVHW041926120322
713152LV00005B/195

9 781944 744274